Ernest Alfred W. Budge, Valerie Susie Meux

Some Account of the Collection of Egyptian Antiquities

In the possession of Lady Meux, of Theobald's Park, Waltham Cross

Ernest Alfred W. Budge, Valerie Susie Meux

Some Account of the Collection of Egyptian Antiquities
In the possession of Lady Meux, of Theobald's Park, Waltham Cross

ISBN/EAN: 9783337330262

Printed in Europe, USA, Canada, Australia, Japan

Cover: Foto ©Andreas Hilbeck / pixelio.de

More available books at **www.hansebooks.com**

EGYPTIAN ANTIQUITIES.

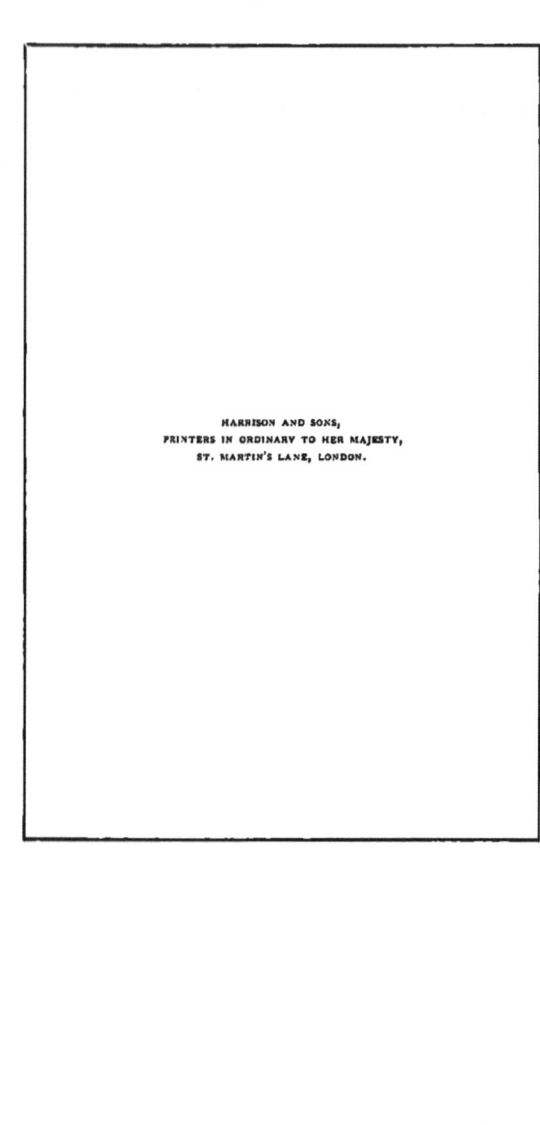

HARRISON AND SONS,
PRINTERS IN ORDINARY TO HER MAJESTY,
ST. MARTIN'S LANE, LONDON.

SOME ACCOUNT

OF THE

Collection of Egyptian Antiquities

IN THE POSSESSION OF

LADY MEUX,

OF THEOBALD'S PARK, WALTHAM CROSS.

BY

E. A. WALLIS BUDGE, Litt.D., F.S.A.,

Formerly Tyrwhitt Hebrew Scholar and Scholar of Christ's College, Cambridge,
Keeper of the Egyptian and Assyrian Antiquities, British Museum.

SECOND EDITION.

WITH THIRTY-FOUR PLATES.

London:
HARRISON & SONS,
Printers in Ordinary to Her Majesty,
St. Martin's Lane.
1896.

PREFACE.

THE collections of Egyptian Antiquities of which some account is given in the following pages were acquired by Lady Meux in 1882, 1895-6. They contain a number of very important objects, among which the following are worthy of special note :—(1.) Limestone slabs from tombs of officials who flourished in the IVth and Vth dynasties, and four fine sepulchral stelæ inscribed with hymns to the Sun-god from Akhmîm. (2.) The rectangular wooden coffin of Ȧn-ḥeru, inscribed in hieratic with Chapters from the Book of the Dead. This coffin was made in the XIth dynasty, about B.C. 2600, or earlier, and belongs to the class represented by the Coffin of Ȧmamu in the British Museum. (3.) A magnificently painted coffin of an unnamed member of the confraternity of the priests of Ȧmen-Rā at

Thebes.   (4.) The mummy and coffin of
Nes-Àmsu, the second prophet of the god
Àmsu, and prophet of the god Khonsu at Àpu
(the Panopolis of the Greeks, represented to-
day by the modern town of Akhmîm in Upper
Egypt), about B.C. 350; they were presented
to Lady Meux in 1886 by the late Walter
Ingram, Esq.   The mummy is interesting as
an example of a body carefully preserved by the
use of bitumen; the coffin is a good specimen
of the work of the funereal craftsman of that
period, and its value is enhanced by its perfect
condition.   There is, moreover, every reason for
believing that Nes-Àmsu was an ancestor of
Nekau, whose sepulchral stele is preserved in
Lady Meux's Collection (see No. 51).   The
designs and colouring and subject matter of the
inscriptions recall the work of a much older
period, and prove that, in spite of the corrupting
influences of the Greek and Persian civilizations,
and the imposition of alien manners and customs
upon Egypt, and the decay which was slowly
undermining her ancient religion, the hand of

the artist had not lost its cunning, that the
worship of the gods of olden time still held
sway, and that the belief in the resurrection of
a spiritual body was no vain thing even to the
educated Egyptian. In the coffins of Ȧn-Ḥeru,
and of the priest of Ȧmen and of Nes-Ȧmsu we
have three of the finest examples of this class of
object belonging to the Ancient and New Em-
pires and to the Ptolemaïc period respectively.
(5.) Double seated limestone figures of Neb-sen
and Nebt-ta, XVIIIth dynasty. (6.) Black
granite kneeling figure of Ȧmen-[em]-ȧpt, a
scribe, XVIIIth dynasty. (7.) Black granite
kneeling figure of Iupa, the scribe and architect
of the Temple of Ȧmen-Rā at Thebes during
the reign of Rameses II., about B.C. 1330.
(8.) Head of a black granite statue of Rameses
III., King of Egypt about B.C. 1200. (9.) Painted
plaster heads with inlaid eyes, of the Roman
period, about A.D. 300. (10.) Wooden boat
containing figures of the captain and his crew,
consisting of one steersman and twenty rowers,
belonging to the Ancient Empire. (11.) A

large bronze seated figure of the goddess
Sekhet. (12.) A fragment of a wooden box
inlaid with ivory, inscribed with the rarely found
prenomen and nomen of Rameses X., King of
Egypt about B.C. 1150. (13.) A hypocephalus
made for Shai-enen, the son of Nes-Nebt-ḥet.
(14.) A collection of about eight hundred scarabs
and amulets from Abydos. (15.) A bronze
libation bucket made for Shashanq, the son of
Thehet-Teḥuti. This fine specimen of bronze
work was probably a votive offering to the
deceased by his daughter Nit-àqert (Nitocris).
(16.) A blue glazed *faïence* figure of Venus
Anadyomene. (17.) Alabaster vase of Pepi I,
King of Egypt about B.C. 3233, etc.

The number of Egyptian Antiquities preserved at Theobald's Park is about eighteen
hundred, and the proportion of first-rate objects
of interest is very considerable.

E. A. WALLIS BUDGE.

LONDON,
July 30, 1896.

LIST OF PLATES.

———

B

CONTENTS.

———◆———

THE FUNERAL OF AN EGYPTIAN.

—•—

THE ancient Egyptian monuments and the hieroglyphic inscriptions cut upon them show us that the
Egyptians, from the earliest dynasties, took the
greatest possible care to preserve the bodies of their
dead from destructive agencies and decay in the tomb.
They learnt, at a very early period, that bodies laid
in the earth which forms the soil of Egypt, were
rotted by the infiltration of the waters of the Nile,
and that to preserve the bodies of their dead from
the attacks of birds and beasts of prey, it was necessary
to bury them in tombs hewn out of the solid rock
in the mountains, on the right and left banks of the
Nile. They attempted to arrest the decomposition
of the body into its natural elements by the use of
drugs, balsams, and aromatic spices; and there is
no doubt that they succeeded admirably in this par-

ticular. At what period of their history the Egyptians began to mummify their dead it is impossible to say, but it is known for a certainty that, as far back as we have any knowledge of them, that is to say about B.C. 4000 or 5000, they possessed the art of mummifying bodies, and also that, in the case of kings and high officials, they made use of an elaborate system of ritual and sepulture. It is possible, but not probable, that the aboriginal inhabitants of Egypt mummified their dead, but it is generally believed that the necessary anatomical knowledge, and the funeral customs, and the systems of sepulture which we now know were made use of by the Egyptians, were brought with them from their home in Asia.

The Egyptian believed that mortal man was composed of a perishable body called 𓂝 *kha*, a genius or "double" 𓂓 *ka*, the soul 𓅽 *ba*, and an intelligence 𓅜 *khu*. The *ka*, or "double," lived in the tomb as long as the body lay there. The soul left the body at death and went wherever it pleased, and passed in and out of the tomb according to its desire. After a period, the length of which is not exactly known, it returned to the body and entered and dwelt therein. It must be understood that only the souls of those who were victorious in the judg-

ment after death could re-enter their bodies; on the
other hand it was absolutely necessary that the body
should be preserved and kept in a perfect state, in
order that it might be a fit dwelling-place for the
"perfect soul" on its return. It is clear then that
the Egyptians mummified their dead because they
believed in the doctrine of the resurrection and im-
mortality, and that they spared neither pains nor
expense in making their "houses of eternity" meet
dwelling-places for the souls who were to live for ever.

The name commonly given to the body of a human
being, animal, bird, fish, or reptile which has been
preserved by bitumen, natron, drugs or spices is
MUMMY, and this name is derived, not from the
old Egyptian word for an embalmed body, but from
the Arabic word for bitumen, *mûmiâ*. The Arabs
seem only to have become familiar with that class
of bodies which had been preserved entirely by
bitumen, and, in consequence, they called every embalmed body *mûmiyya*, *i.e.*, a "bitumenized thing."
From the Arabic the word has passed into all Euro-
pean languages, and it is only from the hieroglyphic
inscriptions that we learn that the ancient Egyptian
word for making a dead man into a mummy was
△ 𓊖 or △ ⸺ *qes*, which means ·literally,

" to bandage a dead body." Another Egyptian word for mummy is *Sāḫu* 𓊪 —𓂋 𓆄 𓅓 𓏛 𓅱.

The Greek historian Herodotus states that the Egyptians mummified the bodies of the dead in three different ways, and that the expense varied according to the system adopted. A later Greek writer, Diodorus Siculus, confirms this statement of Herodotus, and adds that the cost of embalming in the most expensive way was one talent of silver (about £240), that the cost of the second system was twenty minæ (about £80), and that that of the third was very little indeed. The bodies of the poor were merely steeped in natron for seventy days, and were then carried away for burial to holes dug perhaps in the loose sand of the desert, or to a common burial place or cave in the mountains, where they were piled up in heaps or laid in rows similar to those which may be seen in the mountain caves on the western bank of the Nile opposite to Luxor, the site of the ancient Egyptian Diospolis or Thebes. There is some doubt if the bodies of the poor were steeped in natron for as many days as seventy. In Genesis (l. 3) we are told that the physicians embalmed Jacob, and that " forty days were fulfilled for him ; for so are fulfilled the days of embalming ; and the Egyptians wept for him threescore and ten days." Now in an Egyptian document we find it stated that the embalming occupied 16 days, the bandaging 35 days, and the burial 70 days, *i.e.*, 121 days in all. Elsewhere we are told that the embalming occupied 66 days, the arrangements for the funeral 4 days, and the burial 26 days, or 96 days in all; and again we are told that 70 or 80 days are required for embalming and ten months for the burial. It seems nearly certain then that the bodies of the poor were only steeped in natron long enough to dissolve the fleshy parts of the body, and we know that they were buried with a pair of sandals in which to walk in the world beyond the grave, and with a staff or stick to support their steps in the valley of the shadow of death.

The task of describing the details of every scene in the embalmment of the body of an Egyptian king or noble would be endless, for apart from the main facts common to the description of all mummies which were made according to the first and second systems of Herodotus, there are in each mummy a number of peculiarities which arose from individual taste or fancy on the part of the embalmers or the relatives of the dead. These, although extremely interesting to the student, need not be considered in describing the process of mummifying a priestly official, scribe, or gentleman living in Thebes about B.C. 1600. Soon after the death of a man his body was taken to the house of the embalmers, and the friends and relatives decided the details of the process and the price to be paid. It seems that the embalmers either formed a grade of the Egyptian priesthood, or that they were a body of men under the control of the priests ; in either case all the ceremonial observances connected with the embalming of a body would be strictly carried out by them, for upon the performance of these depended the welfare of the deceased in the other world. The body was carefully washed and the brains were removed through the nostrils by an iron rod with a hook at the end, but great care was taken not to break the bridge of the nose in the process. The empty skull was then filled with a mixture of coarse spices and resin, or with pieces of linen which had been either steeped in aromatic or astringent substances, or smeared with unguents. When this process was adopted the hair and teeth were preserved. Skulls filled wholly with resin or bitumen are some-times found. On the left side of the body, just over the groin, a line was then traced, along which an opening was made with a knife of flint or metal, and through it the great intestines and heart, etc., were removed. The interior of the body was then washed

with palm wine, and the whole hollow was filled with
fragrant and preservative spices and gums.　A cheaper
way of ridding the body of its most easily decaying
portions was to inject natron and oil of cedar ; after a
certain time the intestines were dissolved and little
except the skin and bones remained.　In the earlier
dynasties the bodies of the dead were preserved by
means of natron and bitumen, but in the later
dynasties bitumen alone was used.　Bodies preserved
by bitumen lose their hair, teeth and nails, and the
skin and bones become of a dark-brown or black
colour.

Concerning the fate of the intestines Greek writers
have differences of opinion.　According to Herodotus
they were in many cases destroyed by natron ; and
according to Plutarch they were shown to the sun as
the cause of all the sins which the deceased had
committed, and then thrown into the river ; and
Porphyry, confirming the statement of Plutarch,
gives the formula which the embalmers used when
exposing the intestines before the sun, according to
which the deceased begged the sun and the other
gods who grant life to man to allot to him an abode
with the immortal gods, and confessed that he had
worshipped the gods of his country with reverence
and fear from his youth up, and that he had neither

killed nor injured any man. We now know, however,
that after the intestines were taken out of the body
they were washed in palm wine, anointed with
unguents and sprinkled with spices and gums, and
placed in four stone or wooden jars, upon which the
covers were firmly fastened. These four jars are
usually called *Canopic*, and this name has been given
to them because the early Egyptologists compared
them with the jar with small feet, thin neck, swollen
body and round back, under which form it is said
that Canopus, the pilot of Menelaus, who was buried
at Canopus, was worshipped in that city. These jars
were dedicated to four genii of the underworld, who
were under the protection of four deities, and who
represent the four cardinal points; these genii are
called either "children of Osiris," or "children of
Horus." The four genii were called :—

1. 𓅃𓏏𓆓 Mesthá.

2. 𓎛𓊪𓆓 Hāpi.

3. ✶𓂧𓆓 Ṭuamāutef.

4. 𓊪𓈖𓈗𓈖𓆓 Qebḥsennuf.

The first jar had the head of a man, and held the
stomach; the second had the head of an ape, and

held the smaller intestines ; the third had the head
of a jackal, and held the heart ; and the fourth had
the head of a hawk, and held the liver. These jars
were under the protection of Isis, Nephthys, Neith,
and Serqet, and represented the south, north, east,
and west respectively. The greatest care was taken
to preserve the intestines, for the loss of them, or
even of one of them, would deprive the deceased of
life in the world to come.

After the body from which the intestines were
removed had been filled with gums, spices, etc., the
cutting in the side was sewn up, and an amulet of the
utchat 𓂀, or eye of Horus, made of metal, stone,
or porcelain, was laid upon it, and a ring, in the
bezel of which a scarab was inserted, was placed upon
one of the fingers. On the breast of the body,
immediately over the heart, or near the neck, a green
jasper, or green basalt scarab was fixed, either by
bandages or by a torque and chain. This scarab was
set in a frame of gold, and across the back, and down
the back between the wings, were bands of gold.

The scarab, or beetle, is the emblem of the god
Kheperà, who typifies the last moment of night
which immediately precedes the first moment of
the new day, in other words he typifies the state of
matter which is immediately about to come to life,

or to develop itself from one state of existence into
another. The god Kheperâ, 🪲 ⳾ , created himself, and everything that exists in earth, air and sky
from emanations of his own body. He rolled the
egg of the Sun across the sky day by day, and the
custom which the beetle (*Ateuchus Aegyptiorum*)
has of rolling its eggs made up into a ball along
the ground, no doubt suggested this insect as a
pictorial representation of the god. Moreover, this
class of beetles was thought to consist entirely of
males, and this was a further ground for comparing it
with the god Kheperâ.

   The green basalt scarab intended for the breast of
a mummy is inscribed with the 30th chapter of the
Book of the Dead, a composition which is said by
its rubric to be as old as the time of Mycerinus, a
king of the IVth dynasty, about B.C. 3633. This
chapter is called, "Chapter of not allowing the heart
of a man to be repulsed in the underworld," and has
reference to the judgment of a man before Osiris, the
king and judge of the dead, when his heart was
weighed in a balance. Osiris presided over the scene,
and the four children of Horus who protected the
intestines of the deceased, stood before him ; and all
the great gods were present at the trial. The heart
of the man ♡, was placed in one pan of the scales,

and the feather 𝄃, emblematic of right and truth, in the other; a cynocephalous ape 𓃭, sat upon the support of the beam to watch the indicator on behalf of Thoth, the scribe of the gods, and to declare to him whether the beam was exactly straight or not; Thoth himself stood near to register the result for the gods, and Anubis, the god of the dead, also carefully watched the indicator of the balance in order to dispute the result stated if necessary. Behind these gods stood a beast, part crocodile, part lion, part hippopotamus, called Amemit, or "Eater of the dead," *i.e.*, eater of the damned. On the other side of the scales were present the soul of the deceased, his Shai or "luck," an object connected with his birth, and the two goddesses Renenet and Meskhenet, who presided over his birth and childhood and education. When the heart of the deceased exactly counterbalanced the feather of right and truth, Thoth declared to the gods that the weighing was satisfactory, the gods pronounced the deceased victorious, and he was led into the presence of the god by Horus, son of Osiris, and was free to go wherever he pleased in the underworld. Meat and drink were to be given to him daily, an everlasting estate was to be allotted to him in the Sekhet-Aanre or Elysian Fields, together with the necessary corn and barley for sowing it, and he was to be at liberty to come into the presence of the great god Osiris whenever he wished to do so.

The inscription upon the green basalt scarab is an address by the deceased to his heart, and reads :—

"O my heart, my mother! O my heart, my mother!
O my heart of my existence! May there be no
obstacle raised against me in (*or* by) the evidence.
May there be no repulse to me by the children of Horus.*
Mayest thou not be separated from me in the presence
of the Guardian of the Scale. Thou art my double in
my body, the god Khnemu who maketh my limbs sound
    and healthy.
Mayest thou come forth to the felicity to which we
go thither. May the Shenit who make men to be established not overthrow our name. May
the god Setem cause us double joy of heart when
deeds and words are tried in the balance. May
no falsehood be uttered against me near the god in
the presence of the great god, the lord of the underworld. How great art thou rising up in triumph!"

When the amulet *utchat* , the ring, and the large green scarab had been placed upon the body, pieces of obsidian were laid in the sockets of the eyes, the nostrils were plugged with pledgets of linen, and the bandaging of the body began. Each bandage had a special name, and upon each was drawn in ink

---

* Or the deities who attend upon the great gods.

a figure of the god who was believed to take under his protection that part of the body around which it was to be twined, and certain words invoking his aid were written by his side. While the bandaging was going on, one of the embalmers recited formulæ containing addresses to the gods who presided over the different limbs of the body. The bandages were made of linen, and varied in width from three to ten inches; one edge of each was gummed. They were dipped in water and then turned deftly around the fingers and toes, and the gummed edges caused them to adhere to each other. The hands and arms and feet and legs were next treated, and when pads of linen had been laid above the feet to prevent the breaking of the mummy when made to stand upon its feet, and upon other parts of the body, the head and face, the back and shoulders, and the abdomen (upon which the arms and hands had been made to lie) and legs, were bound round with bandages made of many folds of linen, which were kept in their places by narrow strips of linen wound round the body at intervals of six or eight inches. When the body had been bound up in all the horizontal and perpendicular bandages prescribed by the embalmers' directions, it was sewn up in a piece of thick coarse linen over which a pinkish-brown fine linen covering was tied, and the bandaging was complete. Sometimes passages and whole chapters from the Book of the Dead were inscribed upon the bandages, and often amulets were laid between them. The principal amulets were the red jasper buckle ⚭, which typified the blood of the goddess Isis, and which was laid upon the neck; the *tet* ⚱, emblem of the god Osiris; the vulture ⚬, an emblem of the protection of Isis; the collar ⚮, which was laid on the neck of the deceased; the *uatch* sceptre ⚑, emblem of a renewed and vigorous life; the pillow ⚏ ⚒, to "lift up" the head of the mummy; the heart ♡, emblem of the conscience; the *crux ansata* ☥, emblem of life; the two *utchats*, one facing to the right ⚭, and the other to the left ⚮, but both symbolizing "good health"; the *nefer* ⚶, emblem of "good luck"; the *shen* ☉, emblem of the sun's course in the sky; the rising sun in the horizon ⚭, the *menât* ⚭, symbol of joy and health; the *neha* ⚭, emblematic of "protection"; the frog ⚭, meaning "myriads," and "renewed life"; the serpent's head, emblematic of the opening of the mouth and eyes of the deceased in the underworld; and the two fingers.

In the earliest period of the history of Egypt the method of embalming seems to have been less elaborate, and the bandages are neither so numerous, nor are they so well or so carefully put on the body. The greatest perfection in embalming was reached at Thebes about B.C. 1700. The mummies of this period are beautifully made, and all the limbs are pliant and may be handled without breaking. About B.C. 1000 it became the fashion to put the mummy into a brightly painted cartonnage case, which was fastened up the back by sewing. About B.C. 350, the Egyptians began to put the head of the mummy into a gilded mask, and to lay a hollow-work carton- nage pectoral upon the breast. The use of bitumen in the process of embalming became more frequent and extensive, and the decorations consisted of poorly written texts badly copied, and distorted figures of the gods and mythological scenes. In the Græco- Roman period the whole mummy was sometimes covered with a thin layer of plaster upon which imitations of ancient Egyptian mythological scenes were painted in bright colours or gold ; the inscrip- tions are sometimes written in Greek. In the early centuries of this era the outer coverings of mummies of wealthy people were made of silk ; examples of these are found chiefly at Akhmîm (Panopolis).

The mummy of a high priestly official, or gentleman, at Thebes in the XVIIIth dynasty was laid in a

sycamore wood coffin made in the form of a mummy,
i.e., the god Osiris.   The bottom and each side
were made of single pieces of wood pegged together,
and the rounded head-piece was cut out of a solid
block of wood.   A face carved out of very hard wood
and a pair of hands were pegged on to the cover, and
a solid foot-piece was also firmly fastened to it.   In
the face obsidian eyes and bronze eye-lids were
sometimes inlaid.   The inside and outside of the
coffin were covered with a thin layer of plaster, upon
which the artist and scribe painted in bright colours
mythological scenes, figures of the gods, addresses to
the deceased by the gods, and their answers, and
extracts from chapters, or whole chapters of the
Book of the Dead.   The outside of the cover was
ornamented in a similar manner, but the inside was
usually left plain, and in such cases a flat, thin, wooden
covering, made the exact shape of the mummy, and
having a carved face and painted with inscriptions
and mythological scenes, was laid immediately upon
the mummy.   The cover was fastened to the coffin
by wooden dowels, through which pegs were driven,
and the space between the coffin and the cover
was filled up with liquid plaster.   The mummy
with its coffin was then placed in a large, heavy,
wooden coffin, made in the same shape, and

painted much in the same way, and was ready for burial.

The scenes painted upon Egyptian papyri and tombs illustrate with great detail the funeral procession, a brief description of which is as follows :—The coffin containing the mummy was placed in a boat built on a sledge, and, escorted by priests, mourners, wailing women, and attendants carrying funereal furniture, offerings, etc., was drawn to the river bank by oxen. Here the procession embarked, and in a short time arrived at the western bank, in the mountains of which the Egyptians usually built their cemeteries. Then the procession was re-formed and began to make its way to the mountains opposite Thebes. The mummy upon its bier was drawn along by oxen guided by drivers, and in front of it walked the *sem* priest wearing his characteristic dress the panther's skin, burning incense and pouring out libations as he went. Behind followed other priestly officials, and near them came attendants bearing a couch, a chair, vases of unguents, flowers, offerings of meat and drink, sepulchral boxes, and other objects, the number and variety of which depended upon the wealth and position of the deceased. In the company was a band of women who uttered cries of grief, and struck their faces and breasts with their hands.

When the procession had arrived at the tomb, the
mummy or a statue of the deceased was placed in an
upright position before the door in order that the
relatives might take their final farewell of him, and
the ceremony of "opening the mouth" be performed.
Tables loaded with offerings of cakes, beer, fruit,
flowers, *etc.*, were laid out before him, and a bull was
slaughtered; an attendant called the "butcher" then
cut off one of its haunches, and brought it and held it
to the nose of the statue. The *sem* priest next took
four instruments, and with each in its turn touched
its mouth and eyes, while the *kher-ḥeb* priest, having
his hair whitened, read the portions of the funereal
ritual appropriate to each act from a roll of papyrus.
The eyes and the mouth of the deceased had been
closed by the process of embalming, and unless the
use of these members was restored to him he could
neither see nor speak in the netherworld. The *sem*
priest by touching the mouth and the eyes of the
statue with the iron instruments made in the shape
of ⌐, did for the deceased what certain of the
gods did for the dead god Osiris; he thereby regained
the use of his intelligence, and was able to talk with
the gods. After the ceremony of "opening the
mouth" had been performed, the lips of the statue
were anointed with oil, a number of boxes of purifi-

cation and an ostrich feather were offered to it,
and it was draped in the *nemes* cloth ⌡; the *kher-ḥeb*
read meanwhile the proper passages from the liturgical
roll. After the slaughter of another bull and the pre-
sentation of a number of offerings the funereal ceremony was complete.

The form of the Egyptian tomb varied at different
periods. Among the poorest classes it was customary to bury the bodies of the dead in graves dug
in the sand, or in shallow holes made in soft limestone, or in caves, where hundreds of bodies were
laid together. In the early dynasties the Egyptians
built their tombs at Ṣaḳḳârah in the form of heavy
rectangular buildings, the walls of which slanted in-
wards towards their common centre; these structures
vary in size from 170 ft. × 90 feet × 30 ft. to
26 ft. × 20 ft. × 13 ft., and are built of brick and
stone. The name commonly given to a tomb of this
description is *maṣṭaba*, because it resembles the
"bench" upon which Orientals recline and sleep.
The interior of the maṣṭaba tomb consists of three
parts, the upper chamber, the *serdâb*, and the pit.
In the upper chamber, opposite the door, which is
on the east side, is a stele, at the foot of which is
usually a stone altar with offerings upon it. The
serdâb is a hollow, built in the thickness of the wall,

in which a stone statue was placed; sometimes this
hollow is covered up with flat stones, but sometimes
a narrow passage a few inches wide leads from it to
the upper chamber, and it is thought that it was made
intentionally to allow the smoke of the incense to
penetrate to the statue within the hollow in the
masonry. The pit was a perpendicular shaft which
led from the upper chamber to the sarcophagus
chamber, which was hewn out exactly beneath it.
This chamber was approached through a small passage just sufficiently large to allow the sarcophagus to
pass along it. When the mummied body had been
laid in the sarcophagus, with perhaps a pillow 🜨, and
a few vases, the cover was fastened on by cement, the
passage leading to the sarcophagus chamber was
walled up at the end which opened into the pit, and
the pit was filled up with stones and sand. The
walls of maṣṭabas are frequently ornamented with
scenes which had taken place in the life of the
deceased, and with representations of the making of
funereal offerings, which are explained by short hieroglyphic inscriptions.

Other forms of tombs in use among the Egyptians
during the earlier dynasties were the Pyramids, which
were reckoned among the wonders of the world.
The largest or Great Pyramid of Gîzeh was built

by Cheops, the second king of the IVth dynasty, about B.C. 3733; the Second Pyramid of Gizeh was built by Chephren, the third king of the IVth dynasty, about B.C. 3666; and the Third Pyramid of Gizeh was built by Mycerinus, the fourth king of the IVth dynasty, about B.C. 3633. The pyramids at Ṣaḳḳârah, Abuṣîr, Dahshûr and other places usually formed the tombs of kings and of members of the royal families of Egypt.

The tombs of Upper Egypt during the XIIth and following dynasties were built in modified forms of the maṣṭaba, and always contained the equivalents of the upper chamber, *serdâb*, and pit, whatever might be the order of their arrangement. They were usually hewn out of the mountains, but whenever a stony plain was near at hand, as in the case of Abydos, the Egyptians dug tombs therein. The finest examples of tombs hewn out of the solid rock are found at Thebes, and of these the most remarkable are those of the kings of the Middle Empire. They consist of long slanting corridors, terminating in halls and chambers, the walls and ceilings of which are ornamented with inscriptions, mythological scenes, figures of the gods, etc., all painted with admirable taste in bright colours. Of tombs of high officials those of Rekh-mâ-Râ, Nekht, and Peṭā-Âmen-âpt may be taken as excellent examples.

Excavations and discoveries in Egypt have shown that tombs were used over and over again, and that it is possible to find pottery and other objects, which were made at a period after B.C. 550, in a tomb, the walls of which are covered with inscriptions and scenes which prove that it was made for an ancient Egyptian official who lived during the rule of the VIth dynasty, some 3000 years before. It seems to have been the custom not to erase the inscriptions, etc., provided for the first occupant of a tomb, but there is no doubt that his body was removed to another place, and so made way for a successor. The circumstances under which such removals were made are not known, but it is probable that the priests by right took possession of tombs upon the extinction of the family to which the dead who were buried in them belonged, or by purchase when the surviving relatives could not afford to pay for the customary funereal offerings, which it was their duty to present at certain seasons of the year. Another danger which menaced the peace of the occupant of the tomb arose from thieves, who if they did nothing worse, forced open the coffin and carried off all objects made of gold or precious stones, and such

portions of the funereal paraphernalia as could be sold
for other burials. In the XXth dynasty the govern-
ment of Egypt was obliged to prosecute a number of
men who devoted their lives to breaking into the
tombs of the kings at Thebes and robbing them, and
there seems little doubt that the removal of the
bodies of kings and members of royal families to
Dêr el-baḥari arose from the existence of an organized
party of malcontents, whose wish was to loot the
splendid tombs where the kings of old slept their
last sleep. Tombs which were found with com-
parative ease were wrecked and robbed by invaders
of Egypt, the Persians and others, but it is probable
that the greatest harm was done to many of them by
the fanatical Egyptian Christian ascetics who took up
their abode in them. In the mythological scenes
and figures of gods which were painted on the walls
they saw heathen abominations and devils; and in
the statues of the dead which loving friends had
placed in the tombs they saw idols which their
zeal prompted them to destroy utterly. Sometimes
these recluses lived in tombs in which hundreds of
mummies were piled up, either with or without
coffins, and there are legends extant from which
we learn that certain very holy men held con-
versations with mummies, and that they promised

to pray to Christ to release them from the Gehenna
of fire.

On entering an Egyptian tomb one of the first
objects visible was a slab of stone, usually rounded
at the top, upon which was inscribed a figure of the
deceased adoring a god or gods, and below was an
inscription in hieroglyphics setting forth his rank and
position, and containing prayers to the gods Osiris
and Anubis that they would grant to him sepulchral
offerings of food, drink and clothing. Here is a
specimen of a prayer from a stele. "May Àmen-Rā,
lord of the thrones of the North and South, Ptah-
Seker-Osiris, Un-nefer, lord of the passages of the
tomb, grant a royal oblation. May they grant sepulchral meals, and oxen and ducks, and linen bandages,
thousands of all good and pure things, thousands of
all sweet and choice things, the gifts of heaven and
the products of the earth which the Nile bringeth
forth from his storehouses. May they grant the
breathing of the sweet breezes of the north wind, the
eating of bread, the gathering of flowers, and the
receiving of food in felicity from the produce of the
Elysian Fields. May I walk upon the everlasting
road of the beautiful dead, the genii, and the noble
ones, making whatsoever transformations I please
among the followers of Un-nefer, and going in and

coming forth from the underworld. May my soul
be not turned back when it ariseth to come forth,
may it come forth as a living soul, may it drink water
drawn from the depths of the river, may it receive
the cakes of the lord of eternity, may it come into
the presence of the god every day. May my soul
light upon the branches of the trees which I have
planted, may I refresh my face beneath my sycamores,
and may I have my mouth wherewith I may speak
like the followers of Horus." Sepulchral inscriptions are often of the highest importance, for they
record historical facts which would otherwise be
unknown.

Another important object in the tomb was the
ushabti figure, which was placed either in a special
box or upon the floor, and was intended to perform
for the deceased whatever agricultural work he might
be called upon to carry out in the underworld. The
ushabti figure is made of granite, diorite, limestone,
painted terra-cotta, *faïence* glazed blue, green, brown
or white, wood and other substances. It is made in
the form of a mummy with its hands folded upon
its breast; in one hand it holds a mattock, or hoe,
and in the other the cords of a basket, which it
carries over one shoulder. The inscriptions are
either cut or traced upon it in ink in the hieroglyphic

or hieratic characters: the text is that of the VIth
chapter of the Book of the Dead.

In or with the mummy in its coffin, or in a
separate place in the tomb, was placed a roll of
papyrus inscribed in the hieroglyphic or hieratic
characters, with a number of chapters selected from
the great collection of religious texts to which the
name of "Book of the Dead" has been given. In
Egyptian its name is 𓄿𓃀𓊖 *per em
hru* "[The Book of] coming forth by day," and it is
said to be the work of the god Thoth. This book
contains hymns to the gods, formulæ which will
enable him to overcome the beings who would attempt
to impede his progress in the underworld, prayers to
the great gods in that region, and texts to be inscribed
upon amulets, *ushabtiu* figures, *etc.* Extracts from
it were written upon bandages, coffins, sarcophagi,
the walls of the tomb, and other objects, and these
gave the persons for whom they were written power
to overcome all foes and obstacles.

COFFIN OF ÁN-HERU.   XITH DYNASTY. ABOUT B.C. 2500.

FROM KÛRNA.

No. 1.

THE COFFIN OF ÁN-ḤERU.*

1. Rectangular wooden ΄coffin of Án-ḥeru, a high priestly official, who flourished at Thebes about B.C. 2600. The cover and coffin are formed of pieces of wood about three inches thick, which are joined together by pegs, and save for a few marks of the tools which were employed to force open the coffin in modern times, are in a perfect state of preservation. The inscriptions on the outside are in hieroglyphics painted green, and the edges of cover, sides, and ends are decorated with a black and white border. The inside of the cover is quite plain, but that of the coffin is covered with lines of inscriptions in hieroglyphics which contain prayers for funeral offerings ; pictures of objects which form funeral offerings, and articles of personal apparel; and a number of chapters of a very ancient version of the Book of the Dead, written in hieratic. The titles of the chapters are in red. Along the bottom of the

---

* See Plate I.

coffin, painted in blue, flows the celestial Nile ⬚⬚⬚⬚⬚⬚. At the bottom of the right side of the coffin, both inside and outside, are the two *utchats* ⬚⬚. On the cover is a perpendicular line of hieroglyphics which reads :—

suten ṭā	ḥetep	Ánpu	neb	Sepa

May give a royal offering   Anubis, lord of   Sepa,

χent	neter	ḥet	ḥer-áb	Re - sta

dwelling in   the divine house   within   Re - sta.

t'a - f	pet	sam - neſ

May he sail forth   over heaven,   may he unite with

ta	ār - f	en	neter āa	neb

the earth,   may he ascend   to the   great god,   the lord

---

* *I.e.*, the 18th nome of Upper Egypt.

Plate I. A

LEFT SIDE.

RIGHT SIDE.

HEAD.   FOOT.

Length 7 ft. 3 in., width 1 ft. 11 in., depth 1 ft. 11 in.

pet   em   áma𝛘   Án-ḥeru   maá𝛘eru.

of heaven, with veneration, Án-Ḥeru, triumphant.

From Thebes.   6 ft. 3 in. × 1 ft. 10 in. × 1 ft. 6 in.
The inscriptions which decorate the outside of the
coffin contain prayers to Osiris, Isis, Nephthys, and
Anubis for sepulchral offerings, and statements that
the deceased is held in veneration by Seb, Nut, Shu,
" the great god of heaven," and by the four children
of Horus. The hieroglyphics are arranged as on
Plate Iᴀ.

No. 2.

COFFIN OF A PRIEST OF ÀMEN.*

THE COVER.

2. Coffin and cover of an unnamed priest of Àmen-Rā, painted with mythological scenes and explanatory inscriptions, which belong to a period between B.C. 1000 and B.C. 700.

The cover, like the coffin, is ornamented with mythological scenes and inscriptions, usually painted in red, light and dark green upon a yellow ground. The pupils of the eyes and the whiskers are black, the nose is perforated, and the ears are well carved ; the beard is wanting. A heavy head-dress falls on each side of the face, and under the ends are solid wooden hands which are pegged on to the breast ; the pectoral is elaborately painted to imitate rows of

---

* See Plate II.

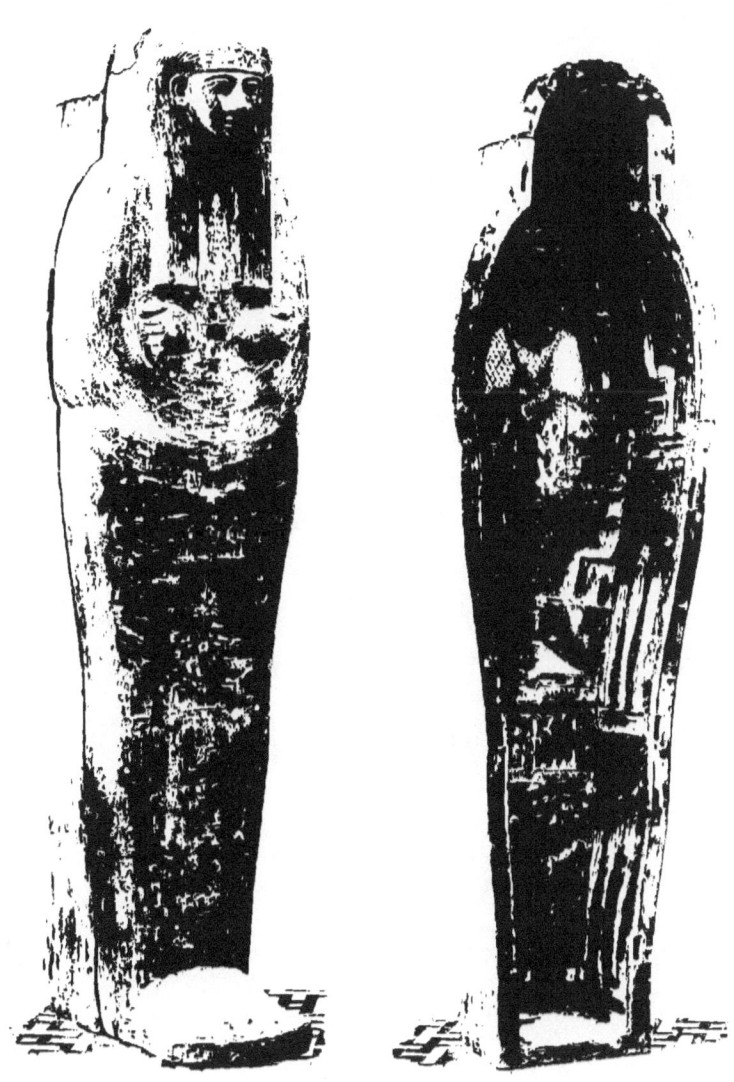

COFFIN OF AN UNNAMED PRIEST OF ÅMEN-RA, WITH MYTHOLOGICAL
SCENES AND EXPLANATORY INSCRIPTIONS.

FROM DÊR EL-BAHARI.   BETWEEN B.C 1000 AND 700.

precious stones or coloured glazed *faïence* beads, a
row of flowers being outermost. Beneath the pectoral
are :—winged disk with uræi ; deities seated on each
side of the beetle, wearing triple crown, with Isis and
Nephthys winged ; the goddess Nut with outstretched
wings, above which are winged uræi ; seated deities
on each side of the beetle wearing the triple crown ;
the god of millions of years holding palm branches ;
the deceased making offerings to Anubis ; and the
spaces between these scenes are filled up with pictures
in which the deceased and his soul are seen in
converse with various deities, and making offerings
unto them.   Immediately beneath are the following
scenes and inscriptions :—

1. Isis, winged, standing before Osiris, who is
seated on a throne.

2. Osiris and Anubis seated one on each side of 🪲.

3. Isis and Nephthys, in the form of winged uræi,
one on each side of the standard emblematic of
Osiris.

4. Two hawk-headed gods seated one on each side
of ▯ .

5. Two apes adoring the sun on the horizon ☉.

6. [hieroglyphs]

[hieroglyphs]

7. [hieroglyphs]

[hieroglyphs]

8, 9. [hieroglyphs]

[hieroglyphs]

[hieroglyphs]

[hieroglyphs]

[hieroglyphs] [Space left blank for name.]

10, 11. The deceased adoring Osiris.

12, 13. The deceased adoring Tmu.

14, 15. A hawk-headed deity with table of offerings.

16, 17. Anubis seated on a throne, and mythological emblems.

The inscriptions in paragraphs 6 and 7 contain

prayers to Rā, Isis, and Nephthys that sepulchral
offerings may be made to the deceased.

On the edges of the cover are two lines of
hieroglyphics which read :—

The above inscriptions are prayers that Râ and Osiris will give to the deceased abundant sepulchral offerings, and they contain some interesting titles of these gods.

THE COFFIN—OUTSIDE.

Beautifully painted coffin of a member of the confraternity of Ámen-Râ, king of the gods, at Thebes, made probably between B.C. 1000 and B.C. 700, in imitation of the coffins in which members of the order in the XVIIIth dynasty were buried. Though exceedingly bright the colours are very harmonious, and the accuracy of the drawing and the excellence of the execution make this beautiful object one of the most striking of its class. The inside of the cover, and both inside and outside of the foot are unpainted. At the head is painted in outline a deity wearing a disk rising out of the top of the buckle ; on each side is a *tet*, surmounted by the crown . The upper edge of the coffin is ornamented by a series

of uræi ⟨hieroglyphs⟩. On the right side, beneath this
line, is an inscription, partly defaced, which reads :

" [May all the gods] dwelling in Hermonthis, and
" Ptaḥ-Seker, the lord of the hidden place, and Isis
" the great lady, the divine mother, the daughter of
" Rā, the mistress of Ámentet, grant thee a following
" of the lords of the underworld, triumphant, as unto
" the followers of Horus. May the underworld and
" the pylons thereof be opened to thee, mayest thou
" go in among the divine company like the shining
" ones who live in Ṭattu, and may they grant thee

" offerings of *tchefa* food, oxen, ducks, incense, linen
" bandages, wax, honey, and every [good] thing of
" heaven and of earth. And may Osiris, the lord of
" eternity, who liveth among those of the east and
" those of the west, grant to the Osiris the libationer
" and reader of the place of truth offerings and
" funeral meals."

The scenes below this line are as follows :—

1. The deceased adoring Osiris.

2. Isis, winged, and a god seated in a shrine ;
the inscription reads :   , "May Râ-Harmachis and Tmu, lord of the
" lands of Heliopolis, grant a royal offering."

3. Nephthys, winged, and a god ; the inscription
reads :   .

4. The deceased, making offerings to a seated
jackal-headed god wearing ; a jackal-headed god
and the goddess of the west making offerings to a
seated god. The inscriptions read : 1. 2.

---

* " Honourable before Ptaḥ-Seker, the lord of the hidden
place " (or underworld).

5. A 𓊽 surmounted by 𓏭, Osiris seated with a table of offerings before him, and a hawk-headed god. The inscriptions read: 1. [hieroglyphs] [hieroglyphs] *. 2. [hieroglyphs] [hieroglyphs] †. 3. [hieroglyphs] ‡.

6. The deceased (?) and a deity standing by a table of offerings placed before a seated god. The inscriptions read: 1. [hieroglyphs] §. 2. [hieroglyphs] ‖.

7. The funeral mountain [hieroglyph], from which comes forth the cow of Hathor, with horns, disk and plumes

---

* "Honourable before Osiris, the lord of eternity, the dweller "in the underworld."

† "Saith Rā-Ḥeru-χuti, 'South and north come to thee: "may the lord of heaven and earth grant thee offerings of "*tchefa* food and oxen.'"

‡ "Honourable before Rā-Harmachis-Tmu, the lord of the "Temple."

§ "Honourable before Ptaḥ-Seker, the lord of the hidden "place."

‖ "Saith Osiris, dweller among those who are in Amentet."

upon her head. By the side of a table of offerings stands the goddess Maāt, ⬭, holding a sistrum; above are four souls carrying ☥. The inscriptions read: 1. 𓃀𓏛𓏤𓏭𓏛𓏤𓏛𓏛*

and 2. 𓃀𓏛𓏤𓏭𓏛𓏤𓏛 [𓈖] 𓏤 [✷],†

written twice.

On the left side, beneath the row of uræi, is an inscription which reads:—

𓃀𓏛𓏭𓃒𓏛𓈖𓏭𓏤𓏛𓏤𓏛𓏛𓏤𓏛𓏛
⬭𓏛☥𓏛𓏤𓏛𓏤𓏛𓏤𓏤𓈖𓏛𓏛𓏤𓏛
𓏛𓏤𓏛𓏛𓏤𓏛☥𓏤𓏛𓏛𓏤𓏛𓏤𓏛𓏛
𓏛𓏤𓏛𓏛𓏤𓏛𓏛𓏛𓏏𓏏𓏏𓏛𓏛𓏤𓏛𓏛
𓏛𓏤𓏛𓏛𓏤𓏛𓏛𓏤𓏛𓏛𓏏𓏏𓏏𓏛
𓏛𓏤𓏛𓏛𓏤𓏛𓏛𓏤𓏛𓏛𓏤𓏛𓏛𓏤𓏛

---

* " May Ptaḥ-Seker, the lord of Ta-tcheser, grant " . . . . .

† " Honoured by Osiris, the lord of eternity, the dweller in " the underworld."

"May Rā-Harmachis-Tmu, dweller in Hermonthis,
"and Ptaḥ-Seker, the lord of the hidden place, dweller
"in the Great House, and Anubis, who dwelleth in
"the divine hall, the chief reader of the hidden place,
"the great god in the town of embalmment, and
"Nephthys the divine sister, and Isis, the great lady,
"the divine mother, the mistress of Âmentet, grant
"[me] sepulchral offerings of *tchefa* food, oxen, ducks,
"incense and wax. May they grant that [my] soul
"may go in and come out to see the disk and to
"follow Seker in his daily festivals round about
"Memphis, and the power of going in and of walking
"about in the presence of the lords of the underworld,
"and may Osiris the lord of eternity, the dweller in
"Âmentet, weave for me a garland of flowers to put
"on my neck on the day of the festival."

The scenes below this line are as follows :—

1. Osiris seated on a throne, Isis, Horus on a
standard, and the deceased (?).

2. Isis, winged, and a god seated in a shrine.

3. Nephthys, winged, and a god seated in a shrine.

4. The deceased making offerings to Anubis, and

the goddess of the West making offerings to a seated god (the deceased?).

5. A relative (?) of the deceased making offerings to the deceased and his wife.

6. The deceased holding the sceptre ⚲ and addressing Rā-Harmachis in the presence of Anubis.

7. A dog-headed ape seated on a throne, before which stand three goddesses wearing disks; the first holds ⋀ , the second ⌐, and the third ⌐ .

The perpendicular inscriptions begin with ⌐ ⌐ and ⌐ ⌐⌐ ⌐⌐⌐ , followed in each case by the name of the god or goddess depicted in the scenes to which they refer.

THE COFFIN—INSIDE.

On the bottom of the coffin are the following scenes :—

1. The heavens ⊏⊐, winged disk, and beetle wearing triple crown; on each side is the legend ⊏⊐ ⌐ ⌐ ⊏⊐, "Beḥuṭet, lord of heaven."

2. Full length figure of a king wearing triple crown and holding flail ⋀ and crook ⌐, and standing on ⌐.

3. On the right, the deceased, Anubis, the deceased (?) seated holding ⚲, dog-headed ape and the legend ⌐ ⌐ ⌐ ⌐ ⌐ ⌐ ⌐ ⌐ ⌐ ⌐ ⌐⌐.

On the left, uræus with disk, vulture, winged uræus, hawk-headed deity (Osiris) seated, and ⟨glyph⟩, ⟨glyph⟩, etc.

4. A heaven of stars, ⟨glyphs⟩, a row of uræi with disks.

5. A standard rising from ⟨glyph⟩ with collar and *menât ;* on one side is Isis and on the other Nephthys.

At the head of the coffin is Horus-beḥuṭet with outstretched wings; on each side is the legend ⟨glyphs⟩.

Right side :—1. Isis the divine mother offering a collar and a *menât* to Rā; the legend reads ⟨glyphs⟩.

2. Row of uræi with disks and three gods, human-headed, hawk-headed and snake-headed respectively; above is the legend ⟨glyphs⟩.

3. A heaven of stars and three gods, human-headed, jackal-headed and dog-headed respectively; above is the legend ⟨glyphs⟩.

Left side :—1. Scene similar to right side No. 1.

2. Three gods with the legend ⟨glyphs⟩.

3. Scene similar to right side No. 3.   From Dêr-el-baḥari, Thebes.   Length 6 ft. 2¼ in.

No. 3.

THE MUMMY AND COFFIN
OF NES-ÀMSU.

Wooden coffin, in the form of a mummy standing upon a pedestal, made for Nes-Àmsu, a priest and prophet of the god Khonsu at Apu,* about B.C. 300.

This fine example of coffin manufacture at Panopolis is decorated with a number of scenes and inscriptions, the greater number of which are painted in red, light and dark green, white, blue and black upon a light yellow ground. The designs are characterized by great freedom and boldness, and the accurate drawing of many of them calls to mind the finest Theban work of the XVIIIth or XIXth dynasty. The hieroglyphics have, at times, almost a cursive

---

* The Panopolis of the Greeks, and Akhmim of the Arabs. This city, which is situated about 320 miles south of Cairo in Upper Egypt, was celebrated for its linen manufacture, and for the skill of its inhabitants in cutting and polishing precious stones.

form, and the greater number of them are traced in
outline.   The head-dress is painted a dark green, the
face and ears are gilded, and the eyelids and eyebrows
are inlaid with that kind of blue glass which is characteristic of the period subsequent to the XXVIth
dynasty.   Over the forehead is painted a beetle, the
wings of which are extended, and they bend down
round the sides of the face ; above the beetle is *shen* Ω,
the emblem of the circuit of the sun, or eternity.   The
beard was broken by the Arabs, but it has now been
repaired.   The breast of the mummy is ornamented
with a pectoral painted to imitate rows of lotus and
other flowers, and pointed pendants, etc., hanging
from a bar which is intended to represent inlaid
work ; from each end of this bar rises a head of the
hawk of Horus surmounted by a disk painted red
and a uræus.

The space to the right and left of the pectoral and
immediately beneath it is filled with the following :—

1. A kneeling figure of Nut with outstretched wings
and arms, wearing a disk upon her head ; in each
hand she holds an ostrich feather $\int$.

2. The *utchat* facing to the left, and the *utchat*
facing to the right (these are typical of the two
eyes of the Sun, for the one is the emblem of the Sun

and the other of the Moon); the ram of Mendes
, wearing horns, disk and plumes , standing
upon a support ; and the emblems of the East
and the West, and .

Arranged in perpendicular lines over the left
breast of the coffin is an inscription which informs
us that the deceased Nes-Ámsu, , held
the dignity of seutcheb, and also that he
was the second priest of the god Ámsu. From the
other texts on the coffin we learn that he was also a
priest of Khonsu. He was the son of Pa-senetchem-áb,
the grandson of Tche-ḥrā, and the great-grandson of
Ara; all these gentlemen had held the same rank and
had performed the same duties in the temple of Ámsu.
His mother's name was Ta-ta-khensu-i, and she was a
sistrum-bearer in the temple of Ámsu. The inscription is an address to the goddess Mer-sekhet, a
form of Hathor (?), and reads: "Hail [to thee], O
mighty one in heaven, daughter of Rā, turner back of
the Fiend, mistress of wrath, [lady of] Manu, regent (?)
in the Mountain of the Underworld, lady (?) of life,
Mer-Sekhet, mistress of sceptres and sistra, lady of
the *menát*,* president of the Great Double House,

---

* The *menát* symbolized "joy," "health," "pleasure."

who maketh protection for her brother with breath
and food (?), and who maketh his body to become
young again every thirtieth day, make thou protection
for Osiris, the *seutcheb*, the second priest of Ámsu,
Nes-Ámsu, triumphant, son of Pa-senetchem-áb (who
held a like office), and the lady, the sistrum-bearer
of Ámsu, Ta-khens-i, triumphant! May his limbs be
gathered together for him, may his body be again
knit together for him, and may he be victorious over
[his] enemies. Come thou, and grant that his soul
may be mighty in his body, do thou overthrow for
him all his enemies, overcome . . . . for him, let
them never rise up against him, let them never come
against him to attack him." The hieroglyphic text
reads :—

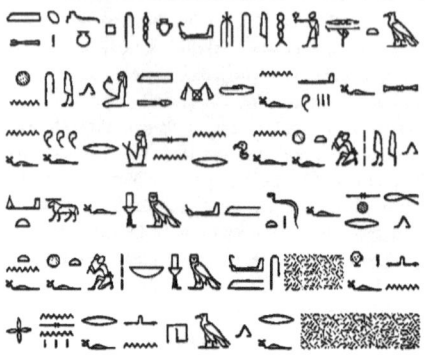

Arranged in perpendicular lines over the right breast of the coffin is an inscription which runs :—
"Behold Osiris, the *seutcheb*, the second prophet [of Ámsu], the prophet of Khonsu, Nes-Ámsu, triumphant, the son of the *seutcheb*, the second prophet of Ámsu, Pa-senetchem-âb-en-āśt, triumphant, the son of the sistrum-bearer of Ámsu, Ta-khens-i, triumphant!

"Stand thou up, Horus grant that thou mayest stand up. May the god Seb grant that he may see his father in thee, in thy name of 'Prince of the Temple.' May Horus grant to thee . . . . . all the gods, may he make thee to ascend to them, and may

they make brilliant thy face.   Horus hath given to
thee thy two eyes that thou mayest see with them.
Horus hath given to thee thy enemies beneath
thee, and he hath raised thee up there.   Through
him thou shalt never be cast down.   Come thou to
thy place [for] the gods have knit thy body together."

The hieroglyphic text reads :—

Immediately beneath the figure of Nut is a horizontal line of inscription which reads :—

án   Àusâr   se-ut'eb   neter ḥen   sen

Behold Osiris, the seutcheb, *the second prophet of*

Amsu   Nes-Âmsu   maāχeru   án - nek

Âmsu, Nes-Âmsu, triumphant! Hath brought to thee

áb - k   en   mut - k   erⱦāt - s   su

thy heart   thy mother, [and] she hath placed   it

ḥer   áuset - s   em   χat - k   maθ - θ

upon   its seat   in   thy body, { *and thou shalt become young.* }

ut'a - k   ḥert   em ḥetep   ṭeḳ - k   Rā
Thou sailest over heaven in peace.   Thou shalt see Rā

em   χut   ȧn   man   t'etta   ḥeḥ
in the horizon without [ceasing] daily for ever and ever.

The next division is occupied by a scene in which the deceased is shown lying upon a bier ⊟; above him hovers his soul in the form of a human-headed bird, having its wings extended and holding ○ *shen*, the emblem of the circuit of the sun in each claw. Beneath the bier stand the four jars which contain his mummied intestines (see above, p. 8). The inscription reads :—

ȧ   baiu   ȧ   ḥesq   enen   χaibit
Hail ye souls !   Hail   slaughterer   of   shadows !

ȧ   neteru   ȧpu   nebu   ṭepu   ānχ,   mā
Hail ye gods   those   all   princes of   life !   I pray

ån · ten   ba   en   Åusår   se - uteb
bring   ye   the soul   to   Osiris,   the seutcheb,

neter ḥen sen   Åmsu   Nes - Åmsu
the second prophet of Åmsu,   Nes - Amsu.

At the head of the bier kneels the goddess Nephthys, with her right hand raised to her face; the inscription referring to her reads :—

ån   Nebt-ḥet   t'eṭ - s   åh   nefer
Behold Nephthys [and] she saith,   "Boy beautiful,

---

* These lines are an extract from a section of the " Lamentations of Isis and Nephthys," the Berlin text (Papyrus No. 1425) of which reads :—

, *etc.*

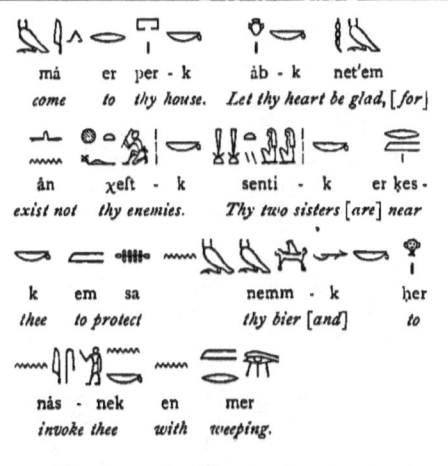

má	er	per - k	áb - k	net'em
come	*to*	*thy house.*	*Let thy heart be glad,* [*for*]

ân	χeſt - k	senti - k	er ḳes -
exist not	*thy enemies.*	*Thy two sisters* [*are*] *near*

k	em sa	nemm - k	her
thee	*to protect*	*thy bier* [*and*]	*to*

nâs - nek	en	mer
invoke thee	*with*	*weeping.*

Behind her stand " Ḥāpi, making protection for Osiris,"[*] and " Ṭuamāutef, making protection for Osiris, the *seutcheb* and second prophet of Ȧmsu, Nes-Ȧmsu, triumphant !"[†]

At the foot of the bier kneels the goddess Isis ,

with her left hand raised to her face ; the inscription
referring to her reads :—

ȧn	Auset	t'ȧ - s	mȧȧ	er
Here is	*Isis* [*and*]	*she saith,*	" *Come*	*to*

per - k	sep sen	Ȧnnu	mȧȧ	er	per - ˈk
thy house,	*twice,*	*Ȧni!*	*Come*	*to*	*thy house,*

ȧn	χefti - k	ȧḥi	nefer	mȧȧ
exist not	*thy enemies.*	*Boy*	*beautiful,*	*come,*

---

* These lines are also an extract from a section of the
" Lamentations of Isis and Nephthys," from a text of which
we are able to correct some mistakes.

† Read . Ȧni is a form of Rȧ.

‡ Read .   § is omitted.

maat - k   sent - k   àn   àbt - k   er - à
let see thee   thy sister,   depart thou not   from me.

à   ḥunnu   nefer   màà   er   per - k
Hail,   boy   beautiful,   come   to   thy house."

Behind Isis stand Àmseth, who says, "I am thy
son, Osiris,"† and "Qebḥsennuf, who maketh protection for Osiris, Nes-Àmsu, the *seutcheb* and second
prophet of Àmsu, triumphant."‡

Below this division is an inscription written in
horizontal lines down the centre of the cover, which
reads:—

I.

àn   Àusàr   seut'eb   neter ḥen sen
Here is Osiris, the seutcheb, the second prophet of

---

* Better

†

‡

I

Ámsu   neter ḥen   ⋋ensu   Nes-Ámsu   maāχeru
Ámsu, the prophet of Khonsu, Nes-Ámsu, triumphant,

sa   seut'eb   neter ḥen   sen   Ámsu
son of   the seutcheb,   the prophet   second of   Ámsu

Pa-senet'em-áb,   sa ennu   neter ḥen   Nes-Ámsu
Pa-senetchem-àb,   son of a like   prophet,   Nes-Ámsu

maāχeru   sa   ennu neter ḥen T'e-ḥrá   maāχeru
triumphant, son of a like prophet, Tche-ḥrà, triumphant,

sa neter ḥen ennu   Qem   sa neter ḥen ennu
son of a prophet the like,   Qem,   son of a prophet the like,

Ára   maāχeru   mes   áḥi
Ára,   triumphant, born of the sistrum-bearer of

Àmsu   Ta - ţā - χensu - i   maāχeru
Àmsu,   Taţā - Khonsu - i,   triumphant.

à   en   baiu   à   ḥesq   enen   χaibit
Hail   ye   souls!   Hail   slaughterer   of   shadows!

à   neteru   àpu   nebu   ţepu   ānχ
Hail   ye gods   those   all   princes   of life!

mā   àn -   ten   ba   en   Àusàr
I pray   bring   ye   the soul   of   Osiris,

seut'eb   neter ḥen   sen   Nes-Àmsu   maāχeru -
the seutcheb,   the priest second,   Nes-Àmsu,   in triumph

net   χnem - f   t'et   en net'em   àb - f
to him.   May he unite with [his] body { according to his heart's desire. }

iu	ba - f	en	t'et - f	seχen
May come	*his soul*	*to*	*his body,*	*may embrace*

t'et - f	ba - f	ân -	sen	nef
his body	*his soul.*	*May*	*bring they*	*him*

neteru	em	Het	Benbenet	em	Ânnu
the gods	*into*	*Het -*	*Benbenet*	*in*	*Heliopolis,*

er ḳes	Śu	sa	Tem	âb - f
near	*the god Shu*	*the son of Tmu.*		*May his heart*

nef	mâ	Râ	âb - f	nef	mâ
be to him	*as [was to]*	*Râ his heart,*		*[and]*	*as [was to]*

---

* This line is written down the cover at the right hand side.

χeperá   āb   sep sen   en   ka - k
Kheperá [his heart].   *Doubly purified*   *be*   *thy ka,*

en   ba - k   en χaíbit - k   en   sāḫ - k
thy soul,   *thy shadow,*   *and*   *thy mummy,*

Ảusár   seut'eb   neter ḫen   sen   Ámsu
O Osiris,   *the* seutcheb,   *the prophet*   *second of*   *Ámsu,*

Nes - Ámsu   maāχeru   sa ennu   neter ḫen
Nes - Ámsu,   *triumphant,*   *son of a like*   *prophet*

Pa - se - net'em - áb
Pa - senetchem - áb.

The four perpendicular lines of inscription contain a speech of the god Kheperá, and read :—

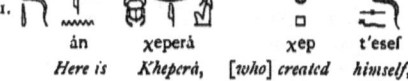

1.   án   χeperá   χep   t'esef
      Here is   *Kheperá,*   *[who] created*   *himself,*

χeperer   āper   t'er maā   mest'er - ſ
{ who cometh into } endowed   ....   his two ears.
    existence

t'eṭ - ſ   i   er per - k   Àusâr   seut'eb
Saith he, " Come   to thy house, Osiris, the seutcheb,

neter ḥen   sen   Àmsu Nes-Àmsu . . . . . . Rā
the prophet second of Àmsu, Nes-Àmsu . . . . Rā

peses' - θ   ḥer - k   2. χu - tuk
extendeth himself over thee,   thou art strengthened,

māki - tuk   erṭāt unen mā sa - k
thou art protected, it is granted that he shall protect thee.

erṭāt - nek   niſut   per   em
May there be given to thee winds coming forth from

Śu   nifti   per   em   neter Tem   er
Shu, and wind coming forth from divine Tmu upon

ut - k   erṭāt - nek   mu   per
thy coffin! May there be given to thee water coming forth

em   ḥāp   Âusâr   seut'eb   neter ḥen
from   the Nile,   O Osiris,   the seutcheb,   the prophet

sen   Nes-Âmsu.   erṭāt - nek   āu
second, Nes-Âmsu. May there be given to thee dilatation

âb   χer   śes (?)   em   Seχet - rat
with boldness   of heart   in   { the Sekhet-Aaru }
                                                 { (Elysian Fields.) }

âb - k   erek   ân   sebeb
Thy heart   shall be to thee   and   shall not depart.

4. χu - tuk Tanen   ι   sa   paut

Protecteth thee the god Tanen,   *O son of the cycle*

neteru - f   per - k   em   χu

of his gods, and thou shalt come forth with splendour."

On the right hand of the horizontal inscription are figures of the gods Harmachis , Seb , and Horus , who "make protection for Nes-Àmsu"; the first holds a crook and whip , and the second and third a whip only. On the left are figures of the gods Tmu , Kheperà , and Osiris , who also "make protection for Nes-Àmsu;" each god holds a whip in his hands.

On the left hand side of the cover are four perpendicular lines of hieroglyphics, which read :—

1.   àn   Àusàr   seut'eb   neter ḥen sen Àmsu

Behold Osiris, the seutcheb, { *the prophet second* }
                                { *of Àmsu,* }

Nes-Ámsu, maāχeru sa seut'eb neter ben

Nes-Ámsu, triumphant, son of the seutcheb, *the prophet*

sen Ámsu Pa-senet'em-áb-āst maāχeru

second of Ámsu, Pa-senetchem-áb-āst, triumphant,

2. mes nebt per en áḥá

born of the lady of the house, the sistrum-bearer

en Ámsu Ta - χens - i maāχeru

of Ámsu, Ta - khens - i, triumphant!

áb en mut-[á] sep sen ḥāt

O heart, my mother, O heart, my mother! O heart of

---

* Here follows a late recension of the 30th chapter of the Book of the Dead.

K

χeper - á   em   seχem   er - á
my existence! May there be no obstacle raised against me

em   met   em   χcsef   er - á   em
by evidence.   May there be no repulse to me   by

3.   t'at'at   em   árit   er - á   em
the children of Horus.   May not be made against me by

neteru   em   req   er - á   em - baḥ
the gods   [thy] separation   from me   in the presence

ári   mãχait   entek   ka - á   er
of the guardian of the scale.   Thou art my ka   in

---

* Read ▯ ⟨⟩ ᴅ.

χat-[â]   χnem   seut'a   ât - â
my body,   *uniting*   *and making sound* *my limbs.*

per - k   er   bu   nefer
Mayest thou come forth   *to*   *the place*   *of happiness*

ḥen - nâ   ţuat   em   seχen   ren - â
[to which] I go in the ţuat.   *May not overthrow my name*

t'at'at   bu   nefer
the children of Horus .... *place of*   *happiness,*

nefer   em   âu   âb   ut'â   meţ
happiness in dilatation of heart at the weighing of words.

em   t'eţ   ḳer   er - â   er ḳes
May there not be spoken falsehood   *against me*   *near*

---

* The text here appears to be corrupt.

neter   nefer   māket   ur - k
the god   *beautiful.* *Verily*   *great shalt thou*

un - θ (sic) Áusár   seut'eb   neter ḥen   sen
be rising up, O Osiris, the seutcheb, *the prophet second*

Ámsu   Nes-Ámsu   maāχeru   t'etta   ḥeḥ
of Amsu, Nes-Ámsu, triumphant for ever and ever.

Over the feet of the cover are painted two pylon-
shaped shrines ⌂, emblematic of Re-stau ⚊
the "passages of the tomb"; upon each sits Anubis
the god of the dead.   The inscription over the
right foot reads :—

án   Ànpu   neb   áat   ári
Behold Anubis, lord of the sarcophagus, making

sa   Áusár.
the protection of Osiris.

and that over the left reads :—

án   Ánpu   χenti   neter   ḥet

Behold Anubis, president of the divine house,

ári   sa   Áusár

making the protection of Osiris.

The line of inscription between the two pylons reads :—

suten   ṭá   ḥetep   en   Áusár   χenti

May give a royal oblation   Osiris,   president of

Ámentet   neter áa   neb   Abṭu

the underworld, the great god, lord of Abydos.

On each side of the feet is a lion ; the name of one is *Sef,* "Yesterday," and that of the other ✕ *Ṭuau,* "To-morrow."

On the front of the pedestal are two lines of hieroglyphics, which read :—

I.

suten   ţā   ḥetep   en   Ḥeru-χuti   neter āa
May give a royal oblation   Harmachis, the great god,

neb   pet   mesk   Śu   per   em
the lord of heaven, offspring of Shu, coming forth from

χut   Seker Àusár   neter āa   ḥer áb
the horizon, and Seker-Osiris   the great god   within

Àpu   2. ţā - f   sośep
Panopolis.   May [they] grant to him   to receive

āu áb   em   bet neſer   em
dilatation of heart   with   happiness   and with

ḥetepu   Seχet - Aru

sepulchral offerings   in the Elysian Fields;

tã - ſ   χut   en   pet   χer   Rã

may [they] give him glory   in   heaven   before   Rã

user   em   ta

and power upon earth!

On the right hand side of the pedestal are two lines
of inscription, which read :

1. án   Áusár   χenti   Ámentet

Behold Osiris, president of the underworld,

neter   âa   neb   Ábṭu   Seker Áusár

the great god,   lord   of Abydos;   and Seker-Osiris,

neter ḥen   ḥer áb   Apu   Ánpu   ḥer
the great god *within* *Panopolis ;* *and Anubis* *upon*

ṭu - f   ṭá - sen   2. per - χeru   áḥ
his hill ; *may they give* *sepulchral offerings,* *oxen,*

apṭ   χet   neb   nefer   áb   en
ducks, *things* *all* *beautiful* *and pure,* *to the*

ka   en   Ausár
ka   *of*   *Osiris.*

On the left hand side of the pedestal are two lines
of inscription, but they are practically a repetition of
those on the right side, and are therefore not given
here.

---

* Read ⸢⸣ neter âa.

† Here follow the titles and genealogy of Nes-Amsu.

On the outside of the coffin under the feet are ten
perpendicular lines of hieroglyphics, which read :—

I.

    án   Ausár   seut'eb   neter ḥen   sen

    Behold Osiris, the seutcheb, *the prophet second,*

Nes-Ámsu   maäχeru   sa   seut'eb   neter ḥen

Nes-Ámsu, triumphant, son of the seutcheb *the prophet*

sen   5.   Sept   ṭä - s   ääui - s

second,   may the goddess Sept†   give her   two hands

er   seśep - k   án   ḥer   en   6.   mut - k

to   receive thee ;   not   may depart   thy mother

---

* Here follow the titles and genealogy (lines 2–4) of Nes-
Ámsu as given in the line of inscription on the coffin near the
coffin near the cover.

† A name of Hathor.

Nut   er - ek   em   ren - s   en   her
Nut   from thee   in   her name   of   Ḥer.

mā   ḥetep - k   em   Nut   mut - k   hru
Mayest   thou rest   in   Nut   thy mother   every

neb   per - k   usten - k   χer - k
day!   Mayest thou come forth, and mayest thou walk

en   ḥeḥ   àn   χeseſ - k   neb - k   er
for   ever.   May not   repulse thee   thy lord   at

āa   nu   ṭuat   er
the doors   of   the underworld . . . . , and

---

* Here there is a play on the words *ḥer* " to depart," and
ḥer " heaven," the " upper regions of the sky."

śem - k   âm Ausâr Nes-Àmsu   maāχeru

mayest thou walk there, Osiris, Nes-Àmsu, triumphant!

Below this inscription is a black and white bull
bearing a mummy upon its back, and below this are
four lines of hieroglyphics containing prayers for
sepulchral offerings; as the text is practically the
same as that given on the right side of the pedestal, it
is not repeated here.

On the inside of the cover are painted in outline :—

1. The winged disk with pendent uræi ,
   emblematic of Rā and Isis and Nephthys.

2. The vulture , emblematic of the goddess
   Mut, holding in each of its claws *shen* Q,
   emblematic of the circuit of the Sun, and
   the feather ῼ, emblematic of Right and
   Truth.

3. The winged scarabæus , emblematic
   of the matter of the dead body of the deceased about to come into a new existence.

4. The vulture of Mut, as described in No. 2.

L 2

On the inside of the lower portion of the coffin is a full-length figure of the goddess Nut drawn in black outline, and on the back is a large figure of *ṭeṭ* 𓊽, wearing plumes and horns 𓊽, emblematic of the god Osiris. Down the edge, on each side, is a line of inscription in which a full genealogy of Nes-Ámsu is given, and the following texts :—

Right side :

á	Án	peḥrer	em
O thou	*god Án,*	*who goest round*	*in*

neter ḥet	en	āa neter	tu - ná	ba - á
the divine house	*of*	*the great god,*	*grant to me*	*my soul*

em	bu	neb	enti	áu - f	men
in	*every*	*place*	*in which*	*it may*	*repose (?)*

ḥeḥ	ua	ṭ'etta	ḥer	śes	Seker - Áusár
for ever and for ever,			*may [it] follow*		*Seker - Osiris*

---

* The Coptic ⲟⲩⲟ ⳉ.

ḫer âb   Âpu   ḥenâ   ka - â   hru   neb
within   Panopolis   and   my ka   every   day.

Left side: tut   âs   âft   neteru   âpu
              Now   behold   four   gods   these,

mesu   Ḥeru   en   teſ - f   Âusâr   seut'eb
children of Horus,   his father Osiris, the seutcheb,

neter ḥen   sen   Âmsu   maâχeru   unen - sen
the prophet second of Âmsu, triumphant, may they be

nek   em   χet - k   ân - sen   nek   χet
to thee   following thee,   may they bring   to thee   things

neſert   em   maâχeru
beautiful,   in   triumph!

The mummy of Nes-Àmsu is 5ft. 5 in. long, and is in a well preserved condition. The head was originally covered with a gilded cartonnage face, and a small, clean-cut, hæmatite scarab was fastened to the breast; the handsome cartonnage face was presented to the British Museum* in 1885, but where the scarab is I know not. The front of the mummy is ornamented with a painted and gilded cartonnage collar and hollow-work pectoral, down the centre of which runs a line of hieroglyphics which record the name, titles and genealogy of the deceased. From Akhmîm.

Length 6 ft., width 1 ft. 8½ in.

---

* Its number is 24,402.

No. 4.

Inner wooden coffin of a lady who probably lived towards the end of the period of the XXVIth dynasty, about B.C. 500. The face, which is painted yellow, is made of a piece of hard wood pegged on the cover; over it falls a heavy head-dress painted in imitation of the handsome examples of an earlier period. The collar, or necklace, is roughly painted, and running down the cover is a line of hieroglyphics containing prayers for funeral offerings; these are almost illegible, and the name of the deceased is quite effaced. To the right and left of this line of hieroglyphics are marks which show that scenes in which the deceased was represented making offerings to the gods of the underworld have been painted there. Between the collar and the inscription is a winged disk with pendent uræi. All other parts of the coffin and cover are uninscribed, and are not ornamented. Preserved within the coffin are the remains of the *cartonnage* case of the mummy which belonged to the coffin. From Thebes.

Length, 6 ft. 2 in.

No. 5.

Cover of a coffin of a lady who probably lived during the Ptolemaïc period, about B.C. 200. The whole style of this object proclaims the very late period to which it belongs, and it is evident that at the time when it was made the art of coffin-making had reached a low ebb. The body is flat instead of being convex at the chest and tapering away to flatness at the feet; the face is large, coarse, and ill-shapen, and the muddy green and red colours used in painting the figures of the gods show that the artist was as little skilled as the carpenter. The hieroglyphics are roughly traced in black upon a yellow ground. Beneath the collar are figures of the four children of Horus, the goddess Nut with outstretched wings, the golden hawks of Horus, a perpendicular line of hieroglyphics containing prayers for funeral offerings of meat and drink, and upright figures of Isis, Nephthys and other deities. From Thebes. Length, 5 ft. 10 in

Nos. 6—10, and 13.

PARTS OF COFFINS.

6. Painted end of a wooden coffin wherein are depicted the deceased adoring a winged disk with pendent uræi, and the goddess Isis standing in adoration before Osiris, and the goddess Nephthys standing in adoration before Rā. On the upper edge is the inscription : [hieroglyphs]

[hieroglyphs]

Græco-Roman Period.   2 ft. by 1 ft. 9 in.

7. Panel from the same coffin, whereon is painted Osiris, holding [glyph] and [glyph], seated on a throne ornamented with [glyph], beneath a winged disk ; behind him, rising from a clump of lotus flowers, is a serpent with the crown of the north, [glyph], on its head. Græco-Roman Period.

1 ft. 9 in. by 1 ft. 2 in.

8. Wooden face from the inner coffin of a man who flourished about the period of the XXVIth dynasty, about B.C. 550; the face is painted red, and the eyebrows blue.

9. Wooden face from the inner coffin of a lady who flourished about B.C. 300; the face is painted black, and the head-dress above is painted with yellow lines.

10. Unpainted wooden face from the coffin of a man who flourished about B.C. 300.

13. Fragment of wood from the coffin of Sheps-ta-Mât; the inscription reads:

Ptolemaïc Period.   9¾ in. by 9 in.

Nos. 11 and 12.

MUMMY PECTORALS.

11. Cartonnage pectoral of Peṭā-Àusâr, the son of the lady Neith, painted in bright colours.

Scene 1. The deceased on a bier by which stands Anubis; at the head stand Isis, Ṭuamāuteḟ and Qebḥsennuḟ, and at the foot Nephthys, Àmset and Ḥāpi.

Scene 2. The deceased adoring four gods.

Scene 3. Winged beetle with disk and ⵡ, two mummies on two biers, and two uræi.

Scene 4. The four children of Horus and a perpendicular line of hieroglyphics, which read:

Ptolemaïc Period. Length, 2 ft. by 4⅝ in.

12. Cartonnage pectoral of Àḟseṭā, painted in bright colours.

M 2

Scene 1.   The deceased on a bier by which stands Anubis: at the head are Isis and a uræus ⸮, and at the foot Nephthys and a uræus ⸮.

Scene 2.   The deceased adoring four gods.

Scene 3.   Winged beetle and ♆ and two uræi.

Scene 4.   The four children of Horus and a perpendicular line of hieroglyphics which read :—

Ptolemaïc Period.   Length, 2 ft. by 4⅜ in.

TUAMAUTEF.   HAPI

SET OF CANOPIC JARS.   XVIIIᵗʰ DYNAST

Nos. 14—17A.

CANOPIC JARS.*

These jars or vases are found in sets of four, and each is dedicated to one of the four gods of the cardinal points—Mesthá, Ḥāpi, Ṭuamāutef and Qebḥsennuf, who are sometimes called the "children of Horus," and sometimes the "children of Osiris." The first of these deities presided over the south and watched over the stomach and large intestines; the second presided over the north and watched over the small intestines; the third presided over the east and watched over the lungs and heart; and the fourth presided over the west and watched over the liver and gall bladder. Sets of Canopic jars have been found with coffins of the XIth dynasty.

14—17. Set of Canopic vases in white limestone ; the eyes are painted in black. From Thebes.

Vase of Ȧmset.	Height, 1 ft. 2½ in.
Vase of Ḥāpi.	Height, 1 ft. 2½ in.
Vase of Ṭuamāutef.	Height, 1 ft. 1½ in.
Vase of Qebḥsennuf.	Height, 1 ft. 2¼ in.

* See above, p. 8, and Plate III.

17A. Limestone vase of Qebḥsennuf inscribed with four lines of text, which read :—

1. [hieroglyphic text]

2. [hieroglyphic text]

3. [hieroglyphic text]

4. [hieroglyphic text]

[hieroglyphic text]

From Thebes.   Height, 1 ft. 2¼ in.

Nos. 18 and 19.

WOODEN MODELS OF
UNGUENT VASES.

18. Wooden jar painted light yellow; fragments of the linen straps by which it was sealed still remain. On the side are two lines of hieroglyphics in black, which read:—1. [hieroglyphs] 2. [hieroglyphs] *âmaχi χer Ausâr neter ḥen ṭep en An-ḥeru Nebseni*, "Nebseni, the first prophet of Ȧn-ḥeru, before Osiris." XXIInd dynasty, about B.C. 900. From Thebes. Height, 6¼ in.

19. Wooden jar painted in black and white to imitate variegated stone; the inscription is in black upon a yellow ground, and is similar to that on No. 18. From Thebes. Height, 6¾ in.

Nos. 20—34.

WOODEN FIGURES OF ISIS, NEPHTHYS, AND PTAḤ-SEKER-ÁUSÁR.

These figures were placed near the coffin of the deceased : Nephthys at the head, and Isis at the foot. The god Ptaḥ-Seker-Áusár, *i.e.*, "Osiris, the Opener and the Closer," was believed to be especially connected with the resurrection.

20. Wooden human-headed bird , emblematic of the soul; it probably stood on the wooden base which supported a figure of Ptaḥ-Seker-Áusár. From Abydos. Height, 5 in .

21. Painted and gilded wooden hawk , wearing disk. It probably stood on the wooden base which supported a figure of Ptaḥ-Seker-Áusár. From Abydos. Height, 6½ in.

23. Painted and gilded wooden figure of Isis kneeling,* with right hand raised. The top of the pedestal is inscribed with three lines of hieroglyphics,

---

* See Plate IV.

NEPHTHYS.   ISIS.

and the sides are ornamented with rosettes. Late
Period. From Abydos.   Height, 1 ft. 4¾ in.

24. Painted and gilded wooden figure of Isis
kneeling, with right hand raised. Late Period. From
Abydos.   Height, 1 ft. 3½ in.

25. Painted and gilded wooden figure of Isis
kneeling, with right hand raised. The three lines of
hieroglyphics on the pedestal are somewhat similar to
those on No. 23, and like them they are merely ornamental. Late Period. From Abydos.
                        Height, 1 ft. 2¾ in.

26. Painted and gilded wooden figure of Nephthys
kneeling,* with right hand raised. The top of the
pedestal is inscribed with three lines of hieroglyphics,
and the sides are ornamented with rosettes. Late
Period. From Abydos.   Height, 1 ft. 5 in.

27. Painted and gilded wooden figure of Nephthys
kneeling, with right hand raised. Late Period. From
Abydos.   Height, 1 ft. 4 in.

28. Painted and gilded wooden figure of Nephthys
kneeling, with right hand raised. The three lines of
hieroglyphics on the pedestal are somewhat similar to

* See Plate IV.

those on No. 26, and like them they are merely ornamental. Late Period. From Abydos.

Height, 1 ft. 3 in.

29. Wooden figure of Ptaḥ-Seker-Àusâr,* with
horns, plumes, and disk, on a pedestal in which is
a cavity that contained an inscribed roll of papyrus.
The face is gilded, the head-dress is blue, and below
the breast-plate is a figure of Nut, painted on a brown
ground. Down the figure and along the pedestal are
three lines of hieroglyphics which do not make sense.
Late Period. From Abydos.   Height, 2 ft. 9½ in.

30. Painted and gilded wooden figure of Ptaḥ-
Seker-Àusâr, with horns, plumes, and disk, on a
pedestal in which is a cavity with cover, that contained a roll of papyrus. This figure was made for
Ta-Àuset, the daughter of Qem-Ḥàpi. The inscriptions on the figure read :—

---

* See Plate V.

PTAḤ-SEKER-AUSÂR.

The second inscription is a prayer to Osiris, Seker-Osiris, and Isis for sepulchral offerings.

On the pedestal is painted a scene in which four souls are standing by a lake, one at each corner, and drinking water; on the right side of the cavity is painted a figure of Isis, and on the left a figure of Nephthys; and on the movable cover is inscribed :—

Late Period.   From Abydos.   Height 2 ft. 7½ in.

31. Painted and gilded wooden figure of Ptah-Seker-Ausâr, with horns, plumes and disk, on a pedestal in which is a cavity containing a portion of the body of the deceased mummified. Below the breast-plate are painted a figure with ∫ in each hand, and three lines of hieroglyphics; the back of the figure is uninscribed. On the top of the pedestal are three lines of hieroglyphics, and its sides are ornamented with the pattern , painted in bright colours. Late Period. From Abydos.   Height 2 ft. 7½ in.

32. Painted wooden figure of Ptah-Seker-Ausâr, with horns, plumes, and disk, on a solid pedestal. Below the breast-plate is painted a pectoral with a *tet* . This figure was made for Petâtä, the son of

Ḥeru-[sa]-Àuset and Shenkhet, and the second inscription is a prayer to Osiris, Seker-Osiris, Isis, Nephthys,
and Anubis for sepulchral offerings. The inscriptions
read :—

1.

2.

Late Period. From Abydos. Height, 2 ft. 5½ in.

33. Wooden figure of Ptaḥ-Seker-Àusàr.

Height, 13 in.

34. Wooden figure of Ptaḥ-Seker-Àusàr on a
pedestal.   Height, 13½ in.

Plate VI.

HYPOCEPHALUS OF SHAI-ENEN.

No. 35.

HYPOCEPHALUS OF
SHAI-ENEN* .†

This interesting object is made of linen covered with plaster, and measures 8 in. in diameter; the inscriptions upon it are traced in black ink upon a yellow ground. The hypocephalus represented the " Eye of Horus," and was placed under the head of the mummy, in which it was supposed to keep warmth until the revivification of the body. The line of inscription around the edge reads :—

---

* See Birch, *Proceedings of the Society of Biblical Archæology*, 1883, pp. 37–40.
† See Plate VI.

"I am the Hidden One in the hidden place. I am
a perfect intelligence among the companions of Râ.
I have gone in and come forth among the perfect
souls. I am the mighty soul of saffron-coloured form.
I have come forth from the underworld at pleasure.
I have come, I have come forth from the eye of
Horus. I have come forth from the underworld with
Râ, from the House of the Great Old Man in Heliopolis. I am one of the beatified dead coming forth
from the underworld; grant thou things for his body,
and grant heaven for my soul and a hidden place for
my mummy! I have come forth from the eye of
Horus."

1. The text in the first division reads :—

"May the god, who himself is hidden, and whose form is concealed, who shineth upon the world in his forms of existence, and in the underworld, grant that my soul may live for ever."

2. In the second division are :—Nehabka offering to Horus-Àmsu, the power of reproduction; a goddess with for a head; the cow of Hathor; the four children of Horus; a leaf (?) and two lions; a pylon surmounted by a ram's head and uræus, and having four rams' heads on each side; Rā and Kheperà.

3. In the third are :—A female figure and a beetle; the boat of the Moon in which are a shrine containing the cynocephalous ape of Thoth, a cynocephalous ape holding , and, at the bows, the god Harpocrates; and the boat of the Sun in which are a shrine containing the gods Horus, Isis, Nephthys, and rowers. Over the boat of the Moon are the names of the deceased and of his mother "Osiris Shai-enen, triumphant for ever, son of Nes-Nebt-het."

4. In the fourth division is a god with two faces, wearing horns, disk and plumes upon his head, and holding a sceptre of Anubis in one hand, and ☥ in the other. The inscription reads :—

"May the great god in his disk give his rays in the underworld of Heliopolis! Do thou grant an entrance and an exit in the underworld without repulse."

On one side of the god is the legend, "Protection, and life, and strength are behind him for ever".

On the right hand of this division are the hawk of Horus or Osiris on a standard in a boat, with Isis and Nephthys making speeches to him, and a second boat in which are Rā, Kheperā and the cynocephalous ape of Thoth holding the *utchat*. On the left hand side are eight rams, three birds of the soul who are described as , and Horus-Sept in a boat. In the centre of the next division a god with four rams' heads is seated ; he wears above them the white crown with

plumes, uræi and horns , and holds the sceptre ⌐.
On each side of the god is an ape wearing crescent,
disk and uræus, making adoration to the god. The
texts are two addresses to the Sun-god, and read :—

I.

II.

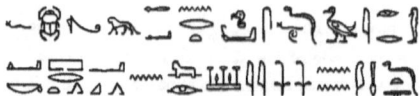

"May the Soul, who begetteth [all] forms of existence, whose body is more hidden than his births, who sendeth forth the light, when the two *utchats* come into existence, his soul cometh into existence, and his body [his] mother, and who is abundant of forms, make the enemies of Shai-enen afraid, and grant that he may come into the underworld with the .... and that he may not be turned back for ever and ever !

"O Soul, mighty of terror, lord of fear, mighty of victory, who makest fire to spring up from the two perfect *utchats*, thou being who art mighty in forms of existence .... who giveth and who hideth his body in life, and whose form cometh into existence as an emanation of ....., the mighty one of victory, who maketh many his forms of existence, grant thou that Shai-enen triumphant may come forth and go into [the underworld] for ever."

Diameter 6½ in.

Nos. 36—39.

PAPYRI.

36. Portion of a hieroglyphic copy of the Book of the Dead which was written during the Ptolemaïc period for ⌒ 𓅃 𓏤 𓎼 𓈖 ⌒ ~~~~ 𓊹 𓏤 𓏤 𓎼 𓆰 Ta-uḳesh, son of the lady of the house Ḥemuȧ. This papyrus is inscribed with part of the 18th chapter of the Book of the Dead, and it contains 51 perpendicular lines of writing, and measures 3 ft. 2 in., by 7 in. The vignettes are traced in outline and represent :—(1) the deceased adoring his soul, (2) the deceased kneeling in adoration before several groups of gods; (3) the *tet* 𓊽, emblem of stability; (4) the buckle 𓎬, emblem of protection; (5) the collar 𓋝, with two hawks' heads; (6) two sceptres in shrines 𓊨𓊨, and the *utchat* winged and walking.

37. Forty fragments of a papyrus inscribed in hieratic with the 17th chapter of the Book of the Dead. At one end is part of a coloured vignette in which the

deceased is represented adoring Rā, who is hawk-
headed and sitting upon a throne, and holding the flail
𖤍, and crook ⌇, emblematic of sovereignty and
dominion. From the remains of a few short lines of
hieroglyphics it seems that the deceased was a "divine
father of Ämen," called Paṭṭā-Khensu ▧ ▱ ●
⌇ (?). XXIInd dynasty.

38. Fragment of papyrus, of a late period, measuring 7 in. × 4 in., upon which are inscribed in
outline the boat of the Sun, a table of offerings, the
emblem of the east ✦, Osiris in the form of a mummy,
wearing the *atef* crown ⌬, and a ṭeṭ ⌷.

39. Fragment of a hieratic papyrus, of a late period,
measuring 8 in. × 4 in.

Nos. 40—55.

INSCRIBED SLABS FROM TOMBS
AND STELÆ.

40. Rectangular limestone slab, from the door of a *maṣṭaba* tomb at Gîzeh, inscribed :—

The deceased flourished during the reign of Khā-f-Rā, king of Egypt, about B.C. 3666. From Gizeh.

Length, 2 ft. 6 in.

41. Rectangular limestone slab, from the door of a *maṣṭaba* tomb at Gîzeh, inscribed :—

The deceased flourished during the reign of Shepses-ka-f, king of Egypt, about B.C. 3600. From Gizeh.

Length, 1 ft. 10 in.

42. Rectangular limestone slab from the door of

the *maṣṭaba* tomb of Uâp at Gîzeh ;* on the slab, in relief, are a seated figure of the deceased, a line of hieroglyphics which record his titles, and a list of funeral offerings. The deceased is seated on a chair with legs in the shape of lions' legs, his right hand is stretched out upon his right leg, and his left, in which he holds an object which falls over his left shoulder, is closed and lies on his left breast; before him stands a table of offerings.

The line of hieroglyphics which record the name and titles of the deceased reads :—

Among the funeral offerings mentioned are :— incense, wine, eye-paint, linen garments, linen cloths, beer, wine, cakes, calves, oxen, gazelle, game, poultry, dates, etc. The seated figure of the deceased, the table of offerings, and the hieroglyphic text are in low relief. From Gîzeh. Length, 2 ft. × 1 ft. 8 in.

43. Rectangular slab of limestone, from the tomb of Tchefâ ,† a superintendent of priests who held the dignities and titles of chancellor, *smer nāt* and

---

* See Plate VII. † See Plate VIII.

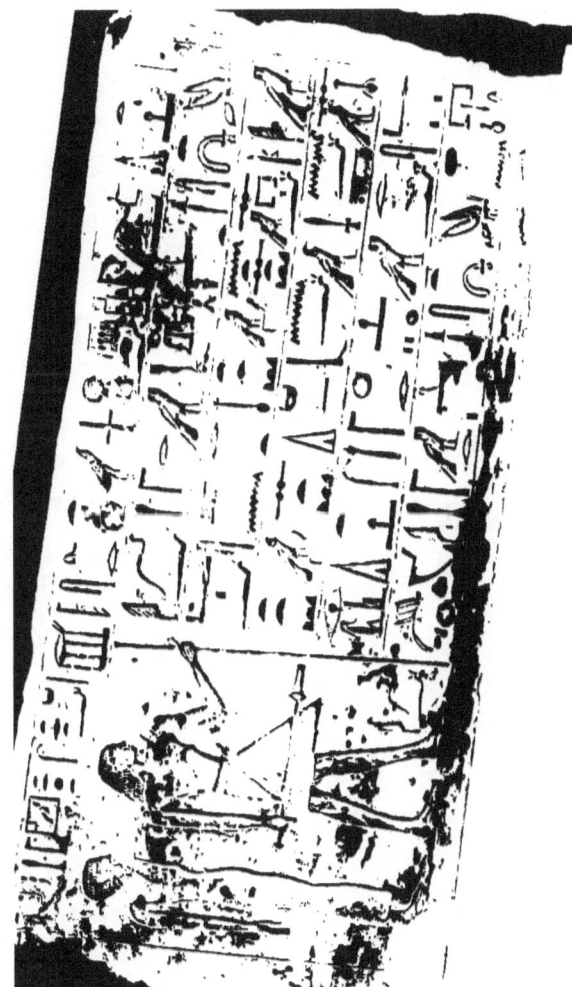

SEPULCHRAL TABLET OF TCHEFA, A HIGH PRIESTLY OFFICIAL

kher ḥeb at El-kab. To the left is a standing figure of the deceased holding a staff in his right hand ⟨figure⟩, and the *kherp* sceptre ⟨figure⟩ in his left; behind him, with her right hand laid upon his right shoulder, stands Ḥentes his loving wife, the kinswoman of the king, and prophetess of Hathor. The inscription, which is cut in fine bold characters, contains prayers to Anubis and Osiris that sepulchral meals may be granted by them to the deceased. The text reads :—

1. ⟨hieroglyphs⟩

2. ⟨hieroglyphs⟩

3. ⟨hieroglyphs⟩

4.

5.

6.

"May Anubis, president of the divine house (*i.e.*, the tomb), the head of the funeral mountain, resident in Ut, give a royal oblation. May Tchefá, the chancellor, the *smer uāt*, the precentor, the president of the prophets, be buried in his tomb in the beautiful Set-Àmenta; may she open his hand. May he be united to the earth and travel over the steely sky. May Set-Àmenta give both her hands to him in twofold peace in the presence of the great god. May Osiris give a royal oblation and sepulchral meals to the chancellor, the *smer uāt*, the president of the prophets!"

Over the heads of the deceased and his wife is the legend :—

"His loving wife, the kinswoman of the king, and prophetess of Hathor, Hentes."

Dr. Wiedemann published, in the *Proceedings Soc. Bibl. Arch.*, 1886, p. 101, a copy of this inscription which he had taken when the slab was in the hands of dealers in Luxor.

VIth Dynasty. Length, 2 ft., width, 1 ft. 2 in.

44. Limestone slab from the door of the *maṣṭaba* tomb of Khā, a royal kinsman, and a high priestly official of Usr-en-Rā, King of Egypt, about B.C. 3200. In the empty cavity, in relief, is the inscription :—

and on each side, in relief, is a figure of the deceased, holding a staff and the ⍭ sceptre.   From Gizeh.

Height, 1 ft. 8 in. × 2 ft.

45. Limestone slab from the door of the *maṣṭaba* tomb of Khā,* a royal kinsman, and a high priestly official of Usr-en-Rā, King of Egypt, about B.C.,3200. The inscription is in relief, and reads :—

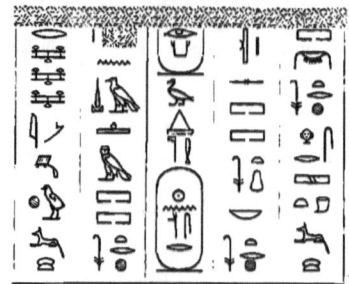

From Gizeh.   Height, 1 ft. 3½ in. × 2 ft. 1 in.

46. Calcareous stone stele with rounded top, upon which are the two *utchats* and *shen* 𓂀𓊪𓂀, ; it was inscribed for a man called Sebek-ḥetep.   In the

---

* See Plate IX.

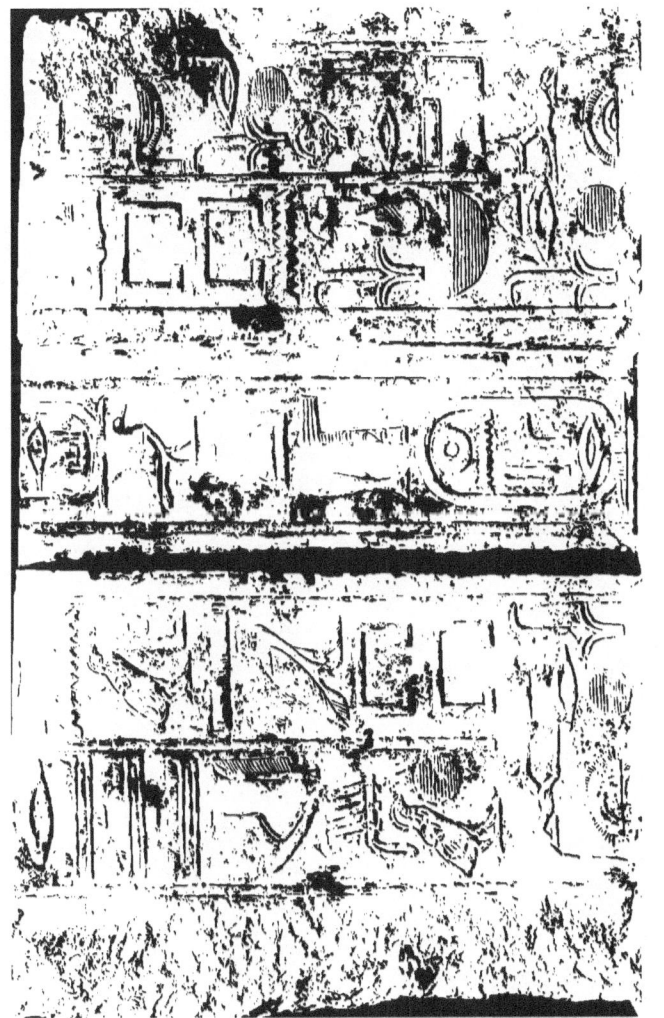

INSCRIBED SLAB FROM THE TOMB OF KHA, A HIGH PRIESTLY OFFICIAL.

first register are four lines of hieroglyphics, which
read :—

1.

2.

3.

4.

"May Osiris, lord of Tattu, the great god, lord of
Abydos, and Anubis, the president of the divine
house (*i.e.*, the tomb) give a royal oblation ! May
they grant sepulchral meals of oxen, ducks, bandages,

wine, wax, offerings of *tchefa* food, and all the pure and beautiful things upon which the gods live, the gifts of heaven, the products of earth, the things which the Nile bringeth forth, and beautiful sepulchral meals, to the *ka* of the superintendent of the temple of Anubis, Sebek-ḥetep, triumphant!"

In the second register Sebek-ḥetep and his wife Nub-em-ḥeb, who held the dignity of ⸗, are seated with a table of offerings before them, and near this stands Sebek-ḥetep's uncle Ṭeṭā-res ⸗ ⸗ who held the office of ⸗.

In the third register, the deceased Ānkhu ⸗, who held the office of ⸗, and his wife ⸗ Nub-em-khāu-s ⸗, stand facing each other; each holds a flower. To the right, seated by a table of offerings, are " his father, superintendent of the divine house, Ṭeṭā-res, triumphant "! ⸗, and " his mother . . . . . Apā " ⸗. A figure seems to have been omitted, for we have the name ⸗ written to the left of the table.

Height, 1 ft. 4½ in.

47. Calcareous stone stele of Ren-senb-buḥáru with rounded top. In the rounded portion are the two *utchats* , and below are four horizontal lines of inscription, which contain the usual prayers that sepulchral meals may be given to the deceased; the text reads :—

Beneath are figures of the deceased and his mother Bebá-res, and two lines of inscription, which read :—

Height, 12½ in.

48. Calcareous stone stele with rounded top, upon which is inscribed the winged disk; beneath is a man standing in front of a table of offerings, and having both hands raised in adoration of the gods "Ptaḥ of the Beautiful Face," and Set.   Height, 9 in.

49. Calcareous stone stele, in the shape of a pylon, with raised border and plumes, painted in red and blue alternately. Length, 1 ft. 9 in., width, 1 ft. 1 in. In the lower part of the stele the deceased, painted red, sits before a table of offerings, and above him are four lines of inscription, which read :—

"May Osiris, lord of Tattu, the great god, lord of Abydos, give a royal oblation; may he give sepulchral meals, and oxen and ducks, and offerings, and *tchefau*

food, and winds of life, and gifts of heaven, and products of earth, and what Hāpi (the Nile) bringeth,
to the *ka* of . . . . Ānkh-sebek-nekht, triumphant,
the son of [the lady of the house] Meri, triumphant!"

50. Altar in fine limestone upon which are cut in
outline altars of offering, etc. On each side is a
libation vase 🝕, from which water flows out towards
the mouth of the altar, and between them are two
tables loaded with offerings of bread, meat, fruit, etc.
Between these tables is a sycamore tree, in the
branches of which stands the goddess Nut, and above
is ☥ "life." Beneath each table is a hollow in the
form of a cartouche wherefrom a human-headed bird,
or soul, receives the water which flows upon his hands.
Above one bird is the legend "Osiris, great god,"
𓊹𓏏, and above the other 𓊹𓏏. The inscriptions, which enclose the whole scene described above,
read :—

I.

2. [hieroglyphics]

The first line shows that the deceased Ausâr-ur, the son of Meḫt-urit, for whom the altar was made, was a high priestly official and a prophet attached to the service of more than one deity, and that his father also held similar ecclesiastical appointments, probably at Apu, the Panopolis of the Greeks, and the Akhmîm of the Arabs. The second line contains a prayer that an abundance of funeral offerings and of "every good thing" may be brought to the tomb of the deceased.

Length, 1 ft. 6¾ in. × 1 ft. 5 in.

50A. Painted limestone stele of Ta-khaâa-en-Bast* with rounded top [symbol], in which is the solar disk, winged, with pendent uræi. In the scene below Horus and Thoth are pouring out libations before the emblem of Osiris [symbol], which rests on [symbol]; behind each god is a figure of the deceased lady with her hands raised in adoration. Beneath are three lines of

* See Plate IXA.

Plate IX<small>A</small>.

STELE OF TA-KHAĀA-EN-BAST, THE SON OF PEBAREMĀ, A SCRIBE OF ĀN-HERU.

FROM ABYDOS.   XXIIND DYNASTY.

Plate IX_{B.}

STELE OF SHASHANQ, THE SON OF PA-KHART-NA-BAST.

FROM ABYDOS. XXIIND DYNASTY.

text in which prayer is made that funeral offerings in abundance may be given to Ta-khaāa-en-Bast, the daughter of Pebaremā .... From Abydos. XXIInd dynasty (?). Height, 12¾ in.

50B. Painted limestone stele of Shashanq,[*] the son of Pa-kharṭ-na-Bast, with rounded top ⌂ , on which are depicted the solar disk, two jackals, and

Beneath are figures of three men with hands raised in adoration of the god Horus, who is standing upright, with a disk and uræus on his head, and a sceptre in his hands, before a table of offerings. The names of the three men and the usual prayer for funeral offerings are traced in black on a yellow ground; some of the characters are illegible. The name of the deceased is given thus .... From Abydos. XXIInd dynasty (?).

Height, 15¾ in.

---

* See Plate IXB.

50c. Limestone tablet of Qu-ka-Ḥeru-sa(?)-Auset,[*] with rounded top ∩, on which are depicted the solar disk, winged, with pendent uræi, jackals, etc.; between the uræi is the legend ⸺⊗⫴⸺. In the scene below the deceased stands in adoration before Osiris, Anubis and Isis, and before Amsu, Ḥeru-netch-àtef-f and Nephthys. Beneath are twelve lines of inscription, which read :—

1.

2.

3.

4.

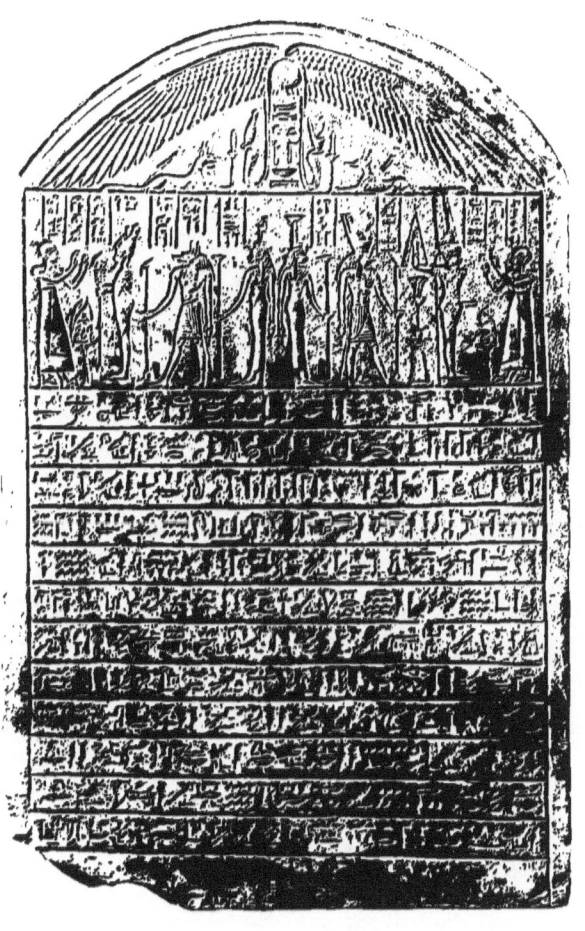

STELE OF QA-KA-HERU-SA-ÁUSET, A PRIESTLY OFFICIAL.

FROM AKHMÎM.   PTOLEMAIC PERIOD.

5. [hieroglyphic text]

6. [hieroglyphic text]

7. [hieroglyphic text]

8. [hieroglyphic text]

9. [hieroglyphic text]

10. [hieroglyphic text]

11.

12.

From Akhmîm.   Ptolemaïc Period.

Height, 1 ft. 9 in.

50D. Limestone stele of Shuamāi* with rounded top ∩. On the upper portion is depicted Osiris holding whip and flail, seated on a throne. Behind him stand Isis, "lady of heaven," and "Horus, the avenger of his father." Before him stand the deceased and his sister Bak-Auset . Above the god are his titles , and above the deceased is the legend :—

---

* See Plate IXD.

STELE OF SHUAMĀI.

XVIIITH DYNASTY.

𓄿𓏏𓎡𓏤 . On the lower part of the tablet the mummy of the deceased is shown being embraced by the god Anubis, and a priest stands before it performing the ceremony of "opening the mouth." Close by stand two attendant priests offering incense and pouring out libations, and two female relatives kneel before it and beat their heads in their grief. To the right are seated the scribe Rā-mes and his sister Meri-Rā, and a male figure makes an offering and pours out a libation before them. In the bottom right hand corner the deceased is seen seated before a tree from out of which the goddess Nut pours water upon his soul ; to the left are five lines of hieroglyphics which contain a prayer that sepulchral offerings may be made to the deceased and that he may enjoy felicity after death. From Abydos. · Height, 2 ft. 10½ in.

No. 51.

STELE OF NEKAU.*

51. Fine limestone stele, with rounded top, ⌂. In the rounded portion are the following :—

1. Winged disk beneath which are two male figures adoring the sun 𓏏; behind each figure is an *utchat* 𓂀.

2. A line of hieroglyphics which reads :—

[hieroglyphic text]

3. The deceased adoring the Sun-god in his morning boat.

4. The deceased adoring the Sun-god in his evening boat.

---

* See Plate X.

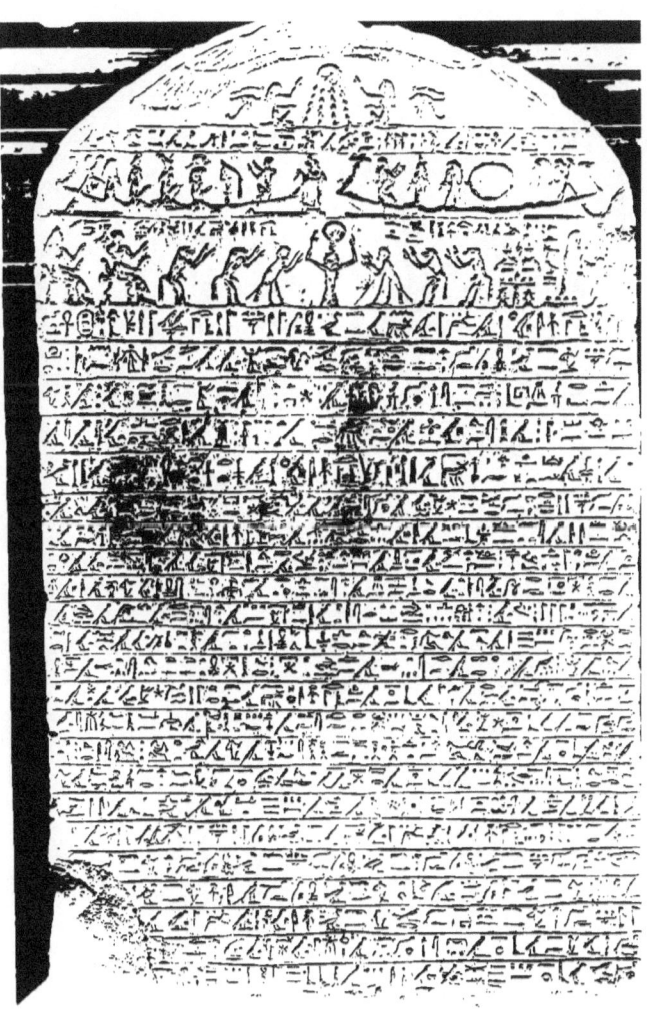

SEPULCHRAL TABLET OF NEKAU, A PRIEST OF PANOPOLIS.

5. The disk of the sun being lifted up out of the waters of the celestial ocean ; on each side are a soul and two apes standing in adoration. To the right stands the deceased pouring out a libation before a table of offerings, and to the left are seated the deceased and his wife.

From the text below we learn that the deceased Nekau was the son of Nes-Ȧmsu, and the grandson of T'eṭ-ḫrȧ, and that all three men held high priestly positions in the town of Ȧpu or Panopolis. In lines 18 ff. Nekau is said to be the son of Nes-Ȧmsu, the son of T'eṭ-ḫrȧ, the son of Nes-Ȧmsu, the son of T'eṭ-ḫrȧ, the son of Ḥeru . . . . . , the son of Ṭȧf-mut-qebt, the son of T'eṭ-Ḥeru-ȧf-ȧnχ, the son of T'eṭ-ḫrȧ, the son of the lady Nes-urt, who was herself the daughter of the *uȧeb* of Panopolis. Thus we know the ancestors from whom Nekau traced his descent for eight generations. Nekau's paternal grandmother was Nes-urt, and he himself is described in his stele as a "royal relative"; he was the *uȧeb* of Panopolis, a prophet of Horus and Isis (?), and he served with the priests monthly in the fourth grade. His father held the like offices, but he seems to have been in addition a "prophet of Osiris and of the two Horus gods, and a prophet of the ceremonials of Pharaoh, may he live for ever"! The greater part of the

inscription on the stele is, however, occupied with
extracts from the hymns to Rā which are usually
found in versions of the XVth Chapter of the Book
of the Dead; the extracts seem to have been chosen
at random and mistakes occur here and there.
Speaking generally, the deceased prays that the gates
of heaven may be opened before him, that his soul
may go into the presence of Rā, that he may be
among the never-setting stars, and that his whole
course of life after death may be like that of Rā.

The text reads :—

4.

5.

6.

7. [hieroglyphic text]

8. [hieroglyphic text]

9. [hieroglyphic text]

10. [hieroglyphic text]

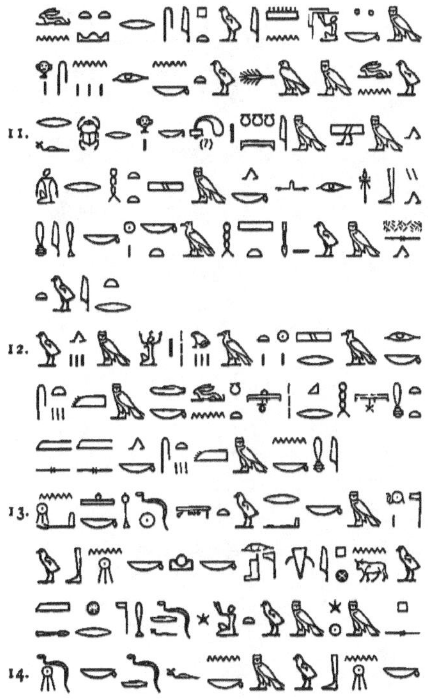
11.
12.
13.
14.

[hieroglyphic text line]

[hieroglyphic text line]

15. *[hieroglyphic text line]*

[hieroglyphic text line]

[hieroglyphic text line]

16. *[hieroglyphic text line]*

[hieroglyphic text line]

[hieroglyphic text line]

[hieroglyphic text line]

17. *[hieroglyphic text line]*

[hieroglyphic text line]

[hieroglyphic text line]

18.

19.

20.

21.

22. [hieroglyphs]

[hieroglyphs]

[hieroglyphs]

23. [hieroglyphs]

[hieroglyphs]

[hieroglyphs]

Ptolemaïc Period.   From Akhmîm.

Height, 2 ft. × 14¼ in.

Plate **XI.**

SEPULCHRAL TABLET OF TA-HEBT, THE DAUGHTER OF HERU-MES.

No. 52.

STELE OF TA-HEBT.*

52. Fine limestone stele, with rounded top, ⬭ .
In the rounded portion are the following :—

Winged disk with pendent uræi and the legend, [hieroglyphs] "Beḥuṭet, great god, lord of heaven." The bone of each wing is in the form of [hieroglyph], thus the two together represent the day sky and the night sky. Immediately beneath the disk is a standard whereon is seated Harpocrates holding ⟨symbol⟩ over his right shoulder. On each side of him is a boat. In that to the right are ⟨symbol⟩ and a disk; in the latter is ⟨symbol⟩, the emblem of the god Kheperà. In that to the left are ⟨symbol⟩ and a disk; in the latter is a ram ⟨symbol⟩. Each boat has an oar or rudder resting, and a standard; each of these is hawk-headed. Both boats are sailing over the sky [hieroglyph].

In the scene below the deceased lady Ta-hebt, the daughter of Ḥeru-mes, and of the lady Kharṭet-Amsu,

---

* See Plate XI.

stands before a table of offerings with both hands raised in adoration of Osiris, who wears ⟨glyph⟩, and holds ⟨glyph⟩ and ⟨glyph⟩. Behind him stand the gods Harpocrates ⟨glyph⟩, Átmu ⟨glyph⟩, Ḥeru-netch-ḥrà-f ⟨glyph⟩, and the goddesses Isis and Nephthys; each god holds the sceptre ⟨glyph⟩ in his left hand, and ⟨glyph⟩ in his right, and each goddess holds a lotus sceptre in her left hand and ⟨glyph⟩ in her right. The legends above the deceased and the deities whom she adores are as follows :—

1. ⟨hieroglyphs⟩ " Osiris Ta-hebt, triumphant, daughter of Ḥeru-mes, triumphant, and of Kharṭet-Ámsu, triumphant.

2. ⟨hieroglyphs⟩ "Saith Osiris, dweller in Ámentet, Unnefer, the great god, the prince of eternity."

3. ⟨hieroglyphs⟩ "Saith Harmachis, the great god, the lord of heaven."

4. ⟨hieroglyphs⟩ "Saith Átmu, the lord of the lands of Ánnu" (Heliopolis).

5. 𓅯𓆓𓏏𓊖𓏺 "Saith Ḥeru-net'-ḥrā-f."

6. 𓃻𓏭𓎡𓏤𓅆 "Saith Isis, the mighty lady, the divine mother."

7. 𓃻𓏭𓊖𓅆 "Saith Nephthys, the divine sister."

The text begins, "May Osiris, the dweller in
" Āmentet, the great god, the lord of Abydos, and
" Seker-Osiris, within Āpu (Panopolis) and Ḥeru-
" χuti · Ātmu, the lord of the lands of Ānnu
" (Heliopolis) and Ḥeru-net'-ḥrāt-f, and Isis, the great
" lady, the divine mother in Āpu (Panopolis), and
" Nephthys, the divine sister, and the great cycle of
" the gods who dwell in Āpu, give sepulchral meals,
" oxen, fowl, incense, libations, unguents, linen
" bandages, and all good, pure, and pleasant things
" which the heavens give, and the earth bringeth
" forth, and the Nile bringeth forth from his store-
" house, and the sweet breeze of the north wind, to
" the *ka* of the lady honourable before Osiris, who
" dwelleth in the underworld, the great god, the lord
" of Abydos, Ta-hebt, the daughter of Ḥeru-mes,
" triumphant, and of the lady Khartet-Āmsu,
" triumphant."

The deceased lady then saith :—

"Hail, Rā-Harmachis, the lord of rays, who shinest
" in the eastern horizon of the sky, shine thou in the
" face of Osiris Ta-hebt, triumphant."

"Ta-hebt singeth hymns of praise to Rā when he
" setteth.   Grant that the soul of Osiris Ta-hebt
" may come forth with Rā into heaven; may it be
" ordained for her to come into his boat when it
" goeth in among the stars which never rest in the
" heavens."

The lady Ta-hebt then praiseth her lord of eternity,
saying, "Hail to thee, Ḥeru-χuti-Kheperá, the
" self-created one !   Thou art doubly beautiful when
" thou shinest in the horizon, thou illuminest the
" world with thy beams, and the gods rejoice when
" they see thee in thy heavens.   The goddess Unnut
" is on thy brow, and the crowns of the south and
" north are upon thy head ; the goddess taketh up
" her place upon thy forehead.   Thoth is established
" upon thy prow to destroy all thine enemies in the
" underworld.   Let me come forth to meet thee and
" to see thy beautiful Form.   I have come to thee
" for I would be with thee, and I would see thy disk
" every day.   Let me not be held back, let me not
" be repulsed, let my limbs be renewed by the sight
" of thy splendours even as are the noble ones who

" are favoured by thee, for I am one of those who
" venerated thee upon earth. Let me arrive at the
" land of eternity, let me attain unto the nome of
" everlastingness. Guide thou me, O Rā, and do
" thou give the sweet breath of life to me."

Following this petition is an address by
Ta-hebt to every priest, and scribe, and official,
entreating them when they pass along the way to her
tomb to make mention of her name so that it may be
proclaimed before the great god, the lord of the
underworld, "for," saith she, "the person whose
" name is mentioned liveth."

Of herself she then says, "My heart was right.
" I never put myself unduly forward; I gave bread
" to the hungry, drink to the thirsty, and clothes to
" the naked. My hand was open to all men. I
" honoured my father and loved my mother, I was
" affectionate to my brethren, and my heart was at
" one with my fellow-citizens. I kept the starving
" folk alive with provisions and clothes each year
" that the inundation of the Nile was low." Nor did
she confine her cares to the living, for she provided
for the ceremonies which were performed for the
benefit of those "whose souls had gone to heaven."
She had trodden the divine path from her earliest
childhood, and having rendered all praise and glory

to her God, and satisfied the priests His servants, she prays that He will establish her children in their places together with those who live for ever and ever.

The text reads:—

7.

8.

9.

10.

[Hieroglyphic text - lines 10-13]

11.

12.

13.

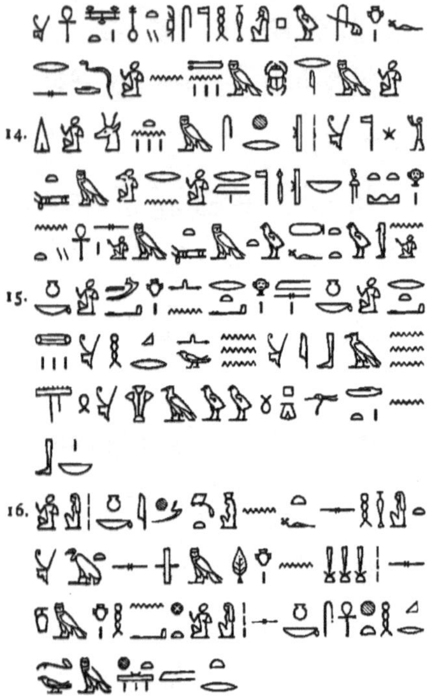

17. [hieroglyphic text]

18. [hieroglyphic text]

19. [hieroglyphic text]

20. [hieroglyphic text]

T

[hieroglyphic text]

21. [hieroglyphic text]

22. [hieroglyphic text]

Ptolemaïc Period.   From Akhmim.

Height, 2 ft. 6 in. × 18 in.

Plate XII.

SEPULCHRAL TABLET OF PET-BAST, A PRIEST OF PANOPOLIS.

No. 53.

STELE OF PET-BAST.*

53. Fine limestone stele, with rounded top, ⌓.
In the rounded portion are the following :—

1. Winged disk, beneath which are two jackals, couchant, one on each side of a standard surmounted by plumes.

2. The deceased adoring Rā-Harmachis, and the inscription :—

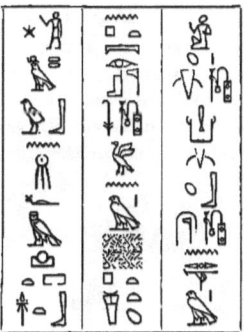

* See Plate XII.

T 2

3. The deceased adoring the Sun-god in the boat of the setting sun, and the legend ✕ 𓀀 ☉ ▱ | ▱ ▱ ▱ ⌇ ▱ 𓎼 ☉ .

The inscriptions on this stele state that Pet-Bast was a royal scribe, and that he was the son of the Ḥeru who was an *ut'eb*, and scribe, and priest of the *ka*, and the *ut'eb* of Seb, and the scribe of the divine hall of Åmsu. The text which covers the lower part of the stele consists of extracts from hymns to the Sun-god; as they are well-known they are not reproduced in type. Ptolemaïc Period. From Akhmîm.

Height, 2 ft. 5 in. ✕ 17¾ in.

54. Sepulchral stele of a woman, on which the deceased is depicted standing by the side of a table of offerings and a libation vase; the workmanship is very rough, and the rudely cut hieroglyphics show that it belongs to a late period. The inscription reads :—

1. 𓏲 𓈖 𓊵 𓈗 𓅆 𓎛

2. 𓏏 𓁐 𓂋 𓏏 𓀒 𓏤𓏤𓏤

3. 𓈗 𓂝 𓏏 ▨▨▨ 𓏥 𓁹 𓂝 𓆓 𓂧 𓏥

By the side of the face is inscribed ,
and lower down we have :—

Late Period. Height, 13 in. × 8½ in.

55. Calcareous stone stele with rounded top, upon which are inscribed the two *utchats;* below is a figure of the deceased standing before a table of offerings. The inscription is of the usual character, and reads :—

1.

2.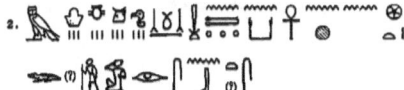

Nos. 57 and 58.

FUNERAL BOAT* AND
WOODEN CLAMP.

57. Wooden model of a boat with a crew of twenty men. In the bows is seated a man, and a man stands in the stern. Probably of the VIth dynasty. From Meir.

58. Hard wood clamp inscribed *neb taui Men-Maät-Rā*, "lord of the two lands, Men-Maät-Rā" (Seti I., King of Egypt, about B.C. 1370). From Abydos.   Length, 16¾ in.

---

* See Plate XIII.

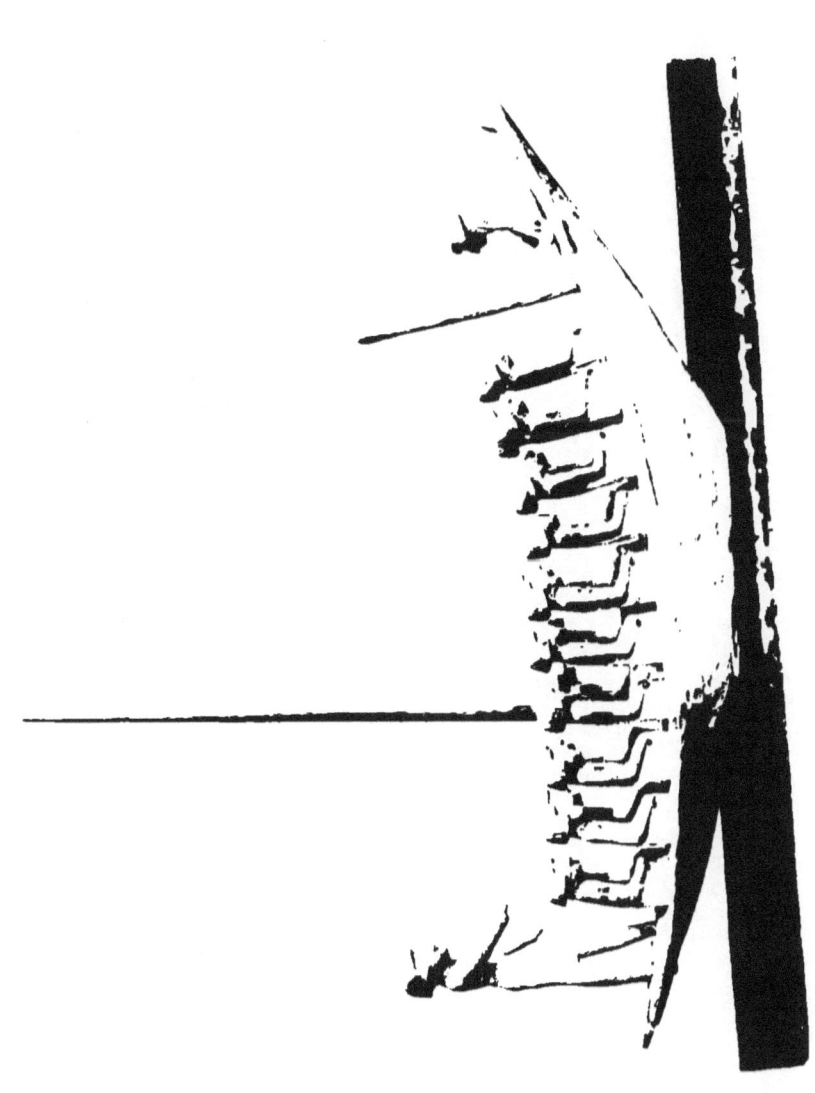

Nos. 56, 59—70.

FIGURES OF PRIESTS, OFFICIALS, ETC.

56. Head from a black granite statue of a priestly official; on the right shoulder is a part of the cartouche of the king whom he served, and on the back the following characters only remain :—

XXth dynasty. From Thebes. Height, 10 in.

59. Black granite statue of Sebek-nekht, the son of the lady of the house Àrit. The two lines of inscription on the sides of the pedestal read :—

Ancient Empire. Height, 7¼ in.

60. Black granite seated statue of a king, bearded, and wearing a square crown; above his forehead is a uræus. His left hand holds the emblem of life ♀, and rests upon his knee. Upon the sides of the throne are the emblems of Upper and Lower Egypt, and between them is the emblem of life ⸢𝄃 ☥ 𝄃⸣. Upon the left arm of the statue is inscribed the pre-nomen of Thothmes III. ⸢◯ ⊙ ▭ 𓎟⸣, King of Egypt, about B.C. 1600. The features of the statue are thick and heavy, and the whole face has the cast of an Ethiopian.   Height, 1 ft. 6 in.

STATUE OF IUPA.

61. Black granite kneeling figure of the scribe Iupa ⸢𓏭 𓃀 𓃠 𓄿⸣,* holding a shrine upon which is the head of a ram.   On the right side of the shrine is the cartouche of the "divine queen, Aāḥmes-nefert-âri,† living [for ever]" ⸢𓇋 ☉ ◯ ━ 𓎛𓏭 ⊙ ⸣ ☥ 𓏏⸣; and on the left side is the prenomen of one of the Amen-ḥetep kings, "lord of diadems, Amen-ḥetep,"‡ ⸢▭ 🏺𓏪 ◯ 𓇋 ▭ ⊙ 𓂋⸣ 𓃠 (*sic*).   In the front of the

---

* See Plate XVI.
† She was the queen of Amāsis I., King of Egypt about B.C. 1700.
‡ The four Ámen-ḥeteps reigned between B.C. 1666–1466.

Plate XVI.

IUPA THE SCRIBE, SUPERINTENDENT OF THE
PALACE OF RAMESES II.

shrine are three lines of inscription containing the
names and titles of :—

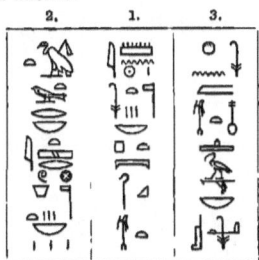

1. "Ȧmen-Rȧ, king of the gods, lord of heaven and
prince of Thebes.

2. "Mut, great lady, the lady of Asheru,* the
mistress of all the gods.

3. "Khonsu in Thebes, Nefer-ḥetep, and Thoth
lord of Hermonthis."

On the back of the statue are two perpendicular
lines of inscription which read :—

1.

---

* A quarter of Thebes.

2.

1. "May Ȧmen-Rȧ, president of the Apts,* grant life, strength, and health to the *ka* of Iupa, triumphant, the highly favoured of the beautiful god, the 'leader' of the festival of Ȧmen."

2. "May Mut, lady of heaven, and Khonsu-Nefer-ḥetep grant a happy span of life to the *ka* of Iupa, triumphant, the royal scribe, the superintendent of the great house, the overseer of the workmen em-ployed in all the buildings of his Majesty."

The four corners of the pedestal, around which runs a line of inscription, are somewhat broken, but the following fragments of the text remain :—

On the front:

---

* The modern Karnak.

FIGURES OF NEB-SEN THE SCRIBE, AND HIS SISTER NEBT-TA,
A LADY OF THE COLLEGE OF ÅMEN-RA AT THEBES.

On left side : [hieroglyphs]

[hieroglyphs]

On right side : [hieroglyphs]

[hieroglyphs]

[hieroglyphs]

From the inscription on the right side it is clear that Ḥāt-āai, the son of Iupa, set up great pillars in the temple of Ȧmen, and from that on the left we learn that the deceased Iupa was employed in the palace of Rameses II.

On the right shoulder of the statue of Iupa is the prenomen of Rameses II.* [cartouche] Usr-Maāt-Rā-setep-en-Rā, and on the left is the nomen [cartouche] "Rā-messu, beloved of Ȧmen."
XIXth dynasty.   Height, 2 ft. 3 in.

FIGURES OF NEB-SEN AND NEBT-TA.

62, 63. Double seated limestone figure of the scribe Neb-sen and his sister Nebt-ta.† Both figures

---

* He reigned about B.C. 1330.   † See Plate XIV.

U 2

wear a linen tunic and necklaces; the left arm of
Neb-sen embraces his sister, and the right arm of
Nebt-ta embraces her brother. The inscription down
the front of the figures reads :—

1. "May there be sepulchral meals in the Apts
upon the table of the lord of the gods to the *ka* of the
scribe of the treasury of the lord of the two lands,
Neb-sen, triumphant!

2. "May there be all sepulchral offerings upon the
table of Mut, the lady of Àsher, to the *ka* of the lady
of the house, the singer of Isis, the divine mother,
Nebt-ta, triumphant!"

On the front of the pedestal is inscribed ![glyph] ![glyph]
![glyph] "Behold their son making their
name to live"; ![glyph] "The

scribe of the treasury of Åmen, Usr-ḫāt; and

"The son, the scribe of the treasury of Åmen, Neb-meḫu, triumphant!"

On the right side of the pedestal, inlaid in blue, are six lines of inscription on behalf of Neb-sen, which read :—

"May Åmen, the establisher of the universe, grant a royal oblation to Neb-sen, the scribe of the Treasury of the lord of the two lands, triumphant before the beautiful god, the lord of eternity. May he grant to him a memorial for good in his town, may his *ka* be nourished upon light, and may his soul be satisfied with the sepulchral meals and with the placing of funeral gifts, and with the constant supply of flowers, fruit and vegetables which shall be brought and laid before him ceaselessly and for ever."

On the left side of the pedestal, inlaid in blue, are five lines of inscription on behalf of Nebt-ta, which read :—

"May Mut, lady of Åsher, the mistress of all the gods, and Isis, the great lady of enchantments . . . . . grant a royal oblation to the *ka* of Nebt-ta, the lady of the house, triumphant! May they grant [to her] sepulchral meals, oxen, ducks, linen bandages, wax, oil, wine and flowers of all kinds regularly upon the altar in the Apts daily"

On the slab at the back of the two figures are the two *utchats* 𓂀𓂀, the *shen* ☉, *etc.*, and five perpendicular lines of hieroglyphics inlaid in blue, which read :—

1. "May Sebek-Rā, lord of Suāanu, grant a royal oblation. May he grant glory, and power, and a

2. "coming forth as a living soul with offerings of *tchefau* food every day to

3. "May Anubis, president of the divine house (*i.e.*, the tomb), grant a royal oblation. May he grant the germination of the dead body in

"4. the underworld, and a going in and a coming out from the passages of the tomb, without repulse of soul, according to the wish of

5. "the *ka* of the scribe of the Treasury of the lord of the two lands, Neb-sen, triumphant! and to his loving sister, the lady of the house, Nebt-ta, triumphant"!

Height, 1 ft. 3 in.

FIGURE OF ÁMEN-EM-ÀPT.

64. Black basalt kneeling figure of Ámen-em-àpt 𓊪𓏤𓈖𓂋𓏏𓀾,* a royal scribe and director of the festivals of Ámen-Rā at Thebes. The inscriptions

---

* See Plate XV.

ÁMEN-EM-ÁPT, A SCRIBE AND DIRECTOR OF THE FESTIVALS
OF ÁMEN RA AT THEBES.

RAMESES III. KING OF EGYPT ABOUT B.C. 1200.

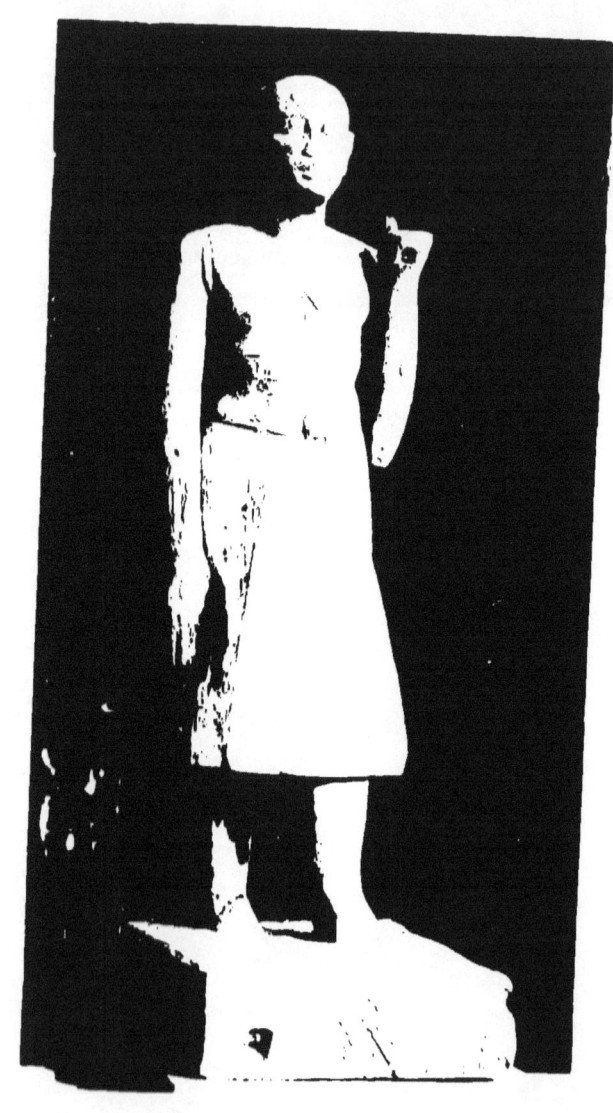

WOODEN FIGURE OF A PRIEST.

EARLY EMPIRE.   FROM GIZEH.

are passages from hymns to the sun in use during the
XVIIIth dynasty. From Thebes. About B.C. 1600.

Height 1 ft. 5½ in.

WOODEN FIGURE OF THE EARLY EMPIRE.

65. Wooden figure of a man on a wooden pedestal;
the left hand is raised to the shoulder. The features
are of the same type as those of the figures found in
the maṣṭaba tombs of the Early Empire. From Gizeh.

Height, 1 ft. 3⅞ in.

65A. Wooden portrait figure of a man.

Height, 8₁⁷₂ in.

RAMESES III.

66. Upper part of a black basalt statue of
Rameses III.,* King of Egypt, about B.C. 1200; the
cartouches of the king are on the arms. From
Thebes.   Height, 1 ft. 3½ in.

67. Black granite figure of the scribe Ápui
𓈖𓊃𓏤𓏥, upon a rounded pedestal; in front is a

---

* See Plate XVII.

figure of the god Osiris in relief.   The deceased was connected with the service of Åmsu and Isis, and the four lines of inscription on the back of the statue record his obedience and love of praising the king his lord, and the great favour with which the king regarded him.   Height, 1 ft. 3½ in.

FIGURES OF PIÅUI AND TAKHARIT.

68. Black granite upright figures of Piåui and his wife Takharit,* a lady of the College of Åmen-Rā at Thebes; on the back are four lines of hieroglyphics containing prayers for sepulchral offerings; they read:—

From Thebes.   Height, 1 ft. 1 in.

---

* See Plate XIX.

FIGURES OF PIAUI AND TAKHARIT, A LADY OF THE COLLEGE OF
ÀMEN-RĀ AT THEBES.

69. Green basalt head of a priest, or high official, with inlaid stone eyes.   XXVIth dynasty.

Height, 6 in.

69A. Brown basalt head from a statue of a royal sistrum-bearer.   From Thebes.   XVIIIth dynasty, about B.C. 1500.   Height, 9 in.

69B. Basalt head from the statue of a prince. About B.C. 800.   Height, 8 in.

70. Upper part of a black basalt figure of a man. Late Period.   Height, 3¼ in.

No. 71.

BRONZE LIBATION BUCKET.*

71. Bronze libation bucket, with handle, made for the hereditary chief of a tribe, the chancellor, the *smer-uāt*, the veritable royal kinsman Shashanq, triumphant, the son of Ḥeru-sa-Áuset, the son of the lady of the house Theheb-Teḥuti, triumphant! Beneath a star bespangled sky are ten perpendicular lines of hieroglyphics, which read :—

1. [hieroglyphics]

2. [hieroglyphics]

3. [hieroglyphics]

---

* See Plate XX.

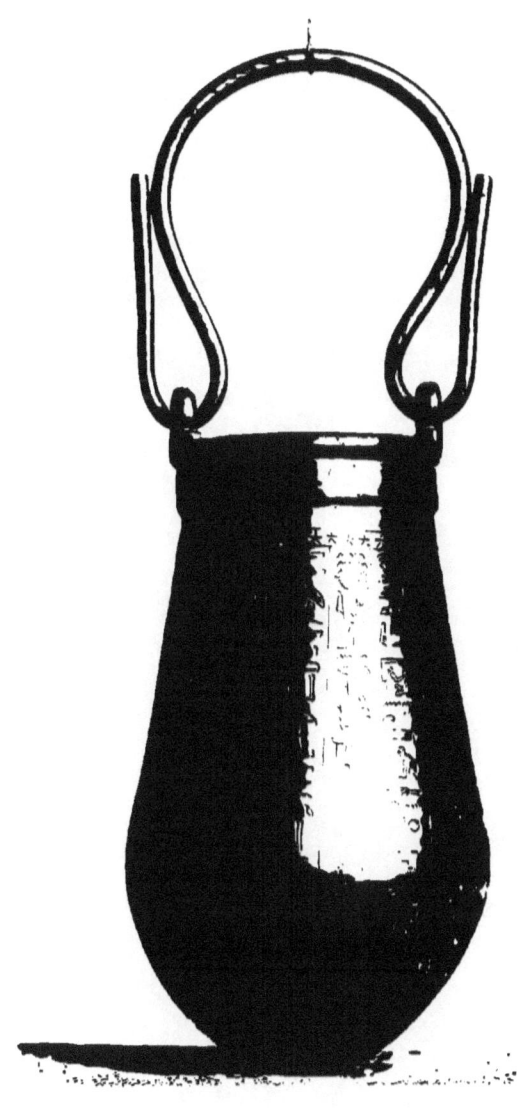

BRONZE VOTIVE LIBATION BUCKET MADE FOR SHASHANQ.

4.

5.

6.

7.

8.

9.

10.

"Behold may this libation be to thee, O Osiris, president of the underworld, great god, lord of Abydos! May this libation be to thee, O Osiris, the hereditary prince, the chancellor, the *smer-uāt,** .... veritable royal relative, loving him, superintendent of the great house of the *neter-ṭuat,*† Shashanq, triumphant, son of the president, the *àm-khent‡* of the *neter-ṭuat,* Ḥeru-sa-Àuset, triumphant! His mother [was] the lady of the house Thehebet-Teḫuti, triumphant! Is brought to thee this thy libation; Isis and Nephthys bring to thee these thy libations, and they are made (?) in the house of Àmen, in which thou art. Mayest thou live through them, mayest thou be strong through them, may libations be poured out [to thee] from choice vessels, O Osiris, the superintendent of the great house of the *neter-ṭuat,* Shashanq, triumphant! Mayest thou come forth at the order (to be said four times). His loving daughter, a singer and a lady of Àmen, Nit-Àqer (Nitocris).   Height, 9½ in.

72. Bronze libation bucket with two handles.

Height, 5¾ in.

73. Bronze model of a libation bucket.

Length, 1⅜ in.

---

* An ancient title of nobility.

† The name of an office held by people of high rank.

‡ The name of a priestly office.

Plate XXI.

BRONZE MIRROR.

Nos. 74, 75.

BRONZE MIRROR* AND *MENÀT*.

74. Bronze mirror having its handle ornamented with heads of Hathor. XXth dynasty.

Length, 10¾ in.

75. Portion of a bronze *menàt* for fixing to a large statue of Ptaḥ or some other god. On the narrow band is a scene in relief in which the goddess Isis, wearing disk and horns, stands in a shrine and suckles Horus or Harpocrates. At the lower part of the band where it joins the oval disk are uræi ; that on the right hand wears the crown of Upper Egypt ⌀, and that on the left the crown of Lower Egypt ⌀. In the centre of the disk, in relief, is Harpocrates wearing the triple crown 👑, and seated on a lotus flower. To the right, with hands raised in adoration, is the goddess Isis, wearing 👑 on her head; and to the left, seated on a throne, is a winged uræus wearing the crown of Upper Egypt. The surface of the bronze was originally gilded. This bronze is an example of a class of objects of considerable interest and rarity.

Length, 8¾ in.

---

* See Plate XXI.

Nos. 75ᴀ—153.

USHABTIU FIGURES
AND BOX.

Ushabtiu is the name given by the ancient
Egyptians to figures made of alabaster, wood, glazed
faïence, etc., which were inscribed with the 6th chapter
of the Book of the Dead, and placed in the tomb to
do for the deceased whatever labours were decreed
for him to perform in the underworld. These figures
are made in the form of the god Osiris, *i.e.*, in the
form of a mummy; the two hands are crossed over
the breast, the one holds a hoe and cord and basket,
the other an instrument for digging. In the text the
deceased addresses the figure, and says, "O *ushabtiu,*
if there be any work apportioned to be done by
Osiris (*i.e.*, the deceased) in the underworld, may all
obstacles be removed for him according to his desire."
To this the figure answers, "Here am I ready whenever ye call." The deceased next says, "O *ushabtiu,*
be ever watchful to labour, to sow the fields, to fill the
canals with water, and to carry sand from the West to

the East." To this the figure answers, " Here am I
ready whenever ye call." The hieroglyphic text
reads :—

à	uśebtiu	àpen	àr	àpt - tu
O	*ushabtiu*	*these,*	*if*	*be decreed*

Àusàr	er	àri	kat	neb	àrit	en	àm
Osiris	*to*	*do*	*work*	*any*	*[which is]*	*to be done*	*there*

em	Neter χert	àu - tu	ḥu	set'ebu
in	*the underworld,*	*be there*	*smitten down*	*obstructions*

àm	em	sa	er	χert - f	makuà
there	*for a person*		*according to*	*his wish.*	*Here am I*

ka - ten	sàp - ten	er	ennu
[when] ye call.	*Watch ye*	*at*	*moment*

Y

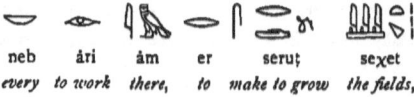

neb	ári	ám	er	seruṭ	seχet
every	*to work*	*there,*	*to*	*make to grow*	*the fields,*

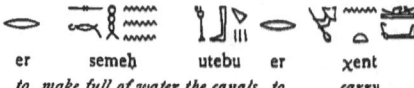

er	semeḥ	utebu	er	χent
to	*make full of water*	*the canals,*	*to*	*carry*

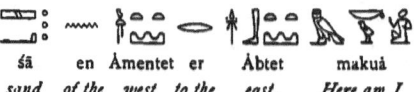

śá	en	Ámentet	er	Ábtet	makuá
sand	*of the*	*west*	*to the*	*east.*	*Here am I*

ka - θen
[*when*] *ye call.*

75A. Wooden *ushabti* figure made for Seti I., King of Egypt, about B.C. 1370, and inscribed with a version of the 6th chapter of the Book of the Dead; it was originally wholly covered with a layer of bitumen. The text reads:—

2. [hieroglyphs]

3. [hieroglyphs]

4. [hieroglyphs]

5. [hieroglyphs]

6. [hieroglyphs]

From Dêr el-baḥari. Height, 8½ in.

75B. Fine alabaster *ushabti* figure of a woman (?). The name is traced in black ink upon the centre of the projecting tunic between two red lines; it is now illegible. The flowing hair, eyebrows, bracelets, etc., are traced in black. From Abydos. Before the XVIIIth dynasty. Height, 7¾ in.

75C. Limestone *ushabti* figure of an unnamed Egyptian official inscribed with Chapter XXXB of the Book of the Dead. The text reads :—

1. [hieroglyphs] [space for name left blank] [hieroglyphs]

2. [hieroglyphic line]

3. [hieroglyphic line]

4. [hieroglyphic line]

5. [hieroglyphic line]

6. [hieroglyphic line]

For an English version of the Chapter, see above, p. 12. From Abydos.   Height, 8½ in.

76. Fine limestone *ushabti* figure made for a female.* The hair, which is beautifully plaited, is ornamented with a fillet of gems, and lotus flowers fall over the brow. The pectoral is painted to imitate precious stones, a linen garment is drawn over the shoulders, and bracelets are on the wrists. XVIIIth dynasty.   Height, 9½ in.

* See Plate XXII., No. 1.

USHABTIU FIGURES.

77. White limestone *ushabti* figure of Ta-bakà ⟨hieroglyphs⟩, inscribed with a version of the 6th chapter of the Book of the Dead.

Height, 7⅝ in.

78. White painted limestone *ushabti* figure of Àâa ⟨hieroglyphs⟩, inscribed with a version of part of the 6th chapter of the Book of the Dead. Height, 7⅝ in.

79. Green basalt *ushabti* figure uninscribed.

Height, 8⅝ in.

80. Painted wooden *ushabti* figure made for Mâḥu ⟨hieroglyphs⟩,* inscribed with a version of the 6th chapter of the Book of the Dead. Height, 12 in.

81. Blue glazed *faïence ushabti* figure of "Pa netchem, the high priest of Àmen," ⟨hieroglyphs⟩ ⟨hieroglyphs⟩, inscribed with the 6th chapter of the Book of the Dead. Pa-netchem lived about B.C. 1040. From Dêr el-baḥari. Height, 6¾ in.

82. Blue glazed *faïence ushabti* figure of "Pa- netchem, the high priest of Àmen," about B.C. 1040. In this example the right hand of the priest-king

---

* See Plate XXII., No. 2.

hangs by his side, and the left hand, holding a flail
⚑, is laid upon the breast.   From Dêr el-baḥari.

Height, 6¾ in.

83. Blue glazed *faïence ushabti* figure of "Pa-
netchem, the high priest of Ámen," about B.C. 1040.
From Dêr el-baḥari.   Height, 6¾ in.

84. Blue glazed *faïence ushabti* figure of Áuset-em-
khebit ⏧, a princess belonging to
the royal priestly family of Thebes, about B.C. 1040.
From Dêr el-baḥari.   Height, 6 in.

85. Blue glazed *faïence ushabti* figure of "King Pa-
netchem" ⏧, about B.C.
1040.   From Dêr el-baḥari.   Height, 4¾ in.

86. Blue glazed *faïence ushabti* figure of "the royal
son,   Tcheṭ-Ptaḥ-áuf-ānkh," ⏧
⏧, the husband of Nesi-ta-neb-asher, about B.C.
1040.   From Dêr el-baḥari.   Height, 4¼ in.

87. Blue glazed *faïence ushabti* figure of Tcheṭ-Ptaḥ-
áuf-ānkh, about B.C. 1040.   From Dêr el-baḥari.

Height, 4¼ in.

88. Blue glazed *faïence ushabti* figure of Tcheṭ-
Ptaḥ-áuf-ānkh, about B.C. 1040.   From Dêr el-baḥari.

Height, 4¼ in.

89, 90. Two blue glazed *faïence ushabtiu* figures of "Tchet-Ptah-àuf-ānkh, the high priest of Àmen," about B.C. 1040.   From Dêr el-baḥari.   Height, 4½ in.

91—93. Blue glazed *faïence ushabtiu* figures of a scribe of the confraternity of Àmen.   The name originally written has been erased.

Height, 5 in.–5¼ in.

94. Blue glazed *faïence ushabti* figure of the priest Pen-Àmen ☐ ⎮ ⎓ 𓀀.   About B.C. 800.

Height, 3¾ in.

95. Blue glazed *faïence ushabti* figure of Pa-maāu 𓀀𓂝 ; about B.C. 800.   Height, 4 in.

96. Painted red terra-cotta *ushabti* figure made for Ta-maāu ⬭ 𓅓 ⎮ 𓀀.   Height, 7¾ in.

97. Calcareous stone *ushabti* figure of Nefer ⎮ ⬭ 𓀀, who held the office ⎮ ⬭ ⬭ ⬭ ⎮ ⬭ ⬭ 𓀀 ; it is inscribed with the 6th chapter of the Book of the Dead.   Height, 8 in.

98. Blue glazed *faïence ushabti* figure inscribed in hieratic with a version of the 6th chapter of the Book of the Dead.   Height, 4 in.

99, 100. Two blue glazed *faïence ushabti* figures of the lady Thet-seshet-Khensu .

Height, 4 in.

101. Blue glazed *faïence ushabti* figure, the name upon which is illegible.   Height, 5 in.

102—109. Eight green glazed *faïence ushabtiu* figures of the lady Nes-Mut .

Height, 3¼ in.

110. Upper part of a green glazed *faïence ushabti* figure. XXVIth dynasty or later.   Height, 1⅞ in.

111. Painted wooden *ushabti* figure made for Kha-nu-meh (?) .   Height, 8½ in.

112—116. Painted wooden *ushabtiu* figures made for Bak-en-seśet . . . . . , a priest of Åmsu.   Height, 6¼ in.–8⅜ in.

117. Brownish-green glazed *ushabti* figure.   Late Period.   Height, 4 in.

118—152. A collection of blue glazed *faïence* and terra-cotta *ushabtiu* figures, uninscribed.

Height, 2½ in.–1⅜ in.

153. Wooden box for holding *ushabtiu* figures. On the cover, painted yellow on a white ground, is a boat with a sail spread , on a green sea. Round the outside of the box, between two red lines, is a hieroglyphic inscription in which the deceased Ȧṭeṭ prays that sepulchral meals may be given to him by the god Osiris. The text reads

Length, 9½ in.

Nos. 154—267.

BRONZE, WOODEN,
AND FAÏENCE FIGURES
OF THE GODS.

154. Gilded stone figure of the god Åmen-Rā; the plumes 𓂉 are wanting. Height, $1\frac{3}{8}$ in.

155. Wooden figure of Åmen·Rā, wearing plumes 𓂉. Height, $4\frac{3}{8}$ in.

Åmen-Rā was called the "king of the gods," and the principal seat of his worship was at Thebes, in the temple of the Åpts (the modern Karnak).

156. Bronze figure of Åmsu, ithyphallic. Height, $2\frac{1}{8}$ in.

Åmsu was a form of Åmen-Rā, and was the power of reproduction deified.

157. Bronze figure of Anubis standing on an uninscribed pedestal. Height, $5\frac{1}{2}$ in.

158. Black and green glazed *faïence* figure of Anubis ⚱, god of the dead.   Height, 1¼ in.

Anubis was the god of the tomb, and he received the mummified bodies of the dead into his charge. He is always present in the "Judgment Scene."

159. Bronze standing figure of Bast, holding an ægis to her breast with her left hand.   Height, 5½ in.

160. Bronze ægis of Bast.   Height, 2⅞ in.

161. Upper part of a lapis-lazuli figure of Bast.
                                                                  Height, ⅝ in.

162. Silver ægis of Bast.   Height, 1½ in.

The chief seat of the worship of the goddess Bast was the city of Bubastis, where she was adored under the form of a cat.

163. Silver figure of Bes.   Length, 1⁹⁄₁₆ in.

164. Green and black glazed *faïence* figure of the god Bes ⚱.   Height, 2¼ in.

165. Blue paste gilded figure of the god Bes.
                                                                  Height, 1⅝ in.

166. Blue paste gilded figure of the god Bes.
                                                                  Height, 1½ in.

167. Blue glazed *faïence* figure of the god Bes.
                                                                  Height, 1½ in.

168. Green glazed *faïence* figure of the god Bes wearing plumes.   Height, $1\frac{1}{2}$ in.

169. Blue paste head of the god Bes.

Height, $\frac{3}{8}$ in.

170—173. Green glazed *faïence* pendent figures of the god Bes.   Height, $\frac{1}{2}$-$\frac{3}{4}$ in.

174. Blue glazed *faïence* figure of the god Bes. Ptolemaïc Period.   Height, $11\frac{1}{4}$ in.

The worship of the god Bes was introduced into Egypt at a very early date from Neter-taui; he was the god of music, pleasure, and war.

175. Bronze figure of the god Harpocrates, wearing the disk and plumes, and the lock of hair on the right side of his head, emblematic of youth.   Height, 6 in.

He typified a form of the morning sun.

176. Green glazed *faïence* pendent figure of the god Harpocrates.   Height, $\frac{6}{8}$ in.

176a. Bronze figure of Harpocrates.

Height, $5\frac{1}{4}$ in.

177. Blue glazed *faïence* figure of Harpocrates; Roman Period.   Height, $1\frac{1}{8}$ in.

Harpocrates, *i.e.*, Ḥeru-pa-khraṭ, , was the son of Osiris and Isis, who was begotten by his father after death ; he typified a form of the morning sun.

178a. Bronze figure of Isis, seated upon a throne and suckling her child Horus.　　Height, 6½ in.

179. Bronze figure of Isis suckling Horus.

Height, 6 in.

180. Green glazed *faïence* figure of the goddess Isis suckling her child Horus. She wears the disk and horns .　　Height, 3 in.

181. Green glazed *faïence* figure of Isis suckling Horus.　　Height, 1¼ in.

182. Green glazed *faïence* figure of Isis suckling Horus ; the goddess has disk and horns upon her head.　　Height, 2 in.

183. Green glazed *faïence* figure of Isis suckling Horus ; the goddess has disk and horns upon her head.　　Height, 2 in.

184. Green glazed *faïence* figure of Isis suckling Horus ; the goddess has disk and horns upon her head.　　Height, 1¹⁄₁₂ in.

185. Green glazed *faïence* figure of Isis suckling Horus ; the goddess has the ⚱ crown on her head.

Height, 2½ in.

186. Light green glazed *faïence* pendent figure of the goddess Isis. Height, ¾ in.

187, 188. Blue glazed pendent *faïence* figures of Isis suckling Horus. Height, ¾ in.

The goddess Isis was the wife of Osiris, the god and judge of the dead.

189. Bronze figure of Khensu-nefer-ḥetep.*

Height, 8⅔ in.

The god Khensu-nefer-ḥetep 𓉔 was worshipped chiefly at Thebes ; he typified a form of the moon-god.

190. Upper part of a lapis-lazuli figure of Khnemu.

Height, ⅞ in.

The god Khnemu 𓉔 was the creator of man, whom he fashioned on a potter's wheel ; the chief seat of his worship was at Philæ, an island at the southern end of the First Cataract.

---

* See Plate XXIII., No. 1.

Plate XXIII.

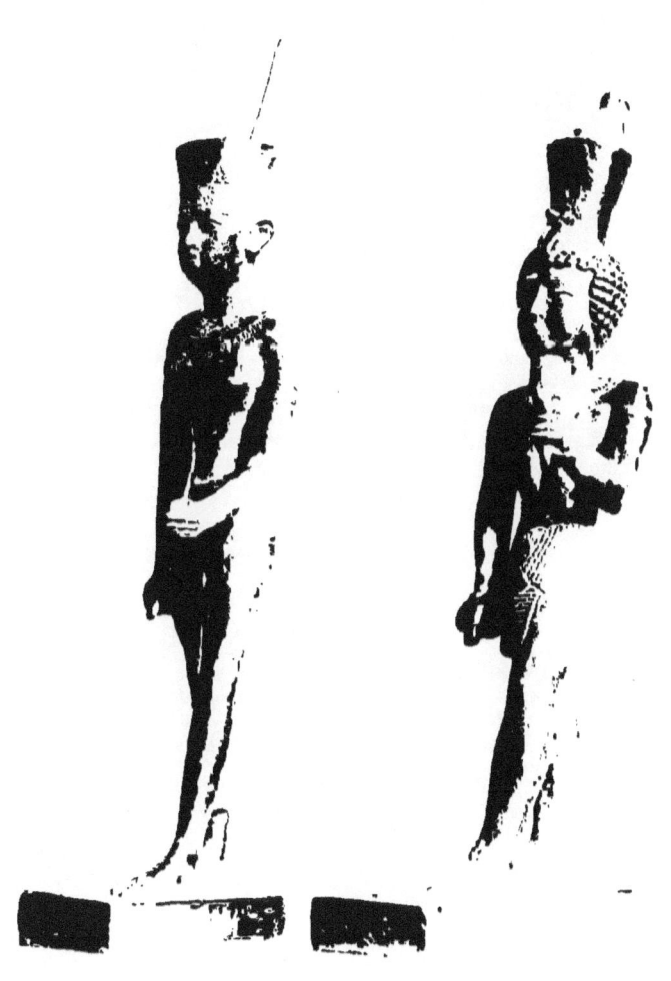

2
NEITH.

1
KHENSU-NEFER-ḤETEP.

191. Blue glazed *faïence* figure of the god Nefer-Tmu. Height, 3 in.

192. Blue glazed *faïence* figure of the god Nefer-Tmu. Height, 2¼ in.

193. Grayish-green glazed *faïence* seated figure of Nefer-Tmu. Height, 1 in.

Nefer-Tmu [hieroglyphs] was the son of Ptaḥ and Sechet or Bast.

194. Bronze figure of Neith.* Height, 9¼ in.

The goddess Nit [hieroglyphs], *i.e.*, the "Shooter" or "Weaver," was identified both with Mut and Hathor; the chief seat of her worship was at Saïs.

195. Blue glazed *faïence* figure of the goddess Nephthys. Height, 2⅞ in.

The goddess Nebt-ḥet [hieroglyphs], the Nephthys of the Greeks, was the daughter of Seb and Nut, and the wife of Set. In funeral scenes she stands at the head of the bier of her brother Osiris, by whom, according to one legend she became the mother of Anubis.

---

* See Plate XXIII., No. 2.

196, 197. Blue glazed *faïence* kneeling figure of the goddess Nut with outstretched wings; she wears on her head the disk and horns ☿. Around the wings and figure are holes whereby it was sewn to the bandage of the mummy. From Abydos.

Lengths, 9⅜ in., 7¾ in.

198. Blue glazed *faïence* figure of the goddess Nut having the double crown ⚜ on her head.

Height, 1⅞ in.

Nut, the goddess of the sky, was the wife of Seb, and was the mother of Osiris, Isis, Set, Nephthys, Anubis, Shu, and Tefnut.

199. Bronze figure of the god Osiris, the judge of the dead and lord of the underworld. Height, 10 in.

200. Bronze figure of Osiris wearing the *atef* crown ⚜, and uræus, and holding in his hands the crook ⚜, and flail ⚜, emblems of sovereignty and dominion. Height, 5 in.

201. Blue glazed *faïence* figure of Ptaḥ-Seker-Àusàr wearing disk and horns; this god was connected with the resurrection. Height, 1⅞ in.

202. Blue glazed *faïence* figure of Ptaḥ-Seker-Àusàr.

Height, 1⅝ in.

Plate XXIV.

THE GODDESS SEKHET.

203. Blue glazed *faïence* figure of Ptaḥ-Seker-Àusár.
Height, 1½ in.

204. Blue glazed *faïence* figure of Ptaḥ-Seker-Àusár.
Height, 1½ in.

205. Blue glazed *faïence* figure of Ptaḥ-Seker-Àusár.
Height, 1½ in.

206. Green glazed *faïence* figure of Ptaḥ-Seker-
Àusár.   Height, 1¼ in.

207. Dark blue glazed *faïence* pendent figure of
Ptaḥ-Seker-Àusár.   Height, ⁷⁄₁₆ in.

The triune god Ptaḥ-Seker-Àusár
was the god of the resurrection.

208. Blue glazed *faïence* figure of Rā with disk.
Height, ¾ in.

209. Silver figure of Rā wearing the double crown
.   Height, 1⅞ in.

Rā , the Sun-god, was probably the
first god worshipped in Egypt.

210. Seated bronze figure of the goddess Sekhet*
with uræus on her head; the badly cut inscription
seems to indicate that it was a votive offering of

---

* See plate XXIV.

Peṭā-Ausár . On the back of the throne are cut a winged hawk with disk, holding plumes, and a cluster of lotus flowers; and on the side is the emblem of the union of the two Egypts, .

Height, 1 ft. 10½ in.

211. Blue glazed *faïence* figure of Sekhet standing on two lions.   Height, 4¼ in.

212. Blue glazed *faïence* standing figure of Sekhet.
Height, 3¾ in.

213. Green glazed *faïence* standing figure of Sekhet.
Height, 2⅞ in.

214. Green glazed *faïence* standing figure of Sekhet.
Height, 2 in.

215. Green glazed figure of Sekhet.   Height, 1⅞ in.

216. Blue glazed *faïence* standing figure of Sekhet.
Height, 1¼ in.

217. Green glazed *faïence* figure of the goddess Sekhet.   Height, 1⅝ in.

218. Blue glazed *faïence* standing figure of Sekhet having on her head disk, horns, and plumes.

Height, 2⅝ in.

219. Blue glazed *faïence* standing figure of Sekhet having on her head disk, horns, and plumes.

Height, 2⅛ in.

220. Blue glazed *faïence* standing figure of Sekhet having on her head disk, horns, and plumes.

Height, $1\frac{2}{3}$ in.

221. Blue glazed *faïence* standing figure of Sekhet wearing the double crown ⚱. Height, $2\frac{1}{8}$ in.

222. Blue glazed *faïence* standing figure of Sekhet wearing the double crown ⚱. Height, 2 in.

223. Blue glazed *faïence* standing figure of Sekhet wearing the double crown ⚱. Height, $1\frac{2}{8}$ in.

224. Green glazed *faïence* standing figure of Sekhet having a uræus over her forehead. Height, $2\frac{1}{4}$ in.

225. Green glazed *faïence* Sekhet with a kitten at her feet. Height, $1\frac{3}{4}$ in.

226. Blue glazed *faïence* standing figure of Sekhet having a uræus over her forehead. Height, $1\frac{3}{8}$ in.

227. Green glazed *faïence* standing figure of Sekhet having a uræus over her forehead. Height, $1\frac{3}{8}$ in.

228. Blue glazed *faïence* seated figure of Sekhet.

Height, $1\frac{5}{8}$ in.

229. Green glazed seated figure of Sekhet.

Height, $1\frac{1}{2}$ in.

230. Blue glazed *faïence* seated figure of Sekhet.

Height, $2\frac{1}{4}$ in.

231. Blue glazed *faïence* seated figure of Sekhet.

Height, 2¼ in.

232. Blue glazed *faïence* seated figure of Sekhet.

Height, 2⅛ in.

233. Blue glazed *faïence* seated figure of Sekhet.

Height, 1½ in.

234. Blue glazed *faïence* seated figure of Sekhet.

Height, 1 7/8 in.

235. Blue glazed *faïence* seated figure of Sekhet.

Height, 7/8 in.

235A. Blue glazed *faïence* seated figure of the goddess Sekhet holding a sistrum.   Height, 2¼ in.

236. Bronze figure of the god I-em-ḥetep, holding an opened roll of papyrus upon his knee.

Height, 3⅝ in.

236A. Bronze figure of I-em-ḥetep.   Height, 6 in.

The god I-em-ḥetep , the Imouthis of the Greek writers, was the son of Ptaḥ and Nut, and the lord of medicine.

237. Light green glazed pendent figure of the goddess Sekhet.   Height, 7/8 in.

237A. Bronze standing figure of the goddess Sekhet.   Height, 5½ in.

238. Gilded lapis-lazuli standing figure of Sekhet.

Height, 1¾ in.

239. Gilded lapis-lazuli seated figure of Sekhet holding an *utchat* in her left hand.

Height, $1\frac{3}{8}$ in.

240. Blue glazed *faïence* figure of the goddess Ta-urt , the Thoueris of the Greek writers, wearing horns and disk .   Height, $2\frac{7}{8}$ in.

241. Portion of a green glazed *faïence* figure of the goddess Ta-urt .   Height, $3\frac{1}{2}$ in.

242. Blue glazed *faïence* figure of the goddess Ta-urt , for fastening to the beadwork covering of a mummy.   Height, $1\frac{1}{2}$ in.

243. Light green glazed Thoueris wearing horns, disk, and plumes on her head.   Height, 2 in.

244. Blue glazed Thoueris wearing horns, disk, and plumes on her head.   Height, $1\frac{7}{8}$ in.

245. Whitish-yellow glazed Thoueris wearing horns, disk, and plumes on her head.   Height, $1\frac{5}{8}$ in.

246. Lapis-lazuli pendent figure of Thoueris.

Height, $\frac{7}{8}$ in.

247-250. The four children of Horus in white, green, and black glazed *faïence*.

247. Åmset, human-headed.   Length, $4\frac{7}{8}$ in.

248. Ḥāpi, dog-headed.   Length, 5 in.

249. Ṭuamāutef, jackal-headed.   Length, 5 in.

250. Qebḥsennuf, hawk-headed.   Length, 4½ in.

251. White, green and black glazed *faïence* figure of Ȧmset.   Length, 4¾ in.

252. White, green and black glazed *faïence* figure of Ṭuamāutef.   Length, 5¼ in.

253. Blue glazed *faïence* plaque with a figure of Ṭuamāutef in relief. The edges are pierced with holes for sewing it to the bandage of the mummy.
                      Length, 1⅝ in.

254. White, green and black glazed *faïence* figure of Qebḥsennuf.   Length, 4⅝ in.

255. Green glazed *faïence* standing figure of Ḥāt-meḥit; she holds an *utchat* in her hands and has a fish on her head.   Height, 3⅜ in.

256. Green glazed *faïence* seated figure of Ḥāt-meḥit; on her head is a fish.   Height, 2¼ in.

The goddess Ḥāt-meḥit was the female counterpart of a form of the Sun-god (*i.e.*, "the living soul of Rā,"), who was worshipped in Mendes.

257. Bronze figure of a double hawk-headed deity (Ḥeru-χuti?) wearing plumes.   Height, 2½ in.

258. Blue glazed *faïence* seated figure of a hawk-headed god wearing plumes ⍐.   Height, 1 in.

259. Dark green glazed *faïence* figure of a god.
        Height, 1½ in.

260. Dark green glazed *faïence* figure of a god.
        Height, 1½ in.

261. Silver head of a goddess with uræus and double crown ⍩ on her head.   Height, 1½ in.

262–266. Five small *faïence* figures of gods.
        Heights, ⅞ in.–⅝ in.

267. Green glazed *faïence* head of a pendent figure of a god.   Length, ⅞ in.

Nos. 268—316.

BIRDS, BEASTS, FISHES,
REPTILES, ETC.,
SACRED TO THE GODS.

268. Lapis-lazuli figure of a ram having four heads.
Length, $1\frac{3}{8}$ in.

269. Lapis-lazuli figure of a ram having four heads.
Length, $\frac{3}{4}$ in.

270. Green glazed steatite ram couchant.
Length, $\frac{5}{16}$ in.

271. Black painted plaster figure of a jackal, sacred to Anubis. Length, $3\frac{7}{8}$ in.

272. Bronze cat, sacred to Bast, lady of Bubastis.
Height, $3\frac{1}{2}$ in.

273. Blue glazed *faïence* cat. Height, 2 in.

274. Blue glazed *faïence* cat. Height, $1\frac{1}{4}$ in.

275. Blue glazed *faïence* cat. Height, $1\frac{1}{4}$ in.

276. Blue glazed *faïence* cat. Height, $1\frac{1}{8}$ in.

277. Blue glazed *faïence* cat with kitten.

Height, $1\frac{1}{8}$ in.

278. Blue glazed *faïence* cat with kitten.

Height, $1\frac{1}{8}$ in.

279-281. Three blue and green glazed *faïence* figures of a cat.   Heights, $\frac{3}{8}$ in. to $\frac{7}{10}$ in.

282. Blue glazed *faïence* mouse inscribed on the base ⟨hieroglyph⟩.   Length, $\frac{9}{10}$ in.

283. Bluish-green glazed *faïence* mouse inscribed on the base ⟨hieroglyph⟩ Ṭā-uat'-meri (?).   Length, $\frac{5}{8}$ in.

284. Green glazed steatite mouse inscribed on the base with winged disk having pendent uræi and ⟨hieroglyph⟩.   Length, $\frac{1}{2}$ in.

285. Green glazed steatite mouse inscribed on the base Unt ⟨hieroglyph⟩.   Length, $\frac{3}{8}$ in.

286. Green glazed steatite double mouse.

Length, $\frac{1}{4}$ in.

287. Green glazed steatite double figure of an animal.   Length, $\frac{3}{8}$ in.

288. Blue glazed *faïence* sow feeding.

Length, $1\frac{3}{8}$ in.

289. Blue glazed *faïence* sow feeding.

Length, $1\frac{1}{4}$ in.

290. Carnelian pendant; head of a lion.

Length, $\frac{7}{10}$ in.

291. Blue glazed *faïence* dog-headed ape, 🐒, sacred to Thoth.   Height, $2\frac{1}{4}$ in.

292. Blue glazed *faïence* figure of the dog-headed ape of Thoth, having on his head crescent and disk.

Length, $1\frac{3}{4}$ in.

293. Green glazed *faïence* pendent dog-headed ape.   Height, $\frac{3}{4}$ in.

294. Bronze dog-headed ape wearing crescent and disk.   Height, $3\frac{1}{4}$ in.

295. Bronze shrew-mouse.   Length, $3\frac{3}{4}$ in.

296. Rectangular bronze case for holding a mummied shrew-mouse; on the top, supported by two pillars, is a shrew-mouse in solid bronze.

Length, $2\frac{1}{16}$ in.

297. Bronze mummied cat case in the form of a cat; in the right ear is a gold earring.

Height, $6\frac{5}{8}$ in.

298. Bronze case, pylon-shaped, for holding the mummies of kittens; on the top are two seated cats in solid bronze.   Length, $4\frac{1}{4}$ in.

299. Bronze ibis with the feather of Maāt .

Height, $1\frac{1}{4}$ in.

300. Lapis-lazuli hawk with pierced projection on the back whereby it was suspended to a collar.

Height, $\frac{6}{8}$ in.

301. Head from a green basalt statue of an official, XXVIth dynasty. Height, $1\frac{11}{12}$ in.

302. Green glazed *faïence* hawk, sacred to Horus, having upon his head the double crown .

Height, $1\frac{1}{2}$ in.

303. Green glazed steatite duck. On the base is inscribed a cruciform ornament with four uræi.

Length, $\frac{1}{2}$ in.

304. Green glazed steatite duck. On the base is inscribed a cruciform ornament with four uræi.

Length, $\frac{7}{12}$ in.

305. Green glazed steatite duck. On the base is a device composed of and lotus flowers.

Length, $\frac{1}{2}$ in.

306. Carnelian duck. Length, $\frac{7}{16}$ in.

307. Bronze uræus wearing disk and horns.

Height, $4\frac{3}{4}$ in.

308. Blue glazed *faïence* frog inscribed on the base "Bast, giver of life," *Bast ṭā ānχ.*

Height, $\frac{1}{2}$ in.

309. Green glazed *faïence* frog inscribed on the base with a floral device.   Height, $\frac{7}{16}$ in.

310. Mother-of-emerald frog.   Height, $\frac{3}{8}$ in.

311. Blue glazed *faïence* frog.   Length, $\frac{1}{2}$ in.

312. Green glazed *faïence* frog.   Length, $\frac{3}{8}$ in.

313. Crystal frog.   Length, $\frac{7}{16}$ in.

314. Carnelian frog.   Length, $\frac{7}{16}$ in.

315. Onyx frog.   Length, $\frac{3}{4}$ in.

316. Green glazed steatite fish; on one side is inscribed the name Ámen-Rā .   Length, $\frac{7}{16}$ in.

Nos. 317—833 and 1392—1785.

SCARABS.

In the south of Egypt, and in Nubia particularly, the traveller may frequently observe a greenish-black or black beetle toiling up a sand-heap, and rolling before it with its hind legs a ball, an inch and a half or two inches in diameter, made of dirt, in which it has wrapped its eggs. Naturalists have called this beetle *Scarabæus sacer*, and they consider it to be the type of *Coprophagi* or "dung-eaters." A remarkable peculiarity exists in the structure and situation of the hind legs, for they are placed very close to the end of the body, and when the beetle rolls its ball of eggs along it seems as if it stands upon its head, and as if its head is turned away from the ball. In this insect the ancient Egyptians saw an emblem of the Sun-god, who rolls his egg across the sky daily. Like him, it was supposed to have produced itself, for all beetles were males, and Horapollo and other writers affirm that a female beetle never existed. It was said to be

only-begotten because it was self-produced ; it represented *generation* because of its supposed acts ; and
father because it was engendered by a father only;
and *world* because in its generation it is fashioned in
the form of a world ; and *man* because there is no
female race among them.   From the Egyptian inscriptions we now know that the beetle, which they
called ⌗⌗⌗ *K'heperà*, was a symbol of the
god ⌗⌗⌗, who was the "father of the
gods," and the creator of all things which exist in
heaven and earth.   He formed himself out of the
matter which he himself produced, and he was
identified with the night-sun at the moment when it
was about to rise for a new day, and thus typified
matter about to change its form of existence, or
matter about to come into existence, and resurrection
and new birth generally.

On the flat base of the scarab the Egyptians en-
graved hieroglyphic texts, the names of gods, kings,
priests, devices, *etc.*   The funeral scarabs made of
green basalt form a distinct class, and are of great
interest.   The finest examples are set in a gold
border and have a horizontal band of gold across the
back ; the division of the wings is marked by a band
of gold running at right angles to the horizontal band

to the end of the body. Green basalt scarabs were attached to the neck by gold or bronze wires, or chains, and they were laid immediately over the heart. The poorer classes of the Egyptians made use of green or blue glazed *faïence* scarabs, which they either sewed upon the bandages, or fastened into pylon-shaped pectorals which they laid upon the breast of the dead. The green basalt scarab is usually inscribed with the text of the 30th chapter of the Book of the Dead, a composition which in its rubric is said to be as old as the IVth dynasty. For a running English translation of this chapter see *supra*, p. 12, and for the hieroglyphic text from the coffin of Nes-Amsu see p. 61 ff.

317. Green basalt scarab in its original gilded copper setting, inscribed with a version of chapter 30B of the Book of the Dead. It is asserted that it belonged to the mummy for whom the coffin without name, which is described on pp. 30–41, was made; parts of the characters in the first line, which contains the name, are covered by the setting, but the signs 𓊪𓏤𓅱𓏥 are clear. Length, 3 in.

318. Black stone funeral scarab made for the scribe 𓅱𓈖𓏏 Sa-Tehuti. It is inscribed with

the 30th chapter of the Book of the Dead, the text
of which as given upon it reads :—

Length 2½ in.

319. Green basalt scarab, inscribed with a faulty
text of parts of the 30th chapter of the Book of the
Dead.   Length, 2¼ in.

320. Green basalt scarab, uninscribed.

Length, 1¾ in.

321. Large bluish-green glazed *faïence* scarab with outstretched wings, pierced on the edges with holes whereby it was sewn to the outer bandage of the mummy. From Abydos.

Length between the tips of the wings, $11\frac{5}{16}$ in.

322. Large bluish-green glazed *faïence* scarab with outstretched wings, pierced on the edges with holes whereby it was sewn to the outer bandage of the mummy. From Abydos.

Length between the tips of the wings, 11 in.

323. Blue paste scarab pierced with seven holes whereby it was sewn to the outer bandages of the mummy. From Abydos.

Length, $3\frac{3}{8}$ in., width, $1\frac{3}{4}$ in.

324. Green *faïence* scarab, uninscribed, for attaching to the bead-work of a mummy. Length, $2\frac{1}{2}$ in.

325. Blue paste scarab, uninscribed, for attaching to the bead-work of a mummy. Length, 2 in.

326. Brown composition scarab, uninscribed, for attaching to the bead-work of a mummy.

Length, $2\frac{1}{8}$ in.

327. Green glazed *faïence* scarab, uninscribed, for attaching to the bead-work of a mummy.

Length, $1\frac{3}{4}$ in.

328. Black terra-cotta scarab, uninscribed, for attaching to the bead-work of a mummy.

Length, 1⅜ in.

329. Pair of blue glazed *faïence* wings from a scarab, for attaching to the bead-work of a mummy.

Length, 2½ in.

330. Blue glazed *faïence* scarab, inscribed with the name Ámen 𓇋𓏠. Length, ¾ in.

331. Green glazed steatite scarab, inscribed with the name Ámen 𓇋𓏠, and a hawk with outspread wings. From Abydos. Length, 1⁹⁄₁₆ in.

332. Yellow glazed steatite scarab, inscribed Ámen-Rā 𓍹𓇋𓏠𓇳𓈖𓍺. Length, 1⁹⁄₁₆ in.

333. Yellow glazed steatite scarab, inscribed Ámen-Rā 𓍹𓇋𓏠𓇳𓈖𓍺. Length, ¾ in.

334. Green glazed steatite scarab, inscribed Ámen-Rā 𓍹𓇋𓏠𓇳𓈖𓍺. Length, ⅝ in.

335. Blue paste scarab, inscribed Ámen-Rā 𓍹𓇋𓏠𓇳𓈖𓍺. Length 1⁹⁄₁₆ in.

336. White marble cowroid, inscribed Àmen-Rā
[glyphs]. From Abydos.   Length $\frac{1}{16}$ in.

337. Green glazed steatite scarab, inscribed Àmen-
Rā [glyphs]. From Abydos.   Length, $\frac{1}{10}$ in.

338. Green glazed steatite scarab, inscribed Àmen-
Rā [glyphs]. From Abydos.   Length, $\frac{1}{2}$ in.

339. Green glazed steatite cowroid, inscribed
Àmen-Rā [glyphs]. From Abydos.   Length, $\frac{1}{16}$ in.

340. Green glazed steatite scarab, inscribed Àmen-
Rā [glyphs]. From Abydos.   Length, $\frac{9}{16}$ in.

341. Green glazed steatite scarab, inscribed
"Favoured of Àmen-Rā," [glyphs] *Amen-Rā ḥes.*
From Abydos.   Length, $\frac{3}{8}$ in.

342. Green glazed steatite scarab, inscribed Àmen-
Rā [glyphs]. From Abydos.   Length, $\frac{3}{8}$ in.

343. Green glazed steatite scarab, inscribed Àmen-
Rā [glyphs]. From Abydos.   Length, $\frac{3}{8}$ in.

344. Green glazed steatite scarab, inscribed Àmen-
Rā [glyphs]. From Abydos.   Length, $\frac{1}{16}$ in.

345. Green glazed steatite scarab, inscribed Åmen-Rå 〔 〕. From Abydos.   Length, $\frac{3}{8}$ in.

346. Green glazed steatite cowroid, inscribed Åmen-Rå 〔 〕. From Abydos. Length, $\frac{1}{2}$ in.

347. Green glazed steatite scaraboid, inscribed Åmen-Rå 〔 〕. From Abydos. Length, $\frac{3}{8}$ in.

348. Black stone scarab on which traces of the name Åmen-Rå 〔 〕 remain. From Abydos.
          Length, $\frac{1}{2}$ in.

349. Rectangular green glazed steatite plaque, pierced, inscribed Åmen-Rå 〔 〕. From Abydos.
          Length, $\frac{1}{2}$ in.

350. Lapis-lazuli scaraboid, inscribed Åmen-Rå 〔 〕. From Abydos.   Length, $\frac{5}{16}$ in.

351. Green glazed steatite scarab, inscribed Åmen-Rå 〔 〕.   Length, $\frac{6}{16}$ in.

352. Green glazed steatite scarab, inscribed with figures of the gods Åmen, Rå, and Anubis; above are two signs which may be 〔 〕, Åmen-Rå. From Abydos.   Length, $\frac{1}{16}$ in.

353. Green glazed steatite scarab, inscribed "Åmen-Rā," etc. . From Abydos.

Length, $\frac{7}{16}$ in.

354. Light blue glazed *faïence* scarab, inscribed "Åmen, the valorous one of all lands," , *Åmen-χepeś-taui*. From Abydos. Length $\frac{7}{8}$ in.

355. Green glazed steatite scarab, inscribed "Beautiful lord, Åmen," *nefer neb Åmen*. From Abydos. Length, $\frac{5}{8}$ in.

356. Green glazed steatite scarab, inscribed "Libationer of Åmen-Rā," .

Length, $\frac{7}{16}$ in.

357. Blue glazed *faïence* scarab, inscribed

Length $\frac{5}{8}$ in.

358. Blue glazed *faïence* scarab, inscribed

Length, $\frac{3}{4}$ in.

359. Green glazed steatite scarab inscribed on the base with a figure of Bes. From Abydos.

Length, $\frac{1}{2}$ in.

360. Green glazed steatite scaraboid, inscribed with a figure of the god Bes. From Abydos.

Length, ⅜ in.

361. Green glazed steatite scarab, inscribed with a figure of the god Bes. From Abydos. Length, ⅝ in.

362. Green glazed steatite cowroid, inscribed with a figure of the god Bes. From Abydos. Length, ⅝ in.

363. Green glazed steatite scarab, inscribed with a figure of Bes being adored by two apes, each of which holds in his fore-paws. From Abydos.

Length, ⅘ in.

364. Green glazed steatite scarab, inscribed with a figure of the god Bes. From Abydos.

Length, 1¼ in.

365. Green glazed steatite scarab, inscribed with a figure of the god Bes. From Abydos.

Length, 1¼ in.

366. Green glazed steatite scarab, inscribed with a figure of the god Bes. From Abydos. Length, $\frac{12}{16}$ in.

367. Green glazed steatite scarab, inscribed with a figure of the god Bes. From Abydos. Length, $\frac{12}{16}$ in.

368. Green glazed steatite scarab, inscribed with a figure of the god Bes. From Abydos. Length, ⅝ in.

369. Rectangular green glazed steatite plaque, set in its original gold frame. On one side in relief is Horus ⟨glyph⟩, standing among lotus flowers, and faced by Thoueris, who wears on her head ⟨glyph⟩; on the other side is the legend ⟨glyphs⟩. From Abydos.

Length, $\frac{9}{16}$ in.

370. Green glazed steatite scarab, inscribed "Horus of the two lands" ⟨glyphs⟩ *Heru taui.* From Abydos. Length, $\frac{9}{16}$ in.

371. Green glazed steatite scarab, mounted in the original gold frame, inscribed Maāt ⟨glyph⟩. From Abydos. Length, $\frac{3}{4}$ in.

372. Green glazed *faïence* scarab, inscribed Kheperà ⟨glyphs⟩. From Abydos. Length, $\frac{1}{2}$ in.

373. Green glazed steatite scarab, inscribed with the name of Unás ⟨glyphs⟩, the last king of the Vth dynasty, about B.C. 3300. From Abydos.

Length, $\frac{9}{16}$ in.

374. Green glazed steatite oval, inscribed on the one side with the prenomen of Usertsen I.

⊙ ⌐☐ *Rā-nub-ka,* and on the other with the name Ámen-ḥetep, 𓏤 ≈ ⌐. From Abydos.

Length, ½ in.

375. Green glazed steatite scarab, inscribed with the prenomen of Usertsen I., ⊙ ⌐☐ *nub-ka-Rā,* king of Egypt about B.C. 2400.   Length, ₁⁷₆ in.

376. Green glazed steatite scarab, inscribed *Au-âb-Rā men ṭā neſer men ṭā ānχ,* "Āu-âb-"Rā, the stable one, the giver of life, the "stable one, the giver of happiness."
From Abydos.   Length, ₁⁹₆ in.

377. Green glazed steatite scarab, inscribed with the prenomen of Ámen-ḥetep I., *Rā-tcheser-kat,* king of Egypt about B.C. 1660. From Abydos.

Length, ½ in.

378. Green glazed steatite scarab, inscribed "Son of the Sun, beautiful god " *Tcheser-ka-Rā* (Ámen-ḥetep I.), " giver of life and power. All life " [to him], and all happiness, and all " good luck, and all stability."
From Abydos.

Length, ⅝ in.

379. Green glazed steatite scarab, in its original ring, inscribed with a sphinx and ⟨hieroglyphs⟩ *neter nefer Maât-ka-Râ*, "Beautiful god, Maât-ka-Râ" (Ḥât-shepset (?)). From Abydos.

Length, $\frac{7}{16}$ in. ; diameter of ring, $1\frac{1}{16}$ in.

380. Yellow glazed steatite scarab, inscribed on the base with the prenomen of Thothmes I., the "beautiful god," ⟨cartouche⟩. Length $\frac{5}{8}$ in.

381. Green glazed steatite scarab, inscribed on the base ⟨hieroglyphs⟩, "Beautiful god, lord of the two lands, Râ-men-kheper" (*i.e.*, Thothmes III., king of Egypt about B.C. 1550). Length, $\frac{5}{8}$ in.

382. Green glazed steatite scarab, inscribed on the base with winged disk and uræi, and a cartouche containing the prenomen of Thothmes III., ⟨cartouche⟩ The cartouche is supported by two uræi on each side.

Length, $\frac{1}{2}$ in.

383. Blue glazed steatite scarab, inscribed on the base with uræus, ⟨hieroglyphs⟩, "Beautiful Horus," and the prenomen of Thothmes III. On the back is inscribed ⟨cartouche⟩, "Beautiful god, Râ-men-kheper."

Length, $\frac{5}{8}$ in.

384. Green glazed scarab, inscribed on the base with a lion-headed sphinx, and ⸻ ⸻, " Beautiful god, lord of the two worlds, Rā-men-kheper, beloved of Åmen-Rā."

Length, ⅝ in.

385. Green stone scarab, inscribed on the base with the prenomen of Thothmes III.

Length, 7/16 in.

386. Dark blue glazed steatite scarab, inscribed with the prenomen of Thothmes III., *Men-kheper-Rā*, king of Egypt about B.C. 1550, and with spirals. From Abydos.

Length, 1⅛ in.

387. Green glazed steatite oval plaque, pierced: on the one side is an *utchat* in relief, and on the other the prenomen of Thothmes III., *Men-kheper-Rā*, and flowers. From Abydos.

Length, ⅞ in.

388. Green glazed steatite scarab, inscribed with the prenomen of Thothmes III.
On each side of the feathers is an uræus,
and on each side of the cartouche *Maāt* .
From Abydos.   Length, $\frac{11}{16}$ in.

389. Green glazed steatite scarab, inscribed with
the prenomen of Thothmes III., , and
*ḥeq Uast neb χepeš meri
Ámen*, "prince of Thebes, lord of might, beloved of
Amen." From Abydos.   Length, $\frac{3}{4}$ in.

390. Green glazed steatite scarab inscribed with
the prenomen of Thothmes III., *Men-kheper-Rā.*
From Abydos.   Length, $\frac{1}{2}$ in.

391. Green glazed steatite scarab, inscribed with the prenomen of Thothmes III.,
Men-kheper-Rā. From Abydos.
                              Length, $\frac{1}{2}$ in.

392. Green glazed steatite scarab, inscribed with
four uræi, having their tails interlaced; in each
space is the prenomen of Thothmes III., .
From Abydos.   Length, $\frac{5}{8}$ in.

393. Green glazed steatite scarab, inscribed with a sphinx, winged serpent, and prenomen of Thothmes III., between uræi.   From Abydos.

Length, ⅝ in.

394. Brown glazed steatite scarab, inscribed with the prenomen of Thothmes III. between winged beetles.   From Abydos.

Length, ¾ in.

395. Green glazed steatite scarab, inscribed with the prenomen of Thothmes III.,   .   To the beetle uræi are attached.   From Abydos.

Length, 1 1/16 in.

396. Green glazed steatite scarab, inscribed with the prenomen of Thothmes III., and winged disk.   From Abydos.

Length, 1⅛ in.

397. Green glazed steatite scarab, inscribed with the prenomen of Thothmes III.,   ; the beetle is winged and has pendent uræi.   From Abydos.

Length, ½ in.

398. Green glazed steatite scarab, inscribed 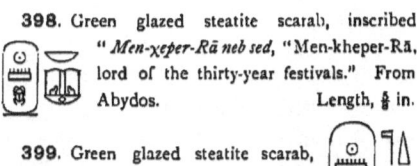 " *Men-χeper-Rā neb sed,* "Men-kheper-Rā, lord of the thirty-year festivals." From Abydos. Length, ⅝ in.

399. Green glazed steatite scarab, inscribed with the prenomen of Thothmes III., etc. From Abydos. Length, 11/16 in.

400. Green glazed steatite scarab, inscribed with the crown , and with the prenomen of Thothmes III.,  which is placed between uræi. From Abydos. Length, ¾ in.

401. Green glazed steatite scarab, inscribed with the prenomen of Thothmes III., etc. From Abydos. Length, ⅝ in.

402. Green glazed steatite scarab, inscribed with the figure of a man kneeling in adoration before the prenomen of Thothmes III., and with a winged uræus. From Abydos. Length, 13/16 in.

403. Green glazed steatite scarab, inscribed with the prenomen of Thothmes III., which is placed between uræi. Below is the emblem of "myriads of years," [figure], resting upon [figure], and between the two palm branches are the signs [figure] *âf ḥrâ*, "Hail to thee." From Abydos.   Length, ⅝ in.

404. Green glazed steatite scarab, inscribed with a sphinx [figure], and [figure], "stability," from each side of which springs an uræus [figure]. The legend reads: [figure] *Men-χeper-Râ neb taui*, "Menkheper-Râ, lord of the north and south." From Abydos.   Length, ⅝ in.

405. Green glazed steatite scarab, inscribed with the prenomen of Thothmes III., [figure], and two winged disks with pendent uræi, . From Abydos.
Length, ¹⁰⁄₁₆ in.

406. Green glazed steatite scarab, inscribed with the prenomen of Thothmes III. From Abydos.   Length, ⅝ in.

407. Green glazed steatite scarab, inscribed with a sistrum surmounted by the prenomen of Thothmes III., ; from each side of the handle springs an uræus . From Abydos. Length, $\frac{11}{16}$ in.

408. Green glazed steatite scarab, inscribed with the prenomen of Thothmes III., , the "beautiful god," *neter nefer.* From Abydos.

Length, $\frac{9}{16}$ in.

409. Green glazed steatite scarab, inscribed with the prenomen of Thothmes III., , and a winged disk. From Abydos.

Length, $\frac{1}{2}$ in.

410. Blue glazed steatite scarab, inscribed, "Beautiful god, lord of the north and south," *Men-xeper-Rā* . From Abydos.

Length, $\frac{3}{4}$ in.

411. Green glazed steatite cowroid, inscribed with the prenomen of Thothmes III., *Men-xeper-Rā.* From Abydos.

Length, $\frac{6}{8}$ in.

412. Rectangular steatite plaque, pierced. On one side are a human-headed lion and the legend [hieroglyphs], "Beautiful god, lord of the north and south, *Men-kheper-Rā.*" On the other is a figure of the king holding [sign]. Before him are the signs [hieroglyphs], *men χeper,* and the name [hieroglyphs] *Amen-Rā.* On each edge is a figure of the god [figure] *Menthu.* From Abydos. Length, $1\frac{1}{8}$ in.

413. Green glazed steatite scarab, inscribed with the prenomen of Thothmes III., [hieroglyphs] *Men-χeper-Rā.* From Abydos.

Length, $\frac{7}{16}$ in.

414. Green glazed steatite scarab, inscribed with the prenomen of Thothmes III., [hieroglyphs], and with "double good luck," [signs].

From Abydos. Length, $\frac{5}{8}$ in.

415. Green glazed steatite scarab, inscribed with the prenomen of Thothmes III., [hieroglyphs], and uræi. From Abydos.

Length, $\frac{5}{8}$ in.

416. Green glazed steatite scarab, inscribed with the prenomen of Thothmes III., , etc. From Abydos.

Length, ⅔ in.

417. Blue glazed steatite scarab, inscribed with the prenomen and titles of Thothmes III., "king of the north and south, the lord of the world, *Men-χeper-Rā.*" From Abydos.

Length, ¹¹⁄₁₆ in.

418. Green glazed steatite scarab, inscribed with the prenomen of Thothmes III., , and with winged disks having pendent uræi. From Abydos.

Length, ⅔ in.

419. Green glazed steatite scarab, inscribed with the prenomen of Thothmes III., and "there is double Maāt and two-fold happiness with Kheper-Rā, the lord." From Abydos.

Length, ¾ in.

420. Green glazed steatite scarab, inscribed with the prenomen of Thothmes III., , etc., and "lord, maker of creation,"

From Abydos. Length, ½ in.

421. Green glazed steatite scarab, inscribed with the prenomen of Thothmes III., ⟨ ◯ ﹏ 月 ⟩, and "life," ♀. From Abydos.   Length, ⅝ in.

422. Green glazed steatite scarab, inscribed with the prenomen of Thothmes III., ☉. From Abydos.   Length, ⅝ in.

423. Green glazed rectangular steatite plaque, inscribed on one side with the prenomen of Thoth-mes III., ☉, and on the other with the prenomen

of Thothmes III. and *Rā-Maāt Rā-men-setep-en-Rā*,

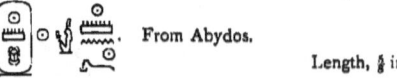. From Abydos.

        Length, ⅔ in.

424. Rectangular green glazed steatite plaque, pierced, and inscribed on one side with the prenomen of Thothmes III., ☉, and winged disk with pendent uræi, and on the other with a hand ⟨═⟩. From Abydos.   Length, ½ in.

425. Green glazed steatite scarab, inscribed with the figure of Thothmes III. slaying an enemy with a club; by the side of his feet is his dog. Behind him is his prenomen, ⊙, and before him is ⊖, "Åmen, my lord." From Abydos. Length ⅝ in.

426. Green glazed steatite scarab, inscribed "*Men-χeper-Rā* (Thothmes III.), beautiful god, lord of every land." From Abydos.

Length, $\frac{9}{16}$ in.

427. Green glazed steatite scarab, inscribed with the figure of a kneeling king; in his right hand he holds ⋀, and in the left 𝄞, and on his head is the crown. The legend reads, ⊙ "*Men-χeper-Rā*, lord of the North and South." From Abydos.

Length, $\frac{11}{16}$ in.

428. Green glazed steatite oval, inscribed on one side with the prenomen of Thothmes III., ⊙, between feathers and uræi, and on the other with four uræi. From Abydos. Length, $\frac{6}{16}$ in.

429. Green glazed steatite scarab, inscribed with a crocodile, and with the legend ⟨hieroglyphs⟩, "Beautiful god, *Men-χeper-Rā*." From Abydos.

Length, $\frac{9}{16}$ in.

430. Green glazed steatite scarab, inscribed ⟨hieroglyphs⟩, "King *Men-χeper-Rā*." From Abydos.

Length, $\frac{3}{4}$ in.

431. Green glazed steatite scarab, inscribed with a sphinx wearing the ⟨hieroglyph⟩ crown, Rā ⟨hieroglyph⟩, ⟨hieroglyphs⟩ *Men-χeper-Rā*, ⟨hieroglyphs⟩, the "living Horus," and ⟨hieroglyph⟩. Abydos.

Length, $\frac{11}{16}$ in.

432. Green glazed steatite scarab, inscribed ⟨hieroglyphs⟩, "Beautiful god, *Men-χeper-Rā*. From Abydos.

Length, $\frac{3}{8}$ in.

433. Green glazed steatite scarab, in its original copper ring, inscribed with the figure of Thothmes III., and the legend ⟨hieroglyphs⟩, "The god, the lord of the world, *Men-χeper-Rā*." From Abydos.

Length, $\frac{3}{4}$ in.

434. Green glazed steatite scarab, inscribed

[hieroglyphs] and [hieroglyphs] , *i.e.*, with prenomens of Thothmes III., and "May the two Horus gods live"! From Abydos. Length, ½ in.

435. Green glazed steatite hollow-work plaque; on one side are the prenomen of Thothmes III., winged uræi, and spiral ornaments, and on the other figures of Râ and Isis.

Length, 1 1/16 in.

436. Green glazed *faïence* scarab, inscribed

[hieroglyphs] , "Beautiful god, *Men-χeper-Râ*."

Length, 1/16 in.

437. Green glazed steatite cowroid, inscribed with the prenomen of Thothmes III., [hieroglyphs].

Diameter, 3/8 in.

438. Green glazed steatite circular object, inscribed with the prenomen of Thothmes III., [hieroglyphs].

Diameter, 1/16 in

439. Rectangular, green glazed steatite plaque, pierced. On one side are inscribed a figure of the god Ptaḥ 🗿 in a shrine, and the legend, 🝣 , "Beautiful Ptaḥ, *Aa-χeperu-Rā*" (*i.e.*, Åmen-ḥetep II., king of Egypt, about B.C. 1450), and on the other a figure of the king holding a hatchet 🝠 in the right hand and a shield in the left; by his side is his prenomen 🝣 . On one edge is inscribed 🝡 , "Giver of beautiful life," and on the other an uræus 🝢 , and an uræus twined round a sceptre 🝟 . From Abydos. Length, ⅝ in.

440. Blue glazed *faïence* scarab, inscribed with the prenomen of Thothmes II., 🝤 *Aa-χeper-Rā*, king of Egypt, about B.C. 1550. From Abydos.
Length, ½ in.

441. Green glazed steatite scarab, inscribed on the base with the prenomen of Åmen-ḥetep III., 🝥 , *Neb-Maāt-Rā*, king of Egypt, about B.C. 1500. Modern imitation. Length, ½ in.

442. Cobalt blue glazed steatite scarab, inscribed with the prenomen of Amenophis III., and with the name of his wife Thi, " Beautiful god, *Neb-Maāt-Rā*, royal wife Thi." From Abydos.   Length, $\frac{1}{16}$ in.

443. Blue glazed *faïence* ring with rectangular bezel of same substance, having two cartouches in hollow-work, XVIIIth dynasty. From Tell el-Amarna.

Diameter, $\frac{13}{16}$ in.

444. Green glazed steatite scaraboid, inscribed " *Men-peh-peh-Rā* " (Rameses I. ?). From Abydos.   Length, $\frac{5}{8}$ in.

445. Blue glazed *faïence* plaque. Obverse, lion and prenomen of Seti I., *Men-Maāt-Rā*, king of Egypt, about B.C. 1400; reverse, winged uræi wearing disks, and prenomen of Seti I.

Length, $\frac{3}{4}$ in.

446. Green glazed steatite scarab, inscribed *neter nefer Men-Maāt-Rā*, "Beauti-

ful god, Men-Maāt-Rā" (Seti I.). On each side of
the cartouche is 𝘫, and below it is the collar 〰.
From Abydos.   Length, ₁₃⁄₁₆ in.

447. Green glazed steatite scarab, inscribed with
the prenomen of Rameses II., ☉ 🪲 *Usr-
χeper-Rā-setep-en-Rā*, king of Egypt, about B.C. 1330.
From Abydos.   Length, ½ in.

448. Green glazed steatite tablet, inscribed with
the figure of Rameses II., ☉ *Usr-Maāt-
Rā-setep-en-Rā* adoring Ptaḥ and Sekhet. From
Abydos.   Length, ₁⁴⁄₁₆ in.

449. Green glazed steatite scarab, set
in its original bronze ring, inscribed,
"Rameses (II.), beloved of Amen, beloved of Rā, subduer of all eastern lands."
From Abydos."

                                          Length, ¾ in.

450. Green glazed steatite scarab, inscribed with
part of the prenomen of Rameses II. (?),
Usr-Maāt-Rā. From Abydos.   Length, ⅝ in.

451. Blue glazed steatite scarab, inscribed with a scene wherein Rameses II. (?) stands in the presence of the god Ptaḥ ; above is the legend, *Usr-Maāt-Ra*. From Abydos. Length, ¾ in.

452. Rectangular blue glazed steatite plaque, pierced. On one side, in relief, are a cartouche and , and on the other *Usr-Māat-Rā*. From Abydos. Length, ¾ in.

453. Green glazed steatite scarab, inscribed with the prenomen of Osorkon II., *Usr-Maāt-Rā-setep* [*Ā*]*men-Rā*, king of Egypt, about B.C. 860. From Abydos. Length, ⁷⁄₁₆ in.

454. Yellow glazed steatite scarab, inscribed , "Beautiful god, lord of the two lands." Length, ⁷⁄₁₆ in.

455. Blue glazed steatite scarab, inscribed with the name Pepâ, a high court official, *àri āt àbu Pepâ*. VIth dynasty. From Abydos. Length 1⁷⁄₁₆ in.

456. Blue glazed steatite scarab, inscribed
āb Åmen-Rā, "priest of Åmen-Rā." From
Abydos.   Length, $\frac{9}{16}$ in.

457. Light green glazed *faïence* pendant, inscribed
on the reverse :—

Seχet	āa	meri	Ptaḥ	meri
Sekhet,	*greatly*	*beloved,*	*of Ptah*	*beloved.*

On the obverse is a faded prenomen of a king with
his titles. XXVIth dynasty. From Gizeh.

Length, $2\frac{3}{4}$ in.

458. Cobalt blue *faïence* scarab, inscribed
suten sa Ḥeru, "royal son, Horus." From Abydos.

Length, $\frac{1}{2}$ in.

459. Green glazed steatite scarab, inscribed
sa Rā men. From Abydos.

Length, $\frac{1}{2}$ in.

460. Green glazed *faïence* scarab, inscribed
"*Men-maut-Rā.*" Modern imitation.

Length, $\frac{3}{8}$ in.

461. Green glazed steatite oval, inscribed
sa Rā men. From Abydos. Length, ₇⁷₈ in.

462. Green glazed steatite scarab, inscribed
Ḥeru sa, " Horus protects," or " under the protection
of Horus." From Abydos. Length, ⅜ in.

463. Green glazed steatite scarab, inscribed with
the head of Horus wearing plumes and uræus and
nefer. From Abydos. Length, ₇⁷₈ in.

464. Green glazed steatite scarab, inscribed
Ḥeru nub, " golden Horus." From Abydos.
Length, ₇⁷₈ in.

465. Green glazed steatite scarab, inscribed
Ḥeru-neb-Maāt, " Horus, the lord of right and truth."
From Abydos. Length, ⅜ in.

466. Green glazed steatite scarab, inscribed
Ḥeru nub-peḥ. From Abydos. Length, ₇⁷₈ in.

467. Greenish-gray stone oval, inscribed
From Abydos. Length, ₇⁴₈ in.

468. Polished green basalt oval, inscribed
From Abydos.   Length, $\frac{7}{16}$ in.

469. Green glazed steatite scarab in its original
gold frame, inscribed ∬ ⌐ *Maāt* (?).   From Abydos.
Length, $\frac{1}{2}$ in.

470. Light blue glazed *faïence* scarab, inscribed
Nit em sa, "Neith is the protectress." From
Abydos.   Length, $\frac{1}{2}$ in.

471. Green glazed steatite oval, inscribed
hes χensu em Uast, "favoured of Khonsu in
Thebes." From Abydos.   Length, $\frac{3}{4}$ in.

472. Blue glazed steatite scarab, inscribed
χensu em Uast sa, "Under the protection
of Khonsu of Thebes." From Abydos.
Length, $\frac{4}{5}$ in.

473. Green glazed steatite scarab, inscribed
χensu em sa, "Khonsu protects." From
Abydos.   Length, $\frac{5}{8}$ in.

474. Green glazed steatite scarab, set in its original bronze ring, inscribed with Rā 🔶, a ram wearing the crown 🔶, and a winged uræus. From Abydos.

Length, $\frac{13}{16}$ in. Diameter, $1\frac{1}{16}$ in.

475. Green glazed steatite oval, inscribed "the lord Åmen," 🔶 *neb Åmen*, or "Rā-Åmen." From Abydos. Length, $\frac{7}{16}$ in.

476. Lapis-lazuli scarab, inscribed 🔶 *Rā-Åmen-peḥ*. From Abydos.

Length, $\frac{3}{8}$ in.

477. Green glazed steatite scarab, inscribed 🔶 *Rā-Ḥeru*. From Abydos. Length $\frac{1}{2}$ in.

478. Light green glazed steatite scarab, inscribed 🔶 *Rā-Ḥeru*. From Abydos. Length, $\frac{1}{2}$ in.

479. Green glazed steatite cowroid, inscribed with 🔶 *Rā-men*, and 🔶. From Abydos.

Length, $\frac{3}{4}$ in.

480. Green glazed steatite scaraboid with the inscription 🔶 *Rā nefer*, "Beautiful Rā," surrounded by a spiral ornament. From Abydos.

Length, $\frac{7}{16}$ in.

481. Green glazed steatite scarab, inscribed with
⊚ *Rā-χeperā* and winged uræi.   From Abydos.
                                   Length, $\frac{9}{16}$ in.

482. Brown glazed steatite scarab, inscribed with
⊚ *Rā χeperā* between two ⱱ crowns.   From Abydos.
                                   Length, $\frac{1}{2}$ in.

483. Green glazed steatite scarab, inscribed
"May Amen open the year happily."   From
Abydos.   Length, $\frac{7}{16}$ in.

484. Lapis-lazuli scarab, inscribed ⇔ *àp Amen*
renpit nefer, "May Amen open the year happily."
From Abydos.   Length, $\frac{3}{8}$ in.

485. Blue paste oval, inscribed ⇔ *àp Amen*
renpit nefer, "May Amen open the year happily."
From Abydos.   Length, $\frac{7}{16}$ in.

486. Green glazed steatite cartouche, inscribed
àp Auset renput neb, " May Isis open all [your]
years happily."   From Abydos.   Length, $\frac{1}{2}$ in.

487. Green glazed steatite scarab, inscribed ꙮ *àp renpit em nefer,* "May [your] year open happily." From Abydos. Length, ½ in.

488. Green basalt oval, inscribed *àp renpit nefer,* "A happy New Year [to you]." From Abydos. Length, ₇/₁₆ in.

489. Green glazed steatite scarab, inscribed *ḥes Rā,* "favoured of Rā." From Abydos. Length, ⅜ in.

490. Green glazed steatite scarab, inscribed *ḥes-à neb Maāt,* "I am favoured by the lord of Maāt." From Abydos. Length, ½ in.

491. Green glazed steatite scarab, inscribed *ḥes Maāt,* "favoured of Maāt." From Abydos. Length, ₇/₁₆ in.

492. Green glazed steatite scarab, inscribed *ḥes Maāt meri Maāt,* "favoured of Maāt, beloved of Maāt." From Abydos. Length, ½ in.

493. Green glazed steatite scarab, inscribed *ḥes neb Uast,* "favoured by the lord of Thebes. From Abydos. Length, ₇/₁₆ in.

494. Polished green stone oval, in its original gold setting, inscribed "Ḥeru-meri-s-Maāt, favoured of Bast." From Abydos.

Length, $\frac{7}{16}$ in.

495. Green glazed steatite cowroid, inscribed ⚲ ⚲ (?) . From Abydos. Length, $\frac{7}{16}$ in.

496. Lapis-lazuli scarab, inscribed *sa ānχ maat Åmen*, "There is protection and life in the eye of Åmen," or "There is protection and life when Åmen watcheth." From Abydos.

Length, $\frac{11}{16}$ in.

497. Green glazed steatite scarab, set in the original gold frame, inscribed , "There is protection and life in the eye of Åmen." From Abydos. Length, $\frac{11}{16}$ in.

498. Lapis-lazuli scarab inscribed "There is protection and life in the eye of Åmen." From Abydos. Length, $\frac{4}{8}$ in.

499. Green glazed steatite scarab, inscribed ⟨glyphs⟩, "There is protection and life in the eye of Åmen." From Abydos. Length, $\frac{7}{16}$ in.

500. Red stone oval, inscribed ⟨glyphs⟩ "There is protection and life in the eye of Åmen." From Abydos. Length, $\frac{1}{2}$ in.

501. Lapis-lazuli scarab, inscribed ⟨glyphs⟩ "The eye of Åmen is without fear," or "Where Åmen watcheth, there is no fear," or "Åmen watcheth, fear not." From Abydos. Length, $\frac{7}{16}$ in.

502. Green glazed steatite oval, inscribed "The eye of Åmen is without fear." From Abydos. Length, $\frac{7}{16}$ in. ⟨glyphs⟩

503. Green glazed steatite scaraboid, inscribed ⟨glyphs⟩ "Åmen watcheth every day." From Abydos. Length, $\frac{9}{16}$ in.

504. Green glazed steatite scarab, inscribed "Åmen watcheth every day." From Abydos. Length, $\frac{9}{16}$ in. ⟨glyphs⟩

505. Dark blue glazed steatite oval, pierced, inscribed "Åmen watcheth every day." From Abydos.

Length, ½ in.

506. Green glazed steatite scarab, inscribed "Åmen watcheth every day." From Abydos.

Length, ⁷⁄₁₆ in.

507. Lapis-lazuli scarab, inscribed "Åmen watcheth every day." From Abydos.

Length, ⅜ in.

508. Lapis-lazuli scarab, inscribed "Åmen watcheth every day." From Abydos.

Length, ⁶⁄₁₆ in.

509. Green glazed steatite scarab, inscribed "Åmen watcheth over Tattu." From Abydos.

Length, ⁷⁄₁₆ in.

510. Green glazed steatite scaraboid, inscribed *Åmen χerp seḫui.* From Abydos.

Length, ⁷⁄₁₆ in.

511. Green glazed steatite scarab, inscribed *Åmen χerp seḫui.* From Abydos.

Length, ⁷⁄₁₆ in.

512. Green glazed steatite scarab, inscribed *Amen χerp . . . . sa.* From Abydos.

Length, $\frac{3}{6}$ in.

513. Green glazed steatite scarab, inscribed *Amen ḥa en àn senṭ.* From Abydos.

Length, $\frac{9}{18}$ in.

514. Green glazed steatite scarab, inscribed *Amen ḥa en àn senṭ.* From Abydos.

Length, $\frac{1}{4}$ in.

515. Lapis-lazuli scarab, inscribed "Amen-ḥetep, Prince of Thebes." From Abydos.

Length, $\frac{1}{4}$ in.

516. Green glazed steatite oval, inscribed *Amen uā mer mer-s.* From Abydos.

Length, $\frac{3}{8}$ in.

517. Blue glazed steatite scarab, inscribed *Amen mer mer-s.* From Abydos.

Length, $\frac{7}{18}$ in.

518. Light green glazed steatite scarab, inscribed
Amen χepēs en uā. From Abydos.

Length, ⅝ in.

519. Light green glazed steatite scarab, inscribed
Amen χepeś en uā. From Abydos.

Length, ½ in.

520. Brown glazed steatite scaraboid, inscribed
Amen χepeś en uā. From Abydos.

Length, ₁₁⁹ in.

521. Green glazed steatite scaraboid, inscribed
Amen χepeś en uā. From Abydos.

Length, ⅜ in.

522. Light green glazed scaraboid, inscribed
Amen χepeś en uā. From Abydos.

Length, ⅝ in.

523. Green glazed steatite scarab, inscribed
Amen χepeś en uā. From Abydos.

Length, ⅗ in.

524. Green glazed steatite scarab, inscribed
Ámen χepeš en uá. From Abydos.

Length, $\frac{9}{16}$ in.

525. Blue glazed steatite oval, inscribed
Ámen χepeš en uá. From Abydos.

Length, $\frac{7}{16}$ in.

526. Green glazed steatite scarab, inscribed
Ámen χepeš en uá. From Abydos.

Length, $\frac{1}{2}$ in.

527. Green glazed steatite scarab, inscribed
ḫeṭ' maa Ámen. From Abydos. Length, $\frac{4}{8}$ in.

528. Lapis-lazuli cartouche, inscribed
ḫeṭ' maa Ámen. From Abydos. Length, $\frac{3}{4}$ in.

529. Green glazed steatite oval, inscribed
ḫeṭ' maa Ámen. From Abydos. Length, $\frac{1}{2}$ in.

530. Green glazed steatite scarab, inscribed
ḫeṭ' Amen ḥetep. From Abydos. Length, $\frac{7}{16}$ in.

531. Green glazed steatite scarab, inscribed
ḫeṭ' Amen ḥetep From Abydos.

Length, $\frac{7}{16}$ in.

532. Green glazed steatite scarab, inscribed
ḥeṭ' Amen ḥetep. From Abydos.   Length, ½ in.

533. Green glazed steatite scarab, inscribed
ḥeṭ' Amen ḥetep. From Abydos.   Length, ⁷⁄₁₆ in.

534. Light green glazed steatite scarab, inscribed
ḥeṭ' maa Amen. From Abydos.
                                        Length, ⁷⁄₁₆ in.

535. Green glazed steatite scarab, inscribed
ḥeṭ' mà ṭefa (?). From Abydos.   Length, ⅜ in.

536. Green glazed steatite scarab, inscribed
ḥeṭ' χeper.   Length, ⁷⁄₁₆ in.

537. Lapis-lazuli cartouche, inscribed (?) .
From Abydos.   Length, ¼ in.

538. Green glazed steatite scarab, inscribed
. From Abydos.   Length, ⁷⁄₁₆ in.

539. Green glazed steatite scarab, inscribed
sab Amen-ḥetep. From Abydos.
                                        Length, 1¾ in.

540. Green glazed steatite scarab, inscribed *sab Amen-ḥetep.* From Abydos.

Length, 1⅙ in.

541. Lapis-lazuli scarab, inscribed *Amen em neter* (?). From Abydos. *āu āb*

Length, ½ in. (?)

542. Lapis-lazuli scarab, inscribed *Amen em neter* (?). From Abydos. *āu āb*

Length, 1⅚ in. (?)

542a. Green basalt oval, inscribed *Amen.* From Abydos. *āmaχ maa*

Length, ½ in.

542b. Green glazed steatite oval, inscribed *āmaχ maa Amen.* From Abydos.

Length, ¼ in.

543. Green glazed steatite scarab, inscribed

āmaχ maa Amen. From Abydos. Length, ½ in.

544. Green glazed steatite scaraboid, inscribed *Ámen àri* (?) *nefer sem,* "Ámen is the . . . . . . of happy travelling." From Abydos.

Length, ⅝ in.

545. Lapis-lazuli scarab, inscribed *Ámen àri* (?) *nefer sem,* "Ámen is the . . . . . . of happy travelling." From Abydos.   Length, ₇⁄₁₆ in.

546. Rectangular steatite plaque, pierced; on one side is inscribed an *utchat* and on the other *Ámen àri* (?) *nefer sem,* "Ámen is the . . . . of happy travelling." From Abydos.

Length, ⅝ in.

547. Blue glazed steatite scarab, inscribed *Ámen àri* (?) *nefer sem,* "Ámen is the . . . . . of happy travelling." From Abydos.

Length, ₁⅟₁₆ in.

548. Green glazed steatite scarab, inscribed "Where there is the eye of Ámen is no fear." From Abydos.   Length, ¾ in.

549. Green glazed steatite scarab, inscribed "Where there is the eye of Àmen is no fear." From Abydos.   Length, $\frac{1}{16}$ in.

550. Green glazed steatite scarab, inscribed *maa Àmen* . . . .   From Abydos.

Length, $1\frac{3}{8}$ in.

551. Green glazed steatite scarab, inscribed with the sign for "good luck" surrounded by annules ; on the back is a smaller scarab in relief. From Abydos.   Length, $\frac{9}{16}$ in.

552. Green glazed steatite scaraboid, inscribed with the name "Kheperà" and "two-fold good luck," .   From Abydos.   Length, $\frac{3}{8}$ in.

553. Green glazed steatite scarab, inscribed "Beautiful is the double Maàt," .   From Abydos.
Length, $\frac{1}{2}$ in.

554. Green glazed steatite scarab, inscribed .   From Abydos.   Length, $\frac{7}{8}$ in.

555. Green glazed steatite scarab, inscribed . From Abydos.
Length, $\frac{7}{8}$ in.

556. Green glazed steatite scarab, inscribed with
"good luck," ⎀ , surrounded by spirals. From Abydos.

Length, ¾ in.

557. Green glazed steatite cowroid, inscribed
⎀⎀⎀⎀ . From Abydos.   Length, ₇/₁₆ in.

558. Green glazed steatite scarab, inscribed with
the emblem of "good luck" surrounded by four

emblems of "gold" ⎀⎀⎀ .   From Abydos.

Length, ½ in.

559. Green glazed steatite scarab, inscribed with
"good luck," ⎀ , and illegible signs. From Abydos.

Length, ₇/₁₆ in.

560. Green glazed steatite scarab, inscribed
⎀⎀⎀ with the name of "Kheperá," and
emblems of "life," "good luck,"
etc. From Abydos.   Length, ₇/₁₆ in.

561. Green glazed steatite scarab, inscribed
⎀⎀⎀ with emblems of "stability," "good
luck," "gold," and the crown of the North. From
Abydos.   Length, ¾ in.

562. Green glazed steatite scarab, inscribed with
the emblem of "stability" ⟨ 𝔍 ⟩.   From Abydos.

Length, ⁴⁄₁₆ in

563. Blue glazed steatite scarab, inscribed with
the emblem of "stability"   .   From Abydos.

Length, ⁹⁄₁₆ in.

564. Green glazed steatite scarab, inscribed with
the emblem of "stability" between two crowns of the
North, ⟨   ⟩.   From Abydos.   Length, ⁴⁄₁₆ in.

565. Cobalt blue glazed *faïence* scarab, inscribed
⟨   ⟩.   From Abydos.   Length, ⁹⁄₁₆ in.

566. Yellow glazed steatite plaque, pierced. On
the one side, in relief, is inscribed 𝕀 *Tet Rā*, and
on the other a clump of lotus flowers. From Abydos.

Length, ⁷⁄₁₆ in.

567. Blue glazed steatite cartouche, inscribed on
one side with the emblems of "beautiful life," 𝕀,
and on the other with ⟨   ⟩.   From Abydos.

Length, ¹²⁄₁₆ in.

568. Green glazed steatite scarab, inscribed with the emblems of "life," "good luck," etc. From Abydos.

Length, $\frac{9}{16}$ in.

569. Green glazed steatite scarab, inscribed "the beautiful *utchat*," *nefer utchat*. From Abydos.

Length, $\frac{1}{2}$ in.

570. Green glazed steatite scarab, inscribed with the emblems of "good luck" surrounded by annules and spirals. From Abydos.

Length, $\frac{1}{2}$ in.

571. Yellow glazed steatite scarab, inscribed [hieroglyphs]. From Abydos.

Length, $\frac{3}{4}$ in.

572. Green glazed steatite scarab, inscribed with the emblems of "life," "growth," and two crowns of the North. From Abydos.

Length, $\frac{9}{16}$ in.

573. Green glazed steatite scarab, inscribed with the emblems of "life" and "fresh youth." From Abydos.

Length, $\frac{1}{2}$ in.

574. Green glazed steatite scarab, inscribed with the emblem of "life" in an oval supported on a winged disk; on each side is an uræus. Below are the emblems of "life," "good-luck," "fresh youth," etc. From Abydos. Length, ⅝ in.

575. Light green glazed *faïence* cartouche, inscribed on one side ☿ *Ānχ-Āmen*, and on the other *χeper-ḥetep*. From Abydos. Length, ₇⁄₆ in.

576. Lapis-lazuli scarab, inscribed "There is life through Osiris," ☿. From Abydos.
Length, ₉⁄₁₆ in.

577. Green glazed steatite oval, pierced, inscribed "life and all protection," ☿. From Abydos.
Length, ₇⁄₁₆ in.

578. Green glazed steatite scarab, inscribed ☿. From Abydos. Length, ½ in.

579. Light green glazed *faïence* scaraboid, inscribed "all life," ☿ *ānχ neb*. From Abydos.
Length, ½ in.

580. Green glazed steatite cowroid, inscribed
with the emblem of "life," etc. From Abydos.
Length, $\frac{5}{8}$ in.

581. Green glazed steatite double scarab, inscribed
"life," ☥ *ānχ*. From Abydos.   Length, $\frac{3}{8}$ in.

582. Green glazed steatite scarab, inscribed with
"life," ☥ *ānχ*, and lotus buds. From Abydos.
Length, $\frac{5}{8}$ in.

583. Green glazed steatite cowroid, inscribed with
the emblem of "growth," . From Abydos.
Length, $\frac{7}{16}$ in.

584. Green glazed steatite scarab, inscribed with
the emblem of "growth" and a winged beetle,

.   From Abydos.   Length, $\frac{5}{8}$ in.

585. Black stone cowroid, inscribed with the
emblems of "growth," "life," , double spiral,
etc. From Abydos.   Length, $\frac{11}{16}$ in.

586. Mother-of-emerald cowroid, inscribed
From Abydos.   Length, $\frac{1}{2}$ in.

587. Green glazed steatite scarab, inscribed with the emblems of "life," "good luck," etc. From Abydos. Length, $\frac{3}{4}$ in.

588. Green glazed steatite scarab, inscribed *men mer mer-s.* From Abydos. Length, $\frac{9}{16}$ in.

589. Lapis-lazuli cartouche, inscribed From Abydos. Length, $\frac{3}{8}$ in.

590. Green glazed steatite scarab, inscribed From Abydos. Length, $\frac{1}{4}$ in.

591. Green glazed steatite scarab, inscribed *neter tet mer Åmen.* From Abydos. Length, $\frac{5}{8}$ in.

592. Blue glazed steatite scarab, inscribed *Åmen ānχ s[enb].* From Abydos. Length, $\frac{9}{16}$ in.

593. Green glazed steatite scarab, inscribed *Åmen ānχ user Åmen.* From Abydos. Length, $\frac{5}{8}$ in.

594. Lapis-lazuli scarab, inscribed *Rā Maāt neter nub.* From Abydos. Length, $\frac{3}{8}$ in.

595. Blue glazed *faience* scarab, inscribed
Nub-Maāt (?)-*Rā*   From Abydos.   Length, ½ in.

596. Green glazed steatite scarab, inscribed with
and a winged disk.   From Abydos.
Length, ⅜ in.

597. Light green glazed scarab, inscribed
From Abydos.   Length, ½ in.

598. Green glazed steatite scarab, inscribed
From Abydos.   Length, ½ in.

599. Semi-transparent dark green stone
scarab, on the base of which traces of the
following characters are visible :—From
Abydos.   Length, ₇⁄₁₆ in.

600. Green glazed steatite scarab, inscribed
.   From Abydos.   Length, 11⁄16 in.

601. Green glazed steatite scarab, inscribed
From Abydos.   Length, ₇⁄₁₆ in.

602. Blue glazed steatite scarab, inscribed
From Abydos.   Length, ₉⁄₁₆ in.

603. Green glazed steatite scarab, inscribed *sem Ámen sa Áuset.* From Abydos.

Length, $\frac{5}{8}$ in.

604. Green glazed steatite scarab, inscribed

. From Abydos. Length, $\frac{3}{4}$ in.

605. Green glazed steatite scarab, inscribed

. From Abydos. Length, $\frac{5}{8}$ in.

606. Green glazed steatite scarab, inscribed

. From Abydos. Length, $\frac{9}{16}$ in.

607. Green basalt oval, inscribed . From Abydos. Length, $\frac{5}{8}$ in.

608. Green glazed steatite scarab, inscribed

. From Abydos. Length, $\frac{5}{8}$ in.

609. Green glazed steatite scarab, with similar inscription. From Abydos. Length, $\frac{9}{16}$ in.

610. Lapis-lazuli scarab, inscribed ⬃. From Abydos.

Length, ½ in.

611. Carnelian cowroid, inscribed, "The giver of light is Rā," *Rā (ā ḥeṭ*. From Abydos.

Length, ₇⁸₈ in.

612. Green glazed steatite cowroid, inscribed . On the back, in rope work, is inscribed *sam*. From Abydos. Length, ¾ in.

613. Green glazed steatite scarab, inscribed From Abydos. Length, ₇⁸₈ in.

614. Green glazed steatite scarab, inscribed "Ámen-ḥetep, prince of Thebes". From Abydos. Length, ½ in.

615. Rectangular, green glazed steatite plaque, pierced; on each side is inscribed *Ámen-ḥetep*. From Abydos.

Length, ⅛ in.

616. Green glazed steatite scarab, inscribed *Amen-ḥetep*. From Abydos.

Length, $\frac{1}{2}$ in.

617. Green glazed steatite oval, inscribed with a hand ⟨⟩. From Abydos. Length, $\frac{7}{16}$ in.

618. Lapis-lazuli oval, inscribed with a hand ⟨⟩. From Abydos. Length, $\frac{6}{16}$ in.

619. Green glazed steatite scarab, inscribed

Length, $\frac{11}{16}$ in.

620. Green glazed steatite scarab, inscribed with and other hieroglyphics characteristic of a very early period.

621. Green glazed steatite scarab, inscribed with and uræi. Length, $\frac{11}{16}$ in.

622. Yellow glazed steatite scarab, inscribed

Length, $\frac{3}{4}$ in.

623. Brown glazed steatite scarab, inscribed with figures of Ámen, Horus, and Rā.   Length, 1½ in.

624. Brown glazed steatite scarab, inscribed with figure of Horus.   Length, ¾ in.

625. Brown glazed steatite scarab, inscribed with figures adoring the emblem of Ámen or of Osiris.
      Length, ¾ in.

626. Blue glazed steatite scarab, inscribed with figures of two crocodiles.   Length, ⅝ in.

627. Green glazed *faïence* scarab, inscribed with figures of a lizard and a human-headed lion .
      Length, ₇⁄₈ in.

628. Blue glazed *faïence* scarab, inscribed with and two uræi.   Length, ⅝ in.

629. Green glazed steatite scarab, inscribed with the figure of a king seated on a throne, and holding a bow; before him is "threefold life."
      Length, ½ in.

630. Green glazed *faïence* scarab, inscribed with lotus flowers , "life" , "strength and power" , *etc.*   Length, 1 in.

631. Green glazed steatite scarab, inscribed with spiral ornaments. Length, 1 in.

632. Yellow glazed steatite scarab, inscribed with spiral ornaments. Length, ½ in.

633. Green glazed steatite scarab, inscribed with "life" ☥, growing out of a branch of lotus flowers. Length, ⅔ in.

634. Green glazed steatite scarab, inscribed with the figure of a man driving an ox. Length, ⅝ in.

635. Grey glazed steatite scarab, inscribed with uræi, and "double good luck". Length, 1¾₆ in.

636. Blue glazed *faïence* scarab, inscribed. Length, ₁₀⁹ in

637. Blue glazed *faïence* scarab, inscribed. Length, 1⅛ in.

638. Green glazed steatite scarab, inscribed with figure of Ta-urt. Length, ₁₂⁹ in.

639. Green glazed steatite scarab, set in the gold bezel of a ring; the inscription is ⏛.
Length, ⅜ in.

640. Green glazed steatite scarab, inscribed with a linear device.   Length, ⅞ in.

641. Blue glazed steatite scarab, inscribed with ⟨⟩.
Length, 11/16 in.

642. Blue paste uræus, inscribed ⚲ ⟨⟩.
Length, ½ in.

643. Green glazed *faïence* scarab, inscribed with ⚲ ⚲ ⚲.   Length, 7/16 in.

644. Green glazed steatite scarab, inscribed with the hawk of Horus ⟨⟩, "life" ⚲, and uræus ⟨⟩.
Length, 11/16 in.

645. Green glazed steatite scarab, inscribed ⟨⟩. Modern imitation.   Length, ½ in.

646. Green glazed steatite scarab, inscribed ⚬ ⟨⟩.   Length, 1¼ in.

647. Green glazed steatite scarab, inscribed ⟨⟩.
Length 1½ in.

648. Green glazed steatite scarab, inscribed ⎶.
Length, ½ in.

649. Green glazed steatite scarab, inscribed with a floral device. Length, $\frac{9}{16}$ in.

650. Blue glazed steatite scarab, inscribed with ⊔ and a floral device. Length $\frac{7}{16}$ in.

651. Green glazed steatite scarab, inscribed with a floral device. Length, $\frac{7}{16}$ in.

652. Green glazed steatite scarab, inscribed with a fish ⋈ and uræi. Length, ½ in.

653. Green glazed steatite scarab, inscribed with a fish ⋈, and beautiful life " . Length, ⅜ in.

654. Green glazed steatite scarab, inscribed with three fishes. Length, $\frac{11}{16}$ in.

655. Blue glazed steatite scarab, inscribed with *ka* ⊔, the buckle (?), and "double good luck,".
Length, ½ in.

656. Yellow glazed steatite scarab, inscribed

Length, $\frac{3}{4}$ in.

657. Green glazed steatite scarab, inscribed

(?)   Length, $\frac{9}{16}$ in.

658. Green glazed steatite scarab, inscribed with
⊔ and uræi.   Length, $\frac{5}{8}$ in.

659. Green glazed steatite scarab, inscribed with
"life" ☥, uræi, ⊔ ⊔, *etc.*   Length, $\frac{1}{2}$ in.

660. Blue glazed steatite scarab, inscribed,
"double good luck," *etc.*   Length, $\frac{3}{4}$ in.

661. Green glazed steatite scarab, with a device.
                                      Length, $\frac{5}{8}$ in.

662. Green glazed steatite scarab.   Length, $\frac{3}{16}$ in.

663. Blue glass scarab, inscribed with head of
Hathor.   ·   Length, $\frac{5}{16}$ in.

664. Green glazed *faïence* scarab, inscribed
⊙ *Sa Rā men.*   Length, $1\frac{1}{16}$ in.

664a. Green glazed, cat-headed scarab, inscribed
on the base with the name Âmen-ḥetep
and papyrus plants .   Length, $\frac{3}{4}$ in.

665. Green glazed steatite cowroid, inscribed with emblems of "life," and "fresh youth," and a winged disk and uræi. From Abydos.

Length, ++ in.

666. Green glazed steatite scarab, inscribed with a ram wearing the crown, Rā, and winged uræus. From Abydos. Length, ++ in.

667. Green glazed steatite scarab, inscribed with the figure of an upright man and two uræi. From Abydos. Length, ⅝ in.

668. Green glazed steatite scarab, inscribed and ♀. From Abydos. Length, ½ in.

669. Light blue glazed *faïence* scarab, inscribed with the figure of a king standing under a canopy between the gods Åmen and Rā, each of whom grasps one of his hands. From Abydos.

Length, ⅞ in.

670. Blue glazed steatite scarab, inscribed with the sun's disk in a boat, and a king kneeling, with both hands raised in adoration before ♀ "life." From Abydos. Length, ⅚ in.

2 K

671. Brown glazed steatite scarab, inscribed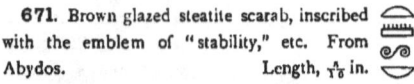
with the emblem of "stability," etc. From
Abydos.   Length, ₁₆⁴ in.

672. Green glazed steatite scarab, inscribed with
the emblem of "life," etc. From Abydos.
                Length, ₁₆⁹ in.

673. Green glazed steatite scarab, inscribed with
winged disk and   . From Abydos.
                Length, ½ in.

674. Green glazed steatite oval, inscribed   .
From Abydos.   Length, ⅜ in.

675. Green glazed steatite scarab, inscribed
From Abydos.   Length, ½ in.

676. Green glazed steatite oval, inscribed   .
From Abydos.   Length, ₁₆⁴ in.

677. Green glazed steatite scarab, inscribed with
a device between ( ). From Abydos.
                Length, ½ in.

678. Green glazed steatite cowroid, inscribed ⟨glyphs⟩. From Abydos. Length, $\frac{5}{8}$ in.

679. Green glazed steatite scarab, inscribed ⟨glyphs⟩. From Abydos. Length, $\frac{1}{2}$ in.

680. Green glazed steatite scarab, inscribed ⟨glyphs⟩. From Abydos. Length, $\frac{9}{16}$ in.

681. Green glazed steatite scarab, inscribed with ⟨glyph⟩ and two illegible signs. From Abydos.
Length, $\frac{9}{16}$ in.

682. Green glazed steatite scarab, inscribed with ⟨glyphs⟩ and two illegible signs. From Abydos.
Length, $\frac{9}{16}$ in.

683. Green glazed steatite scarab, inscribed ⟨glyph⟩ (?) ⟨glyph⟩. From Abydos. Length, $\frac{7}{16}$ in.

684. Green glazed steatite oval, inscribed ⟨glyphs⟩. From Abydos. Length, $\frac{2}{8}$ in.

685. Green glazed steatite scarab, inscribed with the emblem of the union of the two Egypts ⟨glyph⟩ and ⟨glyphs⟩. From Abydos. Length, $1\frac{1}{8}$ in.

686. Green glazed steatite scarab, inscribed with a sphinx ⬛, winged uræus (?), sun's disk ☉, and two captives with their arms tied behind them to ⬛. From Abydos.   Length, ⅞ in.

687. Lapis-lazuli scarab, inscribed ⬛. From Abydos.   Length, ₁₁/₁₆ in.

688. Green glazed steatite scarab, inscribed with ⬛ and a winged uræus. From Abydos.
                    Length, ₁₁/₁₆ in.

689. Red stone scaraboid, inscribed ✳. From Abydos.   Length, ₁₁/₁₆ in.

690. Green glazed steatite scarab, inscribed with ⬛, ⬛, ⬛. From Abydos.   Length, ⅝ in.

691. Blue glazed *faïence* scarab, inscribed with four ⬛. From Abydos.   Length, ₁₀/₁₆ in.

692. Green glazed steatite scarab, inscribed with ⬛, ⬛, and double spiral. From Abydos.
                    Length, ⅝ in.

693. Two yellow glazed steatite scarabs joined together; on one is inscribed ⫯ and on the other ⫰ . From Abydos.   Length, $\frac{3}{8}$ in.

694. Green glazed steatite scarab, inscribed ⫯. From Abydos.   Length, $\frac{1}{2}$ in.

695. Green glazed steatite scarab, inscribed with a human figure astride a sceptre (?), and ⫯(?). From Abydos.   Length, $\frac{9}{16}$ in.

696. Green glazed steatite oval plaque, pierced; on the one side is a disk in relief, and on the other is inscribed ⫯ *neter nefer* and an oryx. From Abydos.   Length, $\frac{5}{8}$ in.

697. Green glazed steatite scarab, inscribed ⫯ . From Abydos.   Length, $\frac{9}{16}$ in.

698. Green glazed steatite cowroid, inscribed ⫯ · From Abydos.   Length, $\frac{7}{16}$ in.

699. Green basalt oval, inscribed ⫯ . From Abydos.   Length, $\frac{1}{2}$ in.

700. Light blue glazed *faïence* oval, inscribed

. From Abydos. Length, $\frac{7}{16}$ in.

701. Green glazed steatite scarab, inscribed

etc. From Abydos. Length, $\frac{3}{8}$ in.

702. Green glazed steatite scarab, inscribed with a sphinx and two uræi. From Abydos.

Length, $\frac{6}{8}$ in.

703. Green glazed steatite scarab, inscribed with the emblem of the union of North and South Egypt.

. From Abydos. Length, $\frac{6}{8}$ in.

704. Blue glazed steatite scarab, inscribed with an *utchat* . From Abydos. Length, $\frac{4}{16}$ in.

705. Green glazed steatite double cowroid, inscribed with an *utchat* , etc. From Abydos.

Length, $\frac{1}{2}$ in.

706. Rectangular green glazed steatite plaque; on one side, in relief, is an *utchat* , and on the other is inscribed . From Abydos. Length, $\frac{6}{8}$ in.

707. Green glazed steatite oval, pierced; on one side, in relief, is an *utchat* 👁, and on the other is inscribed a sistrum with pendent uræi. From Abydos.
Length, $\frac{5}{8}$ in.

708. Light blue glazed *faïence* plaque; on the flat side is an *utchat* 👁, and on the convex side is ⚘ *ḥet'*, "radiance." From Abydos. Length, $\frac{7}{8}$ in.

709. Rectangular green glazed steatite plaque, pierced; on the one side is inscribed an *utchat* 👁, and on the other "Bast, the lady" ⚘. From Abydos. Length, $\frac{3}{8}$ in.

710. Green glazed *faïence* plaque, pierced; on one side is an *utchat* 👁, and on the other ⚘, "the life of Isis." From Abydos. Length, $\frac{7}{8}$ in.

711. Rectangular green glazed steatite plaque, pierced; on one side is inscribed an *utchat* 👁, and on the other ⚘ *Auset*, "Isis." From Abydos.
Length, $\frac{7}{8}$ in,

712. Rectangular blue glazed steatite plaque, pierced; on the convex side is an *utchat* 👁 in relief, and on the flat side is inscribed ⚘ *Nebt-ḥet*, "Nephthys." From Abydos. Length, $\frac{1}{2}$ in.

713. Rectangular green glazed steatite plaque, pierced, inscribed with an *utchat* 👁 on one side, and ⌊ *Nebt-ḥet* on the other. From Abydos.

Length, $\frac{5}{16}$ in.

714. Rectangular green glazed steatite plaque, pierced, inscribed with an *utchat* 👁 on one side, and ⌊ *Nebt-ḥet* on the other. From Abydos.

Length, $\frac{3}{8}$ in.

715. Green glazed steatite plaque, pierced; on one side is an *utchat* 👁, in relief, and on the other is inscribed ☥ (?) *ānχ Rā ṭeṭ*. From Abydos.

Length, $\frac{1}{2}$ in.

716. Green glazed steatite cartouche, pierced; on one side is an *utchat* 👁 (?), and on the other ☥ *ānχ à neb*. From Abydos.   Length, $\frac{7}{16}$ in.

717. Green glazed steatite scarab, inscribed with a hawk wearing the double crown 🦅, and an uræus 🐍. From Abydos.   Length, $\frac{3}{8}$ in.

718. Green glazed steatite scarab, inscribed with the hawk of Horus, with uræus, and *Maāt* 🦅. From Abydos.   Length, $\frac{5}{16}$ in.

719. Green glazed steatite scarab, inscribed with the hawk of Horus with uræus, and Maât 𓅃𓅓𓊪. From Abydos. Length, $\frac{7}{16}$ in.

720. Green glazed steatite scarab, inscribed with the hawk of Horus with uræus, 𓅃𓅓, and an uræus 𓆗. From Abydos. Length, $\frac{7}{16}$ in.

721. Green glazed steatite cowroid, inscribed with the hawk of Horus with uræus, and an uræus above a crocodile 𓅃𓅓𓆗 ; on the back of the cowroid are four uræi. From Abydos. Length, $\frac{5}{8}$ in.

722. Green glazed steatite scarab, inscribed with the hawk of Horus between uræi standing above a crocodile 𓆗𓅓𓆗. From Abydos.

Length, $\frac{5}{8}$ in.

723. Green glazed steatite scarab, inscribed with the hawk of Horus standing between uræi above a crocodile 𓆗𓅓𓆗. From Abydos. Length, $\frac{5}{8}$ in.

724. Green glazed steatite scarab, inscribed with the figure of a lion and two unknown objects. From Abydos. Length, $\frac{9}{16}$ in.

725. Green glazed steatite scarab, inscribed with a hippopotamus, emblem of the goddess Thoueris. From Abydos.   Length,   in.

726. Blue glazed steatite scarab, inscribed with two crocodiles. From Abydos.   Length, $\frac{5}{8}$ in.

727. Blue glazed *faïence* scarab, inscribed with two crocodiles. From Abydos.   Length, $\frac{1}{2}$ in.

728. Green glazed steatite scarab, inscribed with two crocodiles. From Abydos.   Length, $\frac{5}{8}$ in.

729. Green glazed steatite scarab, inscribed with two crocodiles. From Abydos.   Length, $\frac{3}{8}$ in.

730. Green glazed steatite scarab, inscribed with two crocodiles. From Abydos.   Length, $\frac{3}{8}$ in.

731. Green glazed steatite scarab, inscribed with a crocodile , a hand (?), a beetle (?), and a human figure wearing plumes. From Abydos.
                            Length, $\frac{5}{8}$ in.

732. Green glazed steatite scarab, inscribed . From Abydos.   Length, $1\frac{1}{8}$ in.

733. Blue glazed steatite scarab, inscribed with a crocodile and an oval. From Abydos. Length, $1\frac{1}{8}$ in.

734. Green glazed steatite scaraboid, inscribed with a sceptre ⌡ and a crocodile. From Abydos.

Length, $\frac{1}{2}$ in.

735. Green glazed steatite scarab, inscribed with a crocodile and an oryx. From Abydos.

Length, $\frac{7}{8}$ in.

736. Green glazed steatite oval, inscribed with a horse. From Abydos. Length, $\frac{5}{8}$ in.

737. Blue paste oval, inscribed with a horse. From Abydos. Length, $\frac{1}{2}$ in.

738. Blue glazed steatite scarab, inscribed with a hare ✍. From Abydos. Length, $\frac{3}{8}$ in.

739. Green glazed steatite scarab, inscribed with an oryx and a hawk. From Abydos. Length, $\frac{5}{8}$ in.

740. Green glazed steatite scarab, inscribed with a gryphon. From Abydos. Length, $\frac{9}{16}$ in.

741. Green glazed steatite oval, inscribed with a monkey holding *nefer* ⌡. From Abydos.

Length, $\frac{7}{16}$ in.

742. Yellow glazed steatite scarab, inscribed with an ape holding *nefer* ⌡. From Abydos.

Length, $\frac{7}{16}$ in.

743. Lapis-lazuli scarab, inscribed with a monkey holding *nefer* ⌡. From Abydos. Length, ⅝ in.

744. Blue glazed steatite scarab, inscribed with an ape holding *nefer* ⌡. From Abydos.

Length, ₁₆⁹ in.

745. Green glazed steatite scarab, inscribed with an ape holding *nefer* ⌡, and two triangles △ ▽. From Abydos. Length, ₁₆⁹ in.

746. Green glazed steatite scarab, inscribed with a palm tree, on each side of which is a monkey. From Abydos. Length, ¾ in.

747. Brown glazed steatite scarab, inscribed with a jackal's head on legs ꜣ. From Abydos.

Length, ½ in.

748. Blue glazed steatite oval, inscribed with a serpent ₥. From Abydos. Length, ₁₆⁷ in.

749. Cobalt blue glazed *faïence* oval, inscribed with a snake ₥. From Abydos. Length, ½ in.

750. Green glazed steatite cowroid, inscribed with an uræus ⌣. From Abydos. Length, ½ in.

751. Green glazed steatite scarab, inscribed with winged disk having pendent uræi, double ⸶, double ⸷, and cartouche with illegible signs. From Abydos.

Length, ⅝ in.

752. Green glazed steatite scarab, inscribed with three uræi having disks ⸸⸸⸸. From Abydos.

Length, ½ in.

753. Green glazed steatite cowroid, inscribed with four uræi. From Abydos. Length, ⅝ in.

754. Green glazed steatite scarab, inscribed with four uræi, within a ropework border. From Abydos.

Length, $\frac{9}{16}$ in.

755. Green glazed steatite scarab, inscribed with four uræi and four ♀. From Abydos. Length, ¼ in.

755a. Green glazed steatite cowroid, inscribed with four uræi. From Abydos. Length, $\frac{7}{16}$ in.

756. Green glazed steatite cowroid, inscribed with a cruciform ornament and uræi. From Abydos.

Diameter, $\frac{9}{16}$ in.

757. Green glazed steatite cowroid, inscribed with four uræi and a cruciform ornament. From Abydos.

Length, ⅝ in.

758. Green glazed steatite amulet, pierced; on one side is a serpent in relief ⟨figure⟩, and on the other are inscribed four uræi. From Abydos. Length, $\frac{3}{8}$ in.

759. Green glazed steatite cowroid, inscribed with four uræi. From Abydos. Length, $\frac{8}{9}$ in.

760. Green glazed steatite oval, inscribed on one side with a sistrum ⟨figure⟩ having pendent uræi, and on the other with four uræi. From Abydos.

Length, $\frac{1}{2}$ in.

761. Green glazed steatite oval, pierced, inscribed on one side with a sistrum, and on the other with four uræi. From Abydos. Length, $\frac{7}{16}$ in.

762. Green glazed steatite oval plaque, inscribed on one side with a sistrum and uræi, and on the other with four uræi. From Abydos. Length, $\frac{3}{8}$ in.

763. Green glazed steatite double frog (?), each of which is inscribed with four uræi. From Abydos.

Length, $\frac{1}{4}$ in.

764. Blue glazed steatite cowroid, inscribed with a lizard ⟨figure⟩. From Abydos. Length, $\frac{1}{2}$ in.

765. Green glazed steatite scarab, inscribed with a lion and a scorpion ⟨glyph⟩. From Abydos.

Length, $\frac{5}{8}$ in.

766. Rectangular green basalt plaque, pierced, inscribed with a scorpion, etc., ⟨glyph⟩. From Abydos.

Length, $1\frac{1}{8}$ in.

767. Green glazed steatite scarab, inscribed with a fish with lotus buds in its mouth ⟨glyph⟩.
From Abydos. Length, $\frac{9}{16}$ in.

768. Green glazed steatite scarab, inscribed with a fish having a bud in its mouth. From Abydos.

Length, $\frac{9}{16}$ in.

769. Green glazed steatite scarab, inscribed with a fish having a lotus bud in its mouth. From Abydos.

Length, $\frac{1}{2}$ in.

770. Rectangular green glazed steatite plaque; on one side is a fish ⟨glyph⟩ in relief, and on the other ⟨glyph⟩. From Abydos. Length, $\frac{3}{4}$ in.

771. Grayish-blue glazed steatite scarab, inscribed with a sistrum ⟨glyph⟩ and ∘∘. From Abydos.

Length, $\frac{7}{16}$ in.

772. Green glazed steatite scarab, inscribed with a sistrum ♒. From Abydos.　　　　Length, $\frac{7}{16}$ in.

773. Lapis-lazuli cartouche, inscribed with ill-cut hieroglyphics. From Abydos.　　　Length, $\frac{3}{4}$ in.

774. Lapis-lazuli cartouche, inscribed with ill-cut hieroglyphics. From Abydos.　　　Length, $\frac{3}{8}$ in.

775. Green glazed steatite cowroid, inscribed with ✿ and two double uræi. From Abydos.
　　　　　　　　　　　　　　Length, $\frac{5}{8}$ in.

776. Green glazed steatite scarab, inscribed ✿. From Abydos.　　　　Length, $\frac{3}{8}$ in.

777. Green glazed steatite scarab, inscribed with ✠. From Abydos.　　　Length, $\frac{5}{8}$ in.

778. Yellow glazed steatite oval, inscribed ✿. From Abydos.　　　　Length, $\frac{7}{16}$ in.

779. Green glazed steatite scarab, inscribed ✿. From Abydos.　　　　Length, $\frac{3}{4}$ in.

780. Green glazed steatite scarab, inscribed with a line ornament having buds and a spiral. From Abydos.　　　　Length, $\frac{7}{16}$ in.

781. Green glazed steatite scarab, inscribed with a device in lines and spirals. From Abydos.

Length, ⅝ in.

782. Green glazed steatite cowroid, inscribed ⏝. From Abydos. Length, ⅝ in.

783. Green glazed marble scarab, inscribed with spirals, etc. From Abydos. Length, ⅔ in.

784. Green glazed steatite scarab, inscribed with three rows of spiral ornaments. From Abydos.

Length, 1⅛ in.

785. Green glazed steatite scarab, inscribed with an ornament of six spirals united. From Abydos.

Length, ⅝ in.

786. Green glazed steatite scarab, inscribed with double spirals. From Abydos. Length, ¾ in.

787. Green glazed steatite scarab, inscribed with a linear device. From Abydos. Length, ₇₆ in.

788. Green glazed steatite scarab, inscribed with a linear design. From Abydos. Length, 1½ in.

789. Green glazed steatite scarab, inscribed with a linear design within a border of annules. From Abydos. Length, ⅝ in.

790. Green glazed steatite scarab, inscribed with Ỿ, from which spring two buds, and two uræi. From Abydos.   Length, ⅝ in.

791. Green glazed steatite scarab, inscribed with a double clump of lotus flowers . From Abydos.

Length, ⅝ in.

792. Green glazed *faïence* scarab, inscribed with lotus flowers, annules, and a line design. From Abydos.   Length, ₁⁹₆ in.

793. Green glazed steatite scarab, inscribed with lotus flowers. From Abydos.   Length, ₁⁶₆ in.

794. Green glazed steatite scarab, inscribed with a double clump of lotus flowers. From Abydos.   Length, ½ in.

795. Green glazed steatite scarab, inscribed with clumps of lotus flowers. From Abydos.

Length, ₁⁹₆ in.

796. Green glazed steatite scarab, inscribed with a clump of flowers. From Abydos.   Length, ⅜ in.

797. Green glazed steatite scarab, inscribed with lotus flowers. From Abydos.   Length, ₁⁷₆ in.

798. Green glazed steatite scarab, inscribed ⬙.
From Abydos. Length, ⅔ in.

799. Green glazed steatite cowroid, inscribed
◖⬙◗. From Abydos. Length, ⅝ in.

800. Green glazed steatite scarab, inscribed with
two buds. From Abydos. Length, $\frac{5}{16}$ in.

801. Green glazed steatite cowroid, inscribed with
two buds. From Abydos. Length, $\frac{7}{16}$ in.

802. Green glazed steatite cowroid, inscribed with
a double clump of lotus flowers. From Abydos.
Length, ½ in.

803. Green glazed steatite scarab, inscribed with
a double spiral and buds. From Abydos.
Length, ⅔ in.

804. Green glazed steatite scarab, inscribed with
lotus flowers and tables of offerings ⊿ ⊿. From
Abydos. Length, $\frac{9}{16}$ in.

805. Green glazed steatite scarab, inscribed with
a design composed of lotus flowers and ⬙, the
emblem of "union." From Abydos. Length, ⅝ in.

806. Lapis-lazuli scarab, uninscribed. From Abydos. Length, $\frac{3}{4}$ in.

807. Carnelian cowroid, uninscribed. From Abydos. Length, $\frac{7}{16}$ in.

808. Polished whitish-green oval, uninscribed. From Abydos. Length, $\frac{1}{2}$ in.

809. Carnelian cowroid, uninscribed. From Abydos. Length, $\frac{5}{8}$ in.

810. Green glazed steatite scarab, inscribed with rudely formed hieroglyphics. From Abydos. Length, $\frac{5}{16}$ in.

811. Green glazed steatite cowroid, inscribed with badly executed hieroglyphics. From Abydos. Length, $\frac{1}{2}$ in.

812. Green glazed steatite oval, inscribed with illegible signs. From Abydos. Length, $\frac{5}{16}$ in.

813. Green glazed steatite oval, inscribed with illegible signs. From Abydos. Length, $\frac{6}{16}$ in.

814. Green glazed steatite scarab, inscribed with rudely formed hieroglyphics. From Abydos. Length, $\frac{6}{16}$ in.

815. Rectangular mother-of-emerald plaque, pierced, and uninscribed. From Abydos. Length, $\frac{2}{16}$ in.

816. Greenish-gray stone oval, pierced, and uninscribed. From Abydos. Length, $\frac{7}{16}$ in.

817. Black stone scaraboid, uninscribed. From Abydos. Length, $\frac{13}{16}$ in.

818. Amethyst scaraboid, uninscribed. From Thebes. Length, $\frac{7}{9}$ in.

819. Onyx scarab, uninscribed. From Abydos. Length, $\frac{11}{16}$ in.

820. Amethyst scaraboid, uninscribed. From Abydos. Length, $\frac{3}{4}$ in.

821. Amethyst scaraboid, uninscribed. From Abydos. Length, $\frac{7}{16}$ in.

822. Green basalt scaraboid, uninscribed. From Abydos. Length, $\frac{11}{16}$ in.

823. Amethyst scaraboid, uninscribed. From Abydos. Length, $\frac{7}{9}$ in.

824. Amethyst scaraboid, uninscribed. From Abydos. Length, 1 in.

825. Polished fine green basalt scaraboid, uninscribed. From Abydos. Length, $\frac{7}{16}$ in.

826. Carnelian scaraboid.   From Abydos.

Length, ¾ in.

827. Carnelian scaraboid, uninscribed.   From Abydos.

Length, 1 in.

828. Rectangular lapis-lazuli plaque, pierced, and uninscribed.   From Abydos.   Length, ⅜ in

829. Green basalt oval, pierced and uninscribed. From Abydos.   Length, ₁⅝₀ in.

830. Polished green basalt oval, uninscribed. From Abydos.   Length, ₁⅟₄ in.

831. Rectangular plaque of lapis-lazuli, pierced. From Abydos.   Length, ⅝ in.

832. Carnelian oval, uninscribed.   From Abydos.

Length, ₁⅛₀ in.

833. Green basalt oval, uninscribed.   From Abydos.   Length, ½ in.

1392. Large light green glazed *faïence* scarab, inscribed with Chapter XXXʙ of the Book of the Dead; a space for the name of the deceased has been left blank.   As copies of the "Chapter of not allowing the heart to be driven away from him (*i.e.*, the deceased)

in the underworld " on *faïence* scarabs are rare, the text from this rare scarab is given in full.

1. [Blank space for name.]

2. [hieroglyphic text]

3. [hieroglyphic text]

4. [hieroglyphic text]

5. [hieroglyphic text]

6. [hieroglyphic text]

7. [hieroglyphic text]

8. [hieroglyphic text]

9. [hieroglyphic text]

10. [hieroglyphic text]

Length, 2½ in.

1393. Green glazed steatite scarab, inscribed with the name "Ámen-Rā," 𓇳. From Abydos.

Length, ⅝ in.

1394. Light blue glazed steatite scarab, inscribed with the name "Ámen-Rā," 𓇳. From Abydos.

Length, ⅝ in.

1395. Blue glazed steatite scarab, inscribed with a standing figure of Ámen-Rā wearing plumes and holding a sceptre in his left hand. Behind him is a serpent. From Abydos.   Length, 1⅜ in.

1396. Black stone scaraboid, inscribed with the name "Ámen-Rā," 𓇳. From Abydos.

Length, 1⅒ in.

1397. Green glazed steatite grasshopper, on the base of which is inscribed the name "Ámen-Rā," 𓇳. From Abydos.   Length, $\frac{7}{16}$ in.

1398. Green glazed steatite scarab, inscribed with the name "Ámen-Rā," 𓇳. From Abydos.

Length, $\frac{9}{16}$ in.

1399. Green glazed steatite scarab, inscribed with the name "Ámen-Rā," 𓇳. From Abydos.

Length, ⅜ in.

1400. Green glazed steatite cat, inscribed on the base with the name "Åmen-Rā," ⟨hieroglyphs⟩. From Abydos. Length, $\frac{1}{2}$ in.

1401. Green glazed steatite plaque, inscribed on the obverse with a figure of "Åmen-Rā, the lord of valour," ⟨hieroglyphs⟩, and on the reverse with a figure of Ptaḥ "of the beautiful face" ⟨hieroglyphs⟩. From Abydos. Length, $\frac{5}{8}$ in.

1402. Green glazed steatite scarab, inscribed "Åmen maketh brilliance," ⟨hieroglyphs⟩. From Abydos. Length, $\frac{9}{16}$ in.

1403. Green glazed steatite scarab, inscribed "King of the North and South, beloved of Åmen," ⟨hieroglyphs⟩. From Abydos. Length, $\frac{3}{4}$ in.

1404. Green glazed steatite scarab inscribed "Åmen-Rā, lord of might," ⟨hieroglyphs⟩. From Abydos. Length, $\frac{9}{16}$ in.

1405. Green glazed steatite cowroid, inscribed with clusters of flowers and the name "Åmen-Rā," ⟨hieroglyphs⟩. From Abydos. Length, $\frac{3}{4}$ in.

1406. Green glazed steatite scarab, inscribed with the name "Åmen-Rā," 〔figure〕. From Abydos.

Length, ⅝ in.

1407. Green glazed steatite scarab, inscribed with the name "Åmen-Rā," 〔figure〕. From Abydos.

Length, ₇⁄₁₆ in.

1408. Green glazed *faïence* oval, inscribed on one side with 〔figure〕, and on the other with the name "Åmen-Rā," 〔figure〕. From Abydos. Length, ⅝ in.

1409. Blue glazed *faïence* oval, inscribed on one side with a lion and uræus and "beautiful god, lord of the North and South," 〔figure〕; and on the other with the legend "Åmen-Rā, born of Maāt," 〔figure〕. From Abydos. Length, ¾ in.

1410. Green glazed steatite ape (?) inscribed with the name "Åmen-Rā," 〔figure〕. From Abydos.

Length, ₇⁄₁₆ in.

1411. Green glazed steatite scarab, inscribed with the name "Åmen-Rā," 〔figure〕. From Abydos.

Length, ¹⁄₁₆ in.

1412. Blue glazed *faïence* oval plaque, inscribed on one side with the name "Åmen-Rå," and on the other with a cluster of lotus flowers and "Åmen-Rå," . From Abydos. Length, $1\frac{1}{8}$ in.

1413. Green glazed steatite scarab, inscribed with the name "Åmen-Rå," . From Abydos.

Length, $\frac{1}{2}$ in.

1414. Blue glazed *faïence* scarab, inscribed with the name "Åmen-Rå," . From Abydos.

Length, $\frac{3}{4}$ in.

1415. Green glazed steatite oval, inscribed with:—
1, four uræi; and 2, the name "Åmen-Rå," . From Abydos. Length, $\frac{1}{2}$ in.

1416. Green glazed steatite scarab, inscribed with the figure of a king slaying a foe, and the name "Åmen-Rå," . From Abydos.

Length, $\frac{9}{16}$ in.

1417. Blue glazed steatite oval, inscribed with :—
1, the name "Åmen-Rå," , and a breastplate; and 2, a cruciform ornament and four uræi. From Abydos. Length, $\frac{5}{8}$ in.

1418. Green glazed steatite scarab, inscribed "Ámen, president of the double house," . From Abydos.   Length, $\frac{9}{16}$ in.

1419. Green glazed steatite scarab, inscribed "Ámen, the lord of life and health," . From Abydos.   Length, $\frac{11}{16}$ in.

1420. Blue paste scarab, inscribed "Ámen, the gracious guardian (?), the guide," . From Abydos.   Length, $\frac{9}{16}$ in.

1421. Green glazed steatite scarab, inscribed "the radiance (?) of the eye of Ámen," . From Abydos.   Length, $\frac{5}{8}$ in.

1422. Green glazed steatite scarab, inscribed "the radiance (?) of the eye of Ámen," . From Abydos.   Length, $\frac{11}{16}$ in.

1423. Green glazed steatite scarab, inscribed "Ámen watcheth, be not afraid," . From Abydos.   Length, $\frac{11}{16}$ in.

1424. Green glazed steatite scarab, inscribed "Åmen watcheth, be not afraid," . From Abydos. Length, $\frac{14}{16}$ in.

1425. Green glazed steatite scarab, inscribed "Åmen watcheth, be not afraid," . From Abydos. Length, $\frac{9}{16}$ inch.

1426. Lapis-lazuli oval plaque, inscribed "Holy(?) is the eye of Åmen," . From Abydos. Length, $\frac{1}{2}$ in.

1427. Blue glazed *faïence* scarab, inscribed "Åmen [lord of] life and health," . From Abydos. Length, $\frac{5}{8}$ in.

1428. Blue paste scarab, inscribed "Åmen watcheth daily," . From Abydos. Length, $\frac{5}{8}$ in.

1429. Green glazed steatite scarab, inscribed "Åmen watcheth daily," . From Abydos. Length, $\frac{5}{8}$ in.

1430. Green glazed steatite scarab, inscribed "Åmen watcheth daily," . From Abydos.

Length, ⅝ in.

1431. Green glazed steatite oval, inscribed . From Abydos.   Length, ₇⁄₁₆ in.

1432. Green glazed steatite scarab, inscribed "Åmen-Rā, lord of eternity (?)," .

From Abydos.   Length, 1¼ in.

1433. Green glazed steatite scarab, inscribed "Åmen-Rā, born of beautiful Maāt," .

From Abydos.   Length, ½ in.

1434. Green glazed steatite scarab, inscribed (?)

From Abydos.   Length, ₇⁄₁₆ in.

1435. Pinkish-brown rectangular stone plaque inscribed with:—1, figure of An-Ḥeru; 2, *nefer* ; 3, figure of Ptaḥ ; and 4, *nefer* : From Abydos.   Length, ⅝ in.

1436. Light blue opaque glass plaque, inscribed "Bast, the giver of happiness," 𓏏 𓎡 𓃠 𓆙. From Abydos. Length, ₁⁹₆ in.

1437. Green glazed steatite amulet, inscribed with a sistrum 𓏏 having pendent uræi; on the back, in relief, is cut the head of Hathor. From Abydos. Length, ½ in.

1438. Green glazed steatite scarab, inscribed with figures of the gods Râ (?) and Âmen. From Abydos. Length, ⅝ in.

1439. Green glazed steatite scarab, inscribed with the figures of two deities, Âmen and Râ (?). From Abydos. Length, ⅝ in.

1440. Blue paste scarab, inscribed "Beautiful son of Râ" 𓏏 𓅓 𓇳. From Abydos. Length, ⅜ in.

1441. Green glazed steatite scarab, inscribed with a ram wearing plumes, uræi, etc., a winged uræus, and Râ 𓏏. From Abydos. Length, ₁¹³₆ in.

1442. Green glazed steatite rectangular plaque, inscribed with:—1, the figure of Râ and 𓏏𓏏; 2, *nefer* 𓄤; 3, the head of Horus and 𓏏; and 4, *nefer* 𓄤. From Abydos. Length, ₁⁹₆ in.

1443. Green glazed steatite scarab, inscribed with a figure of Râ or Horus, an uræus, and ⌐⌐ "beautiful god." From Abydos.   Length, ⅝ in.

1444. Green glazed steatite scarab, inscribed with a figure of Horus or Râ, an uræus, and "good luck" ↓. From Abydos.   Length, 1⅜ in.

1445. Green glazed steatite scarab, inscribed "Beautiful Râ," (⊙—○) and 𓀃𓏏𓏏𓏏 . From Abydos.   Length, ⅝ in.

1446. Green glazed steatite scarab, inscribed with a king holding a crook ↑, and "Maât Râ ⊙𓏏". From Abydos.   Length, ¾ in.

1447. Green glazed steatite rectangular plaque, inscribed with 𓏏𓅃 "Beautiful Horus," and a winged uræus; and, 2, standing figure of Râ, or Horus, holding a sceptre, and 𓏏𓏏 (?). From Abydos.
          Length, ₁₆⁹ in.

1448. Light green glazed steatite scarab, inscribed with head of Horus, wearing disk and uræus 𓆓, and "good luck" ↓. From Abydos.   Length, ½ in.

1449. Dark glazed steatite scarab, inscribed with
the hawk of Horus and a winged uræus.
From Abydos. Length, $\frac{9}{16}$ in.

1450. Green glazed steatite scarab, inscribed "the
living Horus," . From Abydos.

Length, $\frac{1}{2}$ in.

1451. Green glazed steatite scarab, inscribed
"Favoured of Khonsu in Thebes,".
From Abydos. Length, $\frac{3}{8}$ in.

1452. Green glazed steatite scarab, inscribed
"under the protection of Khonsu". From
Abydos. Length, $\frac{1}{2}$ in.

1453. Green glazed steatite scarab, inscribed
"under the protection of Khonsu of Thebes,"
. From Abydos. Length, $\frac{7}{8}$ in.

1454. Green glazed steatite oval, inscribed
"where the eye of Khonsu is, there is no fear"
. From Abydos. Length, $\frac{3}{8}$ in.

1455. Green glazed steatite scarab, inscribed with

the name "Ptah" and plumes ⌨. From Abydos.   Length, $\frac{4}{16}$ in.

1456. Green glazed steatite scarab, inscribed with a figure of Ptah 🔯 and "beautiful Maāt" 🔯. From Abydos.   Length, $\frac{9}{16}$ in.

1457. Green glazed steatite scarab, inscribed with a winged disk and figures of the gods Ptah, Rā, and Horus (?).   From Abydos.   Length, $\frac{3}{4}$ in.

1458. Blue glazed steatite scarab, inscribed with a winged disk ⌨, and with the figure of a king adoring Ptah and another deity.   From Abydos.
                                              Length, $\frac{6}{8}$ in.

1459. Black glazed stone scarab, inscribed with a figure of Ptah 🔯.   From Abydos.   Length, $\frac{3}{4}$ in.

1460. Carnelian ape, inscribed "Thoth, the lord of Khemennu" ⌨.   From Abydos.
                                              Length, $\frac{6}{8}$ in.

1461. Green basalt rectangular plaque, inscribed on the obverse with a figure of Thoth 🔯, and on the reverse with that of a seated man 🔯.   From Abydos.   Length, $\frac{2}{4}$ in.

1462. Green glazed steatite scarab, inscribed with the figure of the cynocephalous ape (?) of Thoth. From Abydos.   Length, $\frac{1}{2}$ in.

1463. Green glazed steatite scarab, inscribed with a figure of Amen 🝔, the cynocephalous ape of Thoth 🝔, etc.   From Abydos.   Length, $\frac{5}{8}$ in.

1464. Green glazed steatite scarab, inscribed with a figure of the god Bes 🝔.   From Abydos.

Length, $\frac{11}{16}$ in.

1465. Blue glazed steatite scarab, inscribed with a figure of the god Bes 🝔.   From Abydos.

Length, $\frac{11}{16}$ in.

1466. Light blue glazed *faïence* scarab, inscribed with a figure of the god Bes.   From Abydos.

Length, $\frac{7}{8}$ in.

1467. Green glazed steatite scarab, inscribed with a figure of the god Bes.   From Abydos.

Length, $\frac{5}{8}$ in.

1468. Green glazed steatite scarab, inscribed with a figure of the god Bes.   From Abydos.

Length, $\frac{11}{16}$ in.

1469. Blue glazed *faïence* cowroid, inscribed with a figure of the god Bes. From Abydos.

Length, $\frac{6}{8}$ in.

1470. Carnelian ring, the bezel of which is inscribed with a figure of the god Bes 🔺. From Abydos.   Diameter, $\frac{7}{8}$ in.

1471. Blue glazed *faïence* scarab, inscribed with a figure of the god Bes. From Abydos. Length, $\frac{5}{8}$ in.

1472. Green glazed steatite cowroid, inscribed with a figure of the god Bes. From Abydos.

Length, $1\frac{1}{4}$ in.

1473. Green glazed steatite scarab, inscribed with the prenomen of Thothmes III. ☉ 〰 🪲 enclosed within a rope border. From Abydos.

Length, $1\frac{1}{2}$ in.

1474. Rectangular green glazed steatite plaque, inscribed with the prenomen of Thothmes III. 🔲 and four winged solar disks with pendent uræi. 〰 From Abydos.   Length $1\frac{1}{8}$ in. 🪲

1475. Green glazed steatite scarab, inscribed with the prenomen of Thothmes III. 🔲 🪲, and "Ámen-Rā," 🔲. From Abydos. Length, $\frac{1}{2}$ in.

1476. Green glazed steatite scarab, inscribed with the prenomen of Thothmes III., and plumes. From Abydos.

Length ½ in.

1477. Green glazed steatite scarab, inscribed "Men-kheper-Rā, the beautiful god, the lord of the North and South, the conqueror of all foreign lands" From Abydos. Length, ⅝ in.

1478. Yellow steatite scarab, inscribed with the prenomen of Thothmes III. and plumes. From Abydos. Length ₁₀⁹ in.

1479. Grey glazed steatite scarab, inscribed with the prenomen of Thothmes III. and uræi. From Abydos.

Length, ½ in.

1480. Green glazed steatite scarab, inscribed with the prenomen of Thothmes III. enclosed within four linear ornaments. From Abydos.

Length, ⅝ in.

1481. Green glazed steatite scarab, inscribed with the prenomen of Thothmes III., and two crowns of the North, with pendent uræi. From Abydos. Length, ₁₀⁹ in.

1482. Green glazed steatite scarab, inscribed with the winged disk 🪲, the prenomen of Thothmes III. ⟮⊙ 𓆓⟯, and *nefer* with plumes standing between uræi 🪶 . From Abydos.

Length, ⅝ in.

1483. Green glazed steatite scarab, inscribed with a winged disk, and the prenomen of Thothmes III. ⟮⊙ 𓆓⟯, and four uræi. From Abydos.

Length, ⅝ in.

1484. Green glazed steatite scarab, inscribed with the prenomen of Thothmes III. standing between figures of the god Bes and winged uræi; above is a vulture with outspread wings. From Abydos.

Length, 1¼ in.

1485. Green glazed steatite scarab, inscribed with the prenomen of Thothmes III. ⟮⊙ 𓆓⟯, and four uræi. From Abydos.   Length, 1 in.

1486. Green glazed steatite scarab, inscribed with the winged disk 🪲, the prenomen of Thothmes III. ⟮⊙ 𓆓⟯, and a figure of the goddess Maät 🪶. From Abydos.   Length, ¹¹⁄₁₆ in.

1487. Green glazed steatite scarab, inscribed "Men-kheper-Rā, beloved of Amen" ⊙ 🪲 ⌐ 𝕀. From Abydos. Length, ½ in.

1488. Green glazed steatite scarab, inscribed with the winged disk, the prenomen of Thothmes III., and a figure of the goddess Maāt. From Abydos.

Length, ⅒ in.

1489. Blue glazed steatite scarab, inscribed with the figure of a man holding a sistrum (?), and the prenomen of Thothmes III. From Abydos.

Length, ½ in.

1490. Green glazed steatite scarab, inscribed "Men-kheper-Rā, the beautiful god, the lord of the North and South, royally diademed" ⌐⌐. From Abydos. Length, ½ in.

1491. Green glazed steatite scarab, inscribed "Men-kheper-Rā, the beautiful god, the lord of the North and South, royally diademed" ⌐⌐. From Abydos. Length, ⅝ in.

1492. Green glazed steatite scarab, inscribed with the figure of a king holding the crook ⌐, and the legend, "Men-kheper-Rā, [beloved of] Ámen-Rā,"

(hieroglyphs) . From Abydos.

Length, $\frac{11}{16}$ in.

1493. Green glazed steatite scarab, inscribed with the prenomen of Thothmes III., and uræi and plumes, and with a _tet_ having pendent uræi. From Abydos.   Length, $\frac{11}{16}$ in.

1494. Blue glazed steatite scarab, inscribed with a winged disk, _(hieroglyphs)_, the prenomen of Thothmes III., and a _tet_ with pendent uræi.   From Abydos.

Length, $\frac{11}{16}$ in.

1495. Green glazed steatite scarab, inscribed with a human-headed lion standing over a prostrate foe, and the legend, "Men-kheper-Rā, the beautiful god,"

(hieroglyphs) . From Abydos.   Length, $\frac{5}{8}$ in.

1496. Green glazed steatite scarab, set in its original bronze ring, inscribed with the prenomen of

Thothmes III. _(hieroglyphs)_ , and _(hieroglyphs)_ .

From Abydos.   Length, $\frac{5}{8}$ in.

1497. Green glazed steatite scarab, inscribed with

the figure of Thothmes III. and the legend

Behind the king are the signs , *Amen em âpt* (?).
From Abydos.   Length, ⅞ in.

1498. Green glazed steatite scarab,
inscribed with the prenomens of Thothmes III. and his sister Ḥātshepset.
From Abydos.   Length, ⅝ in.

1499. Green glazed steatite oval, inscribed on the
obverse with the prenomen and titles of Thothmes III.

, and the emblem of union, ,
having pendent uræi; and on the reverse with

. From Abydos.   Length, ½ in.

1500. Dark green glazed steatite oval,
inscribed with the prenomen of Thothmes
III. and uræi, and with an uræus and

Maāt, . From Abydos.   Length, ₁₆⁹ in.

1501. Hard green stone rectangular plaque, inscribed with the prenomen of Thothmes III., the figure of the king, etc.   From Abydos.

Length, $\frac{9}{16}$ in.

1502. Green glazed rectangular plaque, inscribed on the obverse with the prenomen of Thothmes III., and on the reverse with the same prenomen, and with the titles of the king and four uræi. From Abydos.   Length, $\frac{1}{2}$ in.

1503. Green glazed steatite scarab, inscribed with the prenomen of Thothmes III., and with the feather of Maät.   From Abydos.   Length, $\frac{3}{8}$ in.

1504. Green glazed steatite scarab, inscribed with the solar disk and uræi, the prenomen of Thothmes III., and the emblem of "life."   From Abydos.

Length, $\frac{1}{2}$ in.

1505. Green glazed steatite scarab, inscribed "Men-kheper-Rā, the beautiful god, the giver of life."   From Abydos.

Length, $\frac{11}{16}$ in.

1506. Green glazed steatite scarab, inscribed with the prenomen of Thothmes III., plumes, emblems of "life," "*ka*," and owls (?). From Abydos. Length ⅟₄ in.

1507. Green glazed steatite scarab, inscribed with the prenomen of Thothmes III., the hawk of Horus, etc. From Abydos. Length, ⅝ in.

1508. Blue glazed steatite scarab, inscribed with the figure of Thothmes III. adoring an obelisk ⌷, emblematic of Ámen; behind him is the name "Ámen", and beneath is the prenomen of Thothmes III. From Abydos. Length, ⅝ in.

1509. Green glazed steatite oval, inscribed on one side with the prenomen of Thothmes III. and on the other, From Abydos. Length, ¾ in.

1510. Green glazed steatite scarab, inscribed with the prenomen of Thothmes III. From Abydos. Length, ₇⁄₁₀ in.

1511. Green glazed scarab, inscribed with the prenomen of Thothmes III. From Abydos.   Length, $\frac{9}{16}$ in.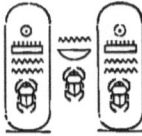

1512. Green glazed steatite rectangular plaque, having upon it in relief the head of Bes; on the back is the prenomen of Thothmes III. From Abydos.

Length, $1\frac{1}{8}$ in.

1513. Green glazed steatite rectangular plaque, inscribed with :—1, the name "Åmen-Rā," and prenomen and titles of Thothmes III. ; 2, cruciform ornament and four uræi; Hathor-headed sistrum, inscribed with the prenomen of Thothmes III, with pendent uræi ; and 4. . From Abydos.   Length, $\frac{6}{8}$ in.

1514. Rectangular copper plaque inscribed "Menkheper-Rā, the beautiful god" and "Åmen-Rā, the king of the gods." From Abydos.

Length, $\frac{1}{2}$ in.

1515. Blue glazed *faïence* scarab, inscribed
with the prenomen of Thothmes III. and a
winged uræus. From Abydos. Length, ⅝ in.

1516. Green glazed steatite scarab, inscribed
with the prenomen of Thothmes III., "life," etc.,
. From Abydos. Length, ⅝ in.

1517. Green glazed steatite oval, inscribed with :—

1, the prenomen of Thothmes III. , and beetle

with pendent uræi; and, 2, a cruciform ornament
and four uræi. From Abydos. Length, ₁⁹₆ in.

1518. Green glazed steatite rectangular stone
plaque, inscribed with :—1, a figure of Ån-Ḥeru and
; 2, the prenomen of Thothmes III. ;
3, the prenomen of Thothmes III. and two deities;
and 4, standing figure of a deity. From Abydos.
Length, ⅝ in.

1519. Green glazed steatite oval, inscribed on one
side with the prenomen of Thothmes III. ,
between plumes and uræi, and on the other with the

figure of the king and "Men-kheper-Rȃ, beautiful prince," ⊙ ▭ 🪲 ‡ ↑. From Abydos.

Length, ⅝ in.

1520. Green glazed steatite scarab, inscribed with a sphinx, ▱, "life" ⚡, and the prenomen of Åmen-ḥetep III. (⬭). From Abydos. Length, ₁⁷₆ in.

1521. Green glazed steatite amulet, inscribed on one side with 🦅 and an uræus, and on the other with the prenomen of Åmen-ḥetep III. From Abydos. Length, ⁹₈ in.

1522. Cobalt blue glazed *faïence* oval plaque, inscribed on one side with the name "Åmen-ḥetep," ▭ ▱, and on the other with the prenomen of Amenophis III. ⊙ ▱, etc. From Abydos.

Length, ₁⁹₆ in.

1523. Green glazed rectangular steatite plaque, inscribed on one side with a sphinx and winged uræus, and on the other with the figure and prenomen of Åmen-ḥetep III. ⊙ ▱. From Abydos.

Length, ⅝ in.

1524. Blue glazed steatite scarab, inscribed with the prenomen of Åmen-ḥetep III. ⊙ ⌣. From Abydos. Length, $\frac{9}{16}$ in.

1525. Green glazed *faïence* duck, inscribed with the prenomen of Åmen-ḥetep III. From Abydos. Length, $\frac{1}{2}$ in.

1526. Green glazed steatite scarab, inscribed with the prenomen of Åmen-ḥetep III. From Abydos. Length, $\frac{9}{16}$ in.

1527. Green glazed steatite scarab, inscribed with the prenomen of Åmen-ḥetep III. ⊙ ⌣. From Abydos. Length, $\frac{5}{8}$ in.

1528. Green glazed steatite scarab, inscribed with the prenomen of Åmen-ḥetep III. (⊙ ⌣), and , "diademed with Maāt." From Abydos. Length, $\frac{9}{16}$ in.

1529. Blue glazed steatite scarab, inscribed "Åmen-ḥetep, prince of Thebes," . From Abydos. Length, $\frac{11}{16}$ in.

1530. Blue glazed *faïence* scarab, inscribed "Åmen-ḥetep, prince of Thebes," [hieroglyphs]. From Abydos.
Length, 1⅜ in.

1531. Green glazed steatite scarab, set in its original copper ring, inscribed "Åmen-ḥetep, prince of Thebes," [hieroglyphs]. From Abydos. Length, 1⅟₁ in.

1532. Green glazed steatite scarab, inscribed "Åmen-[ḥetep], prince of Thebes," [hieroglyphs]. From Abydos. Length, ⅜ in.

1533. Gray glazed steatite scarab, inscribed "Beautiful god, Åmen-ḥetep," etc. From Abydos. Length, 1½ in.

1534. Green glazed steatite scarab, inscribed with the name "Åmen-ḥetep," [hieroglyphs]. From Abydos. Length, ₁⁹₆ in.

1535. Green glazed steatite cartouche, [hieroglyph], inscribed with the name "Åmen-ḥetep," [hieroglyphs]; on the back, in relief, is a fish. From Abydos.
Length, ₁⁹₆ in.

1536. Green glazed steatite rectangular plaque, inscribed with the name "Åmen-ḥetep," ; on the back, in relief, are ten scarabs. From Abydos.

Length, ½ in.

1537. Green glazed steatite hollow-work scarab, inscribed with the name "Åmen-ḥetep," From Abydos.

Length, ½ in.

1538. Green glazed steatite scarab, inscribed with the name "Åmen-ḥetep," From Abydos.

Length, ⅝ in.

1539. Green glazed steatite cowroid, inscribed "Royal wife Thi," From Abydos.

Length, ¾ in.

1540. Blue glazed steatite scarab, inscribed "Royal wife Thi," From Abydos.

Length, ⅝ in.

1541. Blue glazed rectangular plaque, inscribed with the prenomen and nomen of Ḥeru-em-Ḥeb, a king of the XVIIIth dynasty, about B.C. 1400. From Abydos.

Length, 1¼ in.

1542. Green glazed steatite scarab, inscribed with the prenomen of Seti I, ⊙ ⫯. From Abydos.

Length, $\frac{7}{16}$ in.

1543. Green glazed steatite scarab, inscribed with a figure of the god Set, and the prenomen of Seti I, king of Egypt about B.C. 1373. From Abydos. Length, $\frac{5}{8}$ in.

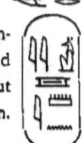

1544. Green glazed steatite scarab, inscribed with the prenomen and nomen of Rameses II. From Abydos.

Length, $\frac{3}{4}$ in.

1545. Green glazed steatite scarab, inscribed "libationer of Ȧmen-Rā," From Abydos. Length, $\frac{1}{2}$ in.

1546. Blue glazed steatite scarab, inscribed "libationer of Ȧmen-Rā,". From Abydos. Length, $\frac{11}{16}$ in.

1547. Green glazed steatite scarab, inscribed "Libationer of Ȧmen-Rā,". From Abydos. Length, $\frac{1}{2}$ in.

1548. Green glazed steatite scarab, inscribed "Libationer of Åmen-Rā," [hieroglyphs]. From Abydos. Length, ¾ in.

1549. Blue paste oval, inscribed "May the New Year be happy." From Abydos. [hieroglyphs] Length, ₁⁰₆ in.

1550. Purple glazed *faïence* frog, inscribed on the base "good luck," [hieroglyph]. From Abydos. Length, ⅜ in.

1551. Brown glazed steatite scarab, inscribed with the figure of a woman smelling a flower, and "good luck," [hieroglyph]. From Abydos. Length, ⅝ in.

1552. Green glazed steatite scarab, inscribed with the boat of the sun, on each end of which a hawk is perched; within it are the signs for "millions of years," [hieroglyph], and "life and happiness," [hieroglyphs]. From Abydos. Length, ⅝ in.

1553. Green glazed steatite scarab, inscribed with the animal symbolic of Set, "good luck," and [hieroglyph]. From Abydos. Length, ⅝ in.

1554. Green glazed steatite scarab, inscribed "double life" and "happiness." From Abydos.   Length, ½ in.

1555. Copper scarab, inscribed "life," and "double power," . From Abydos.
                                        Length, $\frac{9}{16}$ in.

1556. Green glazed steatite scarab, inscribed "good luck," , etc. From Abydos. Length, $\frac{9}{16}$ in.

1557. Green glazed steatite duck, inscribed on the base , Ḥeru-à, "Belonging to Horus." From Abydos.   Length, ⅝ in.

1558. Yellowish-green glazed steatite scarab, inscribed , *Ḥeru-à*, "Belonging to Horus." From Abydos.   Length, ⅝ in.

1559. Green glazed steatite scarab, inscribed Ḥeru-à, "Belonging to Horus," . From Abydos.
                                        Length, ⅝ in.

1560. Green glazed steatite scarab, inscribed Nub-ka-Rā. From Abydos.   Length, ½ in.

1561. Green glazed steatite scarab, inscribed
⟨glyphs⟩. From Abydos. Length, ½ in.

1562. Green glazed steatite scarab, inscribed
⟨glyphs⟩. From Abydos. Length, ⅝ in.

1563. Green glazed steatite scarab, inscribed with
"Beautiful Horus" ⟨glyphs⟩ and an uræus (?). From
Abydos. Length, $\frac{9}{16}$ in.

1564. Green glazed steatite scarab, inscribed
⟨glyphs⟩. From Abydos. Length, $\frac{7}{16}$ in.

1565. Green glazed steatite scarab, inscribed
"Favoured of the lord of Thebes, ... life"
⟨glyphs⟩. From Abydos. Length, ¾ in.

1566. Green glazed steatite scarab inscribed
⟨glyphs⟩. From Abydos. Length, ½ in.

1567. Blue glazed steatite scarab, inscribed
⟨glyphs⟩. From Abydos. Length, $\frac{9}{16}$ in.

1568. Green glazed steatite scarab, inscribed
From Abydos.   Length, ⅝ in.

1569. Green glazed steatite scarab, inscribed
. From Abydos.   Length, ⁷⁄₁₆ in.

1570. Blue glazed steatite scarab, inscribed
From Abydos.   Length, ⁹⁄₁₆ in.

1571. Blue glazed steatite scarab, inscribed
. From Abydos.   Length, ⁷⁄₁₆ in.

1572. Green glazed steatite scarab, inscribed
"Favoured of Rā, the lord of Thebes". From
Abydos.   Length, ⅝ in.

1573. Green glazed steatite scarab, inscribed
From Abydos.   Length, ⅝ in.

1574. Green glazed steatite scarab, inscribed
From Abydos.   Length, ½ in.

1575. Blue glazed steatite scarab, inscribed
From Abydos.   Length, ⅝ in.

1575a. Blue paste scarab, set in original bronze
ring, with similar inscription.   From Abydos.
                    Length, ⁹⁄₁₆ in.

1576. Green glazed steatite scarab, inscribed with a vulture and "life," ☥ ⌐ 𓅢. From Abydos.

Length, $\frac{9}{16}$ in.

1577. Green glazed steatite scarab, inscribed with the figure of an ape holding *nefer* 𓀾, and the signs ▢ (?) ⌐ △. From Abydos. Length, $\frac{5}{8}$ in.

1578. Green glazed steatite scarab, inscribed 𓃛 . From Abydos. Length, $\frac{1}{2}$ in.

1579. Green glazed steatite scarab, inscribed 𓅢 From Abydos. Length, $\frac{7}{16}$ in. 𓎬

1580. Blue glazed steatite scarab, inscribed 𓇼 From Abydos. Length, $\frac{3}{8}$ in. 𓄿

1581. Yellow glazed steatite scarab, set in its original gold frame, inscribed From Abydos. Length, $\frac{3}{8}$ in.

1582. Green glazed steatite triple scarab, inscribed
⳾⳾⳾. From Abydos.   Length, ½ in.

1583. Green glazed steatite scarab, in its original
setting, inscribed ⳾⳾. From Abydos.
                                                    Length, ₇⁄₈ in.

1584. Blue glazed *faïence* scarab, inscribed
⳾⳾⳾. From Abydos.   Length, ⅝ in.

1585. Green glazed steatite oryx, inscribed on
the base ⳾⳾. From Abydos.   Length, ₁⁹⁄₆ in.

1586. Green glazed *faïence* oval, inscribed "the
. . . . . . Åmen-ḥetep," ⳾ (?) ⳾. From Abydos.
                                                    Length, ⅝ in.

1587. Green glazed steatite scarab, inscribed " . . . . Ṭeṭ, beloved of Åmen."
From Abydos.   Length, ⅝ in.

1588. Green glazed steatite scarab, inscribed
From Abydos.   Length, ₇⁄₈ in.

1589. Green glazed steatite scarab, inscribed "lord
of life (?)" ⳾ ⳾. From Abydos.   Length, ½ in.

1590. Amethyst scarab, inscribed "Isis protecteth her servant (?)," ⌇⌇⌇. From Abydos.

Length, $\frac{11}{16}$ in.

1591. Yellow glazed steatite scarab, inscribed ⌇⌇⌇ From Abydos.   Length, $\frac{9}{16}$ in. ⌇⌇⌇

1592. Green glazed steatite scarab, inscribed with a bee ⌇⌇. From Abydos.   Length, $\frac{1}{2}$ in.

1593. Green glazed *faïence* scarab, inscribed ⌇⌇ From Abydos.   Length, $\frac{1}{2}$ in.

1594. Green glazed steatite scarab, inscribed ⌇⌇⌇. From Abydos.   Length, $\frac{3}{4}$ in.

1595. Green glazed steatite scarab, inscribed. From Abydos. Length, $\frac{9}{16}$ in.

1596. Green glazed steatite scarab, inscribed From Abydos.   Length, $\frac{11}{16}$ in.

2 R

1597. Green glazed steatite scarab, inscribed with ⟨hieroglyphs⟩, etc. From Abydos. Length, ⅝ in.

1598. Green glazed steatite scarab, inscribed ⟨hieroglyphs⟩ From Abydos.   Length, $\frac{7}{16}$ in.

1599. Green glazed steatite scarab, inscribed ⟨hieroglyphs⟩ From Abydos.   Length, ⅝ in.

1600. Blue   paste   cowroid,   inscribed ⟨hieroglyphs⟩ From Abydos.   Length, $\frac{7}{16}$ in.

1601. Green   glazed   steatite   scarab,   inscribed ⟨hieroglyphs⟩. From Abydos.   Length, ⅝ in.

1602. Green   glazed   steatite   scarab,   inscribed ⟨hieroglyphs⟩. From Abydos.   Length, $\frac{9}{16}$ in.

1603. Green glazed steatite scarab, inscribed ⟨hieroglyphs⟩ ".......Amen-ḥetep." From Abydos.   Length ⅝ in.

1604. White glazed steatite scarab, inscribed ⟨hieroglyphs⟩ ".....Amen-ḥetep." From Abydos.   Length, ½ in.

1605. Green glazed steatite scarab, inscribed "life," ☥. From Abydos. Length, ½ in.

1606. Yellowish-green stone oval plaque, inscribed "Ámen-ḥetep, overseer of ....." From Abydos. Length, $\frac{10}{16}$ in.

1607. Green glazed steatite scarab, inscribed ⟨glyphs⟩. From Abydos. Length, $\frac{11}{16}$ in.

1608. Green glazed steatite cowroid, inscribed. From Abydos. Length, ¾ in.

1609. Green glazed steatite scarab, inscribed ⟨glyphs⟩ From Abydos. Length, ½ in. (?)

1610. Green glazed steatite scarab, inscribed ⟨glyphs⟩. From Abydos. Length, $\frac{7}{16}$ in.

1611. Green glazed steatite scarab, inscribed ⟨glyphs⟩ (?) From Abydos. Length, ⅝ in.

1612. Green glazed steatite scarab, inscribed ⟨glyphs⟩ From Abydos. Length, $\frac{9}{16}$ in.

1613. Green glazed steatite cowroid, inscribed
From Abydos.
        Length, $\frac{1}{1\frac{1}{8}}$ in.

1614. Green glazed steatite scarab, inscribed
From Abydos.   Length, $\frac{7}{16}$ in.

1615. Green glazed steatite scarab, inscribed
((?)).   From Abydos.   Length, $\frac{5}{8}$ in.

1616. Green glazed steatite scarab, inscribed
From Abydos.   Length, $\frac{3}{4}$ in.

1617. Green   glazed   steatite   scarab,
inscribed
From Abydos.   Length, $\frac{5}{8}$ in.

1618. Green glazed steatite scarab, inscribed
From Abydos.   Length, $\frac{5}{8}$ in.

1619. Green glazed steatite scarab, inscribed
From Abydos.   Length, $\frac{9}{16}$ in.

1620. Blue glazed *faïence* scarab, inscribed

From Abydos.   Length, ⅝ in.

1621. Green glazed steatite fish, on one side of which is inscribed

From Abydos.   Length, ⅝ in.

1622. Green glazed steatite scarab, inscribed

. From Abydos.   Length, ⅞ in.

1623. Brown steatite scarab inscribed

From Abydos.   Length, ⅝ in.

1624. Brown glazed steatite scarab, inscribed

From Abydos.   Length, ⅜ in.

1625. Green stone amulet , inscribed

From Abydos.   Length, 1¼ in.

1626. Blue glazed *faïence* scarab, inscribed

From Abydos.   Length, ½ in.

1627. Green glazed steatite scarab, inscribed
"favoured of the god beloved of Thebes."
From Abydos.   Length, ⅝ in.

1628. Green glazed steatite scarab, inscribed
⬚⬚⬚ (?). From Abydos.   Length, ⅜ in.

1629. Green glazed steatite cowroid,
inscribed. From Abydos.   Length, ¾ in.

1630. Green glazed steatite scarab, inscribed
From Abydos.   Length, ⅝ in.

1631. Green glazed steatite scarab, inscribed
"favoured of the lord of the North and South,"
⬚⬚⬚⬚. From Abydos.   Length, 7/16 in.

1632. Blue glazed steatite cynocephalous ape, on the base of which are inscribed
From Abydos.   Length, ¾ in.

1633. Green glazed steatite scarab, inscribed
with the figure of a king slaughtering an animal.
From Abydos.   Length, 9/16 in.

1634. Green glazed steatite scarab, inscribed
[glyphs]. From Abydos.   Length, $\frac{9}{16}$ in.

1635. Green glazed steatite scarab, inscribed
[glyphs]. From Abydos.   Length, $\frac{6}{8}$ in.

1636. Green glazed steatite scarab, inscribed
[glyphs]. From Abydos.   Length, $\frac{1}{2}$ in.

1637. Green glazed steatite scarab, inscribed
[glyphs], etc. From Abydos.   Length, $\frac{4}{8}$ in.

1638. Green glazed steatite scarab, inscribed
[glyphs]. From Abydos.   Length, $\frac{11}{16}$ in.

1639. Green steatite scarab, inscribed
From Abydos.   Length, $\frac{6}{8}$ in. [glyphs]

1640. Green glazed steatite scarab, inscribed [glyphs]
From Abydos.   Length, $\frac{7}{16}$ in.

1641. Green glazed steatite scarab, inscribed
"stability" [glyphs]. From Abydos.   Length, $\frac{1}{2}$ in.

1642. Green steatite scarab, inscribed [glyphs]
From Abydos.   Length, $\frac{11}{16}$ in.

1643. Green glazed steatite fish, inscribed
From Abydos.   Length, ⅜ in.

1644. Green glazed steatite scarab, inscribed
(?) .   From Abydos.   Length, ⅜ in.

1645. Green glazed steatite scarab,
inscribed
From Abydos.   Length, ⅜ in.

1646. Green glazed steatite scarab, inscribed
From Abydos.   Length, ₇⁄₁₆ in.

1647. Yellow glazed steatite scarab, in its original
silver setting, inscribed   , etc. From Abydos.
                                       Length, ⅞ in.

1648. Green glazed steatite scarab, inscribed
From Abydos.   Length, ₁⁹⁄₁₆ in.

1649. Bezel of a carnelian ring,
inscribed
From Abydos.   Length, ¾ in.

1650. Green glazed steatite amulet, inscribed with : 1. [figure] ; and, 2. [figure]. From Abydos.

Length, ½ in.

1651. Green glazed steatite scarab, inscribed [figure]. From Abydos.

Length, ⅝ in.

1652. Blue glazed steatite scarab, inscribed [figure], etc. From Abydos.

Length, ¾ in.

1653. Green glazed steatite scarab, inscribed
From Abydos.

Length, ₁₆⁹ in.

1654. Mother-of-emerald scarab, inscribed "Overseer of the temple, chief chancellor, Ḥetep-á (?)." From Abydos.

Length, 1½ in.

1655. Blue paste scarab, inscribed "Âmen leadeth to the seat of the heart (?)." From Abydos.

Length, ₁₆⁹ in.

1656. Green glazed steatite scarab, inscribed with
and two double spirals enclosed within ovals.
From Abydos. Length, $\frac{7}{16}$ in.

1657. Green glazed steatite scarab, inscribed
From Abydos. Length, $\frac{9}{16}$ in.

1658. Green glazed steatite scarab, inscribed
From Abydos. Length, $\frac{5}{8}$ in.

1659. Green glazed steatite scarab, inscribed
From Abydos. Length, $\frac{11}{16}$ in.

1660. Green glazed steatite scarab, inscribed
From Abydos. Length, $\frac{3}{4}$ in.

1661. Green glazed steatite scarab, inscribed
From Abydos. Length, $\frac{11}{16}$ in.

1662. Green glazed steatite scarab, inscribed ⬚⬚
From Abydos.   Length, ⅝ in. ⬚ (?)

1663. Green glazed steatite scarab, inscribed with two illegible signs. From Abydos.   Length, ½ in.

1664. Blue glazed *faïence* scarab, with illegible inscription. From Abydos.   Length, ⅜ in.

1665. Green glazed steatite scarab, inscribed with a beetle and "double life." ⬚⬚⬚. From Abydos.
                                   Length, ⅝ in.

1666. Cobalt blue glazed steatite scarab, inscribed with two sandals and a scorpion ⬚⬚⬚. From Abydos.   Length, ⅝ in.

1667. Green glazed steatite scarab, inscribed with the figure of a hippopotamus holding a knife. From Abydos.   Length, ½ in.

1668. Green glazed steatite scarab, inscribed with the hawk of Horus ⬚⬚⬚. From Abydos.
                                   Length, ⅝ in.

1669. Green glazed steatite scarab, inscribed with the figure of a lion. From Abydos.   Length, ½ in.

1670. Green glazed steatite scarab, inscribed with the figure of a dog and the signs . From Abydos.   Length, ⅝ in.

1671. Green glazed steatite rectangular plaque, inscribed with the figure of a horse; on the back in relief is an *utchat*, . From Abydos.
Length, ⅝ in.

1672. Green glazed steatite cowroid, inscribed with the figure of a woman holding a papyrus sceptre. From Abydos.   Length, $\frac{9}{16}$ in.

1673. Green glazed steatite cowroid, inscribed with a fish having two lotus buds in its mouth . From Abydos.   Length, ¾ in.

1674. Green glazed steatite mouse, inscribed on the base with a fish. From Abydos. Length, $\frac{7}{16}$ in.

1675. Blue glazed steatite grasshopper, inscribed on the base with the sign of "life," . From Abydos.
Length, ⅜ in.

1676. Yellow glazed steatite scarab, inscribed with the figure of a horse, etc. From Abydos.
Length, $\frac{11}{16}$ in.

1677. Blue paste frog, inscribed on the base "good luck," ⌇. From Abydos. Length, ⅝ in.

1678. Opaque red glass frog, inscribed on the base with a hare. From Abydos. Length, ¾ in.

1679. Blue glazed steatite plaque, inscribed with two crocodiles; on the back, in relief, is a fish. From Abydos. Length, ⅞ in.

1680. Green glazed steatite cat, inscribed on the base with a cat. From Abydos. Length, ⅜ in.

1681. Green glazed steatite scarab, inscribed ⌇. From Abydos. Length, ½ in.

1682. Blue paste scarab, in its original gold setting, inscribed with a hawk, etc. From Abydos. Length, ¾ in.

1683. Green glazed steatite scarab, inscribed with a hawk-headed kneeling figure and two animals. From Abydos. Length, ¾ in.

1684. Gray stone oval, inscribed with a sphinx and a hare ⌇. From Abydos. Length, 1½ in.

1685. Green glazed steatite scarab, inscribed with a hawk , crocodile , and two uræi . From Abydos. Length, $1\frac{1}{4}$ in.

1686. Green glazed steatite scarab, inscribed with the figure of a man and two beetles . From Abydos. Length, $\frac{7}{8}$ in.

1687. Blue glazed steatite plaque, inscribed with the figure of a man holding a bow, and a linear pattern composed of diamonds and annules. From Abydos. Length, $\frac{3}{4}$ in.

1688. Blue glazed steatite scarab, inscribed with a dog, or lion, and . From Abydos. Length, $\frac{3}{4}$ in.

1689. Green glazed steatite scarab, inscribed with the figures of a man and an animal (?). From Abydos. Length, 1 in.

1690. Green glazed steatite searab, inscribed with a sistrum, etc. From Abydos. Length, $\frac{7}{10}$ in.

1691. Yellow glazed steatite scarab, inscribed with a winged disk , *nefer* , etc. From Abydos. Length, $\frac{3}{4}$ in.

1692. Green glazed steatite scarab, inscribed with the figures of a lion and a prostrate man. From Abydos. Length, ⅝ in.

1693. Green glazed steatite scarab, inscribed with a Hathor-headed sistrum, from the handle of which projects two hands grasping ⧘⧘ , the emblems of renewed youth. From Abydos. Length, ¹⁰⁄₁₈ in.

1694. Green glazed steatite scarab, inscribed with a human figure (?). From Abydos. Length, ½ in.

1695. Green glazed steatite scarab, inscribed with a beetle ⬗ , and four ornamental designs. From Abydos. Length, ⅝ in.

1696. Green glazed steatite scarab, inscribed with a crocodile and an uræus. From Abydos.
Length, ½ in.

1697. Green glazed steatite scarab, inscribed with a male figure embracing two females (?). From Abydos. Length, ¾ in.

1698. Green glazed steatite duck on a base in the shape of a cartouche ⬄ ; the inscription reads, "beautiful life" ⧍ ⧎ . From Abydos.
Length, ¹⁰⁄₁₈ in.

1699. Green glazed steatite scarab, inscribed "beautiful life" 𓋹 𓋹 . From Abydos.

Length, ½ in.

1700. Cobalt blue glazed steatite scarab, inscribed with a human head. From Abydos.   Length, ⅝ in.

1701. Green glazed steatite circular seal, inscribed with figures of a lion and a lizard, double spiral, etc. From Abydos.   Length, 1 in.

1702. Blue glazed *faïence* scarab, inscribed with a sphinx and a winged uræus. From Abydos.

Length, ¾ in.

1703. Green glazed steatite scarab, inscribed with a crocodile and a snail (?). From Abydos.

Length, ⅝ in.

1704. Green glazed steatite scarab, inscribed with a sistrum and two cats, or lions. From Abydos.

Length, ⁹⁄₁₆ in.

1705. Green glazed steatite scarab, inscribed with figures of a king, a man (?), "life" 𓋹, etc. From Abydos.   Length, ⅞ in.

1706. Green glazed steatite amulet, part fish and part *utchat*, inscribed with "good luck" 𓄤, etc. From Abydos. Length, 9/16 in.

1707. Green glazed steatite scarab, inscribed with a lion, scorpion, *nefer* 𓄤, etc. From Abydos. Length, 3/4 in.

1708. Green glazed steatite scarab, inscribed with  enclosed within a border of spirals; on the back of the scarab, in hollow-work, are a cluster of lotus flowers , and a head , and two uræi. From Abydos. Length, 5/8 in.

1709. Green glazed steatite scarab, inscribed with a ram wearing horns, plumes and uræi, a beetle, etc. From Abydos. Length, 3/4 in.

1710. Dark green scarab, inscribed with 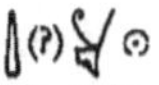 and a winged uræus. From Abydos. Length, 5/16 in.

1711. Green glazed steatite frog, inscribed on the base with a sistrum  having pendent uræi. From Abydos. Length 6/16 in.

1712. Blue glazed steatite scarab, inscribed with the figure of a man holding an uræus, and an uræus. From Abydos. Length, $\frac{3}{4}$ in.

1713. Blue glazed steatite scarab, inscribed with a sistrum ♀ having pendent uræi. From Abydos.

Length, $\frac{5}{8}$ in.

1714. Blue glazed *faïence* scarab, inscribed with a sistrum having pendent uræi, etc. From Abydos. Length, $\frac{1}{2}$ in.

1715. Blue glazed *faïence* scarab, inscribed with three uræi. From Abydos. Length, $\frac{5}{8}$ in.

1716. Green glazed steatite scarab, inscribed with four uræi. From Abydos. Length, $\frac{3}{4}$ in.

1717. Green glazed steatite scarab, inscribed with the head of a hawk, having on it a disk and uræus. From Abydos. Length, $\frac{7}{16}$ in.

1718. Blue paste scarab, set in its original gold ring, inscribed with a sistrum having pendent uræi. From Abydos. Length, $\frac{9}{16}$ in.

1719. Green glazed steatite scarab, inscribed with five uræi wearing plumes, etc. From Abydos.

Length, $1\frac{1}{4}$ in.

1720. Blue glazed *faïence* scarab, inscribed with three uræi wearing plumes, etc. From Abydos.

Length, ¾ in.

1721. Green glazed steatite cowroid, inscribed with a cruciform ornament and four uræi. From Abydos. Length, ₁₁₆ in.

1722. Green glazed steatite scarab, inscribed with a sphinx and a winged uræus. From Abydos.

Length, ⅝ in.

1723. Green glazed steatite scarab, inscribed with ☥ and two uræi. From Abydos. Length, ⅝ in.

1724. Green glazed steatite scarab, in its original silver setting, inscribed with two winged disks having pendent uræi, and 🪲 . From Abydos.

Length, ⅔ in.

1725. Green glazed steatite scarab, inscribed with 🪲 and a winged uræus. From Abydos.

Length, ½ in.

1726. Green glazed steatite scarab, inscribed with a sistrum having pendent uræi. From Abydos.

Length, ₁₆⁹ in.

1727. Green glazed steatite hare, inscribed on the base with four uræi.   From Abydos.   Length, ½ in.

1728. Brown glazed steatite mouse (?), inscribed on the base with four uræi.   From Abydos.

Length, ⅜ in.

1729. Green glazed steatite fish, inscribed on one side with four uræi.   From Abydos.   Length, $\frac{7}{16}$ in.

1730. Green glazed steatite scarab, inscribed with four uræi.   From Abydos.   Length, $\frac{11}{16}$ in.

1731. Blue glazed steatite scarab, inscribed with a cluster of lotus flowers.   From Abydos.

Length, $\frac{7}{16}$ in.

1732. Green glazed steatite scarab, inscribed with cluster of lotus flowers, .   From Abydos.

Length, $\frac{9}{16}$ in.

1733. Green glazed steatite scarab, inscribed with "stability," lotus flowers, etc.   From Abydos.

Length, ½ in.

1734. Blue glazed steatite oval, inscribed on one side with , and on the other with a fish having a lotus flower in its mouth.   From Abydos.

Length, $\frac{9}{16}$ in.

1735. Green glazed steatite scarab, inscribed with lotus flowers. From Abydos. Length, $\frac{1}{2}$ in.

1736. Green glazed steatite scarab, inscribed with a cluster of lotus flowers and two uræi. From Abydos. Length, $\frac{9}{16}$ in.

1737. Green glazed steatite scarab, inscribed with a lotus flower, etc. From Abydos. Length, $\frac{9}{16}$ in.

1738. Brownish-yellow opaque glass scaraboid, inscribed with a cluster of lotus flowers. From Abydos. Length, $\frac{9}{16}$ in.

1739. Green glazed steatite scarab, inscribed with a cluster of lotus flowers. From Abydos.

Length, $\frac{1}{2}$ in.

1740. Green glazed steatite scarab, inscribed with two lotus flowers, etc. From Abydos.

Length, $\frac{9}{16}$ in.

1741. Green glazed steatite scarab, inscribed with a cluster of lotus flowers. From Abydos.

Length, $\frac{5}{8}$ in

1742. Green glazed steatite scarab, inscribed with a lotus flower. From Abydos. Length, $\frac{5}{8}$ in.

1743. Green glazed steatite scarab, inscribed with a cluster of lotus flowers . From Abydos.

Length, $\frac{6}{8}$ in.

1744. Blue glazed steatite scarab, inscribed with a cruciform floral design. From Abydos.

Length, $\frac{11}{8}$ in.

1745. Green glazed steatite plaque, inscribed with a cruciform ornament ; on the back, in relief, is a fish. From Abydos. Length, $\frac{1}{2}$ in.

1746. Green glazed steatite scarab, inscribed with a cruciform floral design. From Abydos.

Length, $\frac{5}{8}$ in.

1747. Green glazed *faïence* cowroid, inscribed with a cruciform ornament and four uræi. From Abydos.

Length, $\frac{6}{8}$ in.

1748. Green glazed steatite scarab, inscribed with a cruciform floral ornament. From Abydos.

Length, $\frac{7}{16}$ in.

1749. Blue glazed steatite scarab, inscribed with a cruciform ornament and four uræi. From Abydos.

Length, $\frac{6}{8}$ in.

1750. Green glazed steatite cowroid, inscribed with a cruciform ornament and four uræi. From Abydos. Length, $\frac{3}{4}$ in.

1751. Yellow glazed steatite scarab, inscribed with a cruciform floral ornament. From Abydos.
Length, $\frac{9}{16}$ in.

1752. Green glazed steatite scarab, inscribed with a cruciform ornament, one end of which terminates in *tet* . From Abydos. Length, $\frac{1}{2}$ in.

1753. Green glazed steatite scarab, inscribed with a cruciform floral ornament. From Abydos.
Length, $\frac{9}{16}$ in.

1754. Green glazed steatite scarab, inscribed with a cruciform design. From Abydos. Length, $\frac{9}{16}$ in.

1755. Green glazed steatite scarab, inscribed with a design composed of spirals. From Abydos.
Length, $\frac{3}{8}$ in.

1756. Dark green glazed steatite scarab, inscribed with annules. From Abydos. Length, $\frac{5}{8}$ in.

1757. Green glazed steatite scarab, inscribed with a linear design. From Abydos. Length, $\frac{3}{4}$ in.

1758. Light blue glazed steatite scarab, inscribed with a linear design. From Abydos.   Length, $\frac{7}{8}$ in.

1759. Green glazed steatite scarab, inscribed with a linear device. From Abydos.   Length, $\frac{15}{16}$ in.

1760. Green glazed steatite scarab, inscribed with a floral design and spirals. From Abydos.

Length, $\frac{9}{16}$ in.

1761. Green glazed steatite scarab, inscribed with a design composed of annules and spirals. From Abydos.   Length, $\frac{5}{8}$ in.

1762. Green glazed steatite scarab, inscribed with a linear device. From Abydos.   Length, $\frac{7}{16}$ in.

1763. Amethyst scarab inscribed with a linear device. From Abydos.   Length, $\frac{7}{8}$ in.

1764. Green glazed steatite cat, inscribed on the base with a floral design. From Abydos.

Length, $\frac{1}{2}$ in.

1765. Green glazed steatite scarab, inscribed with linear ornaments. From Abydos.   Length, $\frac{11}{16}$ in.

1766. Green glazed steatite scarab, inscribed with a twisted double-line ornament. From Abydos.

Length, $\frac{9}{16}$ in.

1767. Green glazed steatite scarab, inscribed with a linear device. From Abydos. Length, $\frac{1}{2}$ in.

1768. Brown glazed steatite cowroid, set in its original copper ring, incribed with an *utchat* 𓂀, and a line of annules. From Abydos.

Length, $\frac{14}{8}$ in.

1769. Green glazed steatite scarab, inscribed with a design formed of short lines and annules. From Abydos. Length, $\frac{5}{8}$ in.

1770. Green glazed steatite scarab, inscribed with a floral device and spirals. From Abydos.

Length, $\frac{1}{2}$ in.

1771. Green glazed steatite scarab, inscribed with a floral design. From Abydos. Length, $\frac{1}{2}$ in.

1772. Green glazed steatite rectangular plaque; on one side, in relief, is a fish, and on the other six annules 🆚 . From Abydos. Length, $\frac{3}{4}$ in.

1773. Green glazed basalt scaraboid, uninscribed. From Abydos. Length, $\frac{5}{8}$ in.

1774. Amethyst scaraboid, uninscribed. From Abydos. Length, $\frac{3}{4}$ in.

1775. Carnelian scaraboid, uninscribed. From Abydos. Length, $\frac{5}{8}$ in.

1776. Mother-of-emerald scaraboid, uninscribed. From Abydos. Length, $1\frac{1}{4}$ in.

1777. Light green stone oval, uninscribed. From Abydos. Length, $\frac{1}{2}$ in.

1778. Mother-of-emerald scaraboid, uninscribed. From Abydos. Length, $\frac{1}{2}$ in.

1779. Agate scarab, uninscribed. From Abydos Length, $\frac{5}{8}$ in.

1780. Green glazed *faïence* scarab, uninscribed. From Abydos. Length, $\frac{9}{16}$ in.

1781. Green glass scarab, uninscribed. From Abydos. Length, $\frac{3}{4}$ in.

1782. Gray stone oval plaque, uninscribed. From Abydos. Length, $\frac{9}{16}$ in.

1783. Dark stone scarab, uninscribed. From Abydos. Length, $\frac{3}{8}$ in.

1784. Dark green polished stone oval plaque, uninscribed. From Abydos. Length, $\frac{1}{2}$ in.

1785. Large steatite scarab, inscribed with a record of the slaughter of one hundred and two lions by Åmen-ḥetep III. during the first ten years of his reign; the text reads:—

1.

ānχ   Ḥeru   ka   neχt   χā   em

May live the Horus, bull powerful, diademed with

2.

maāt   . . . . .   semen   hepu   sekerḥ

law, { *lord of North and South* }*, establisher of laws,   pacifier of*

3.

taui   Ḥeru nub   ān   χepeś

the two lands, Horus the golden, mighty of valour,

ḥu   sati   4.   suten net

smiter of foreign lands,   { *King of the North and South,* }

Neb-maāt-Rā   sa Rā   en   χat - f

Neb-maāt-Rā,   son of the sun,   of   body his,

5.

Amen-ḥetep ḥeq Uast   ṭā   ānχ
Amenḥetep, prince of Thebes,   giver   of life, [*and*]

suten   ḥemt   Θi   er χet   mau   ān
royal   spouse   Thi.   In respect of   lions,   brought

en   ḥen · f   em   satet - f   t'esef   śaā
      majesty his   from   shooting his   own,   beginning

7.

em   renpit   uā   neferit   er   renpit   met   mau
from   year   first   up   to   year   tenth,   lions

8.

ḥesau   śaā   sen
fierce,   one hundred and two.

XVIIIth dynasty.   About B.C. 1500.   Length, 3⅝ in.

1786. Green glazed *faïence ṭeṭ* , emblem of
stability, surmounted by horns, plumes, etc.   From
Tūna.   Height, 4¹⁄₁₆ in.

1787. Blue glazed *faïence* fragment of a vase with figure of a fish, flowers, etc., in relief. Very fine work. From Tûna. Length, 1⅜ in.

1788. Green glazed *faïence* fragment of a vase with the figure of man, papyrus plants, etc., in relief. Very fine work. From Tûna. Length, 2⅝ in.

Nos. 834-1310.

AMULETS, ETC.

834. Onyx *utchat* 👁, inscribed ⬚. Length, $\frac{7}{16}$ in.

835. Onyx *utchat* 👁, inscribed. Length, $\frac{1}{2}$ in.

836. Green glass *utchat* 👁. Length, $\frac{9}{16}$ in.

837. Blue glazed *faïence utchat* 👁. Length, $2\frac{1}{2}$ in.

38. Blue glazed *faïence utchat* 👁. Length, $2\frac{1}{8}$ in.

839. Blue glazed *faïence utchat* 👁.* Length, $1\frac{3}{4}$ in.

---

* Originally inlaid with red colour.

840. Blue glazed *faïence utchat* ⟨eye⟩.*

Length, 1⅞ in.

841. Blue glazed *faïence utchat* ⟨eye⟩.

Length, 1⅝ in.

842. Blue glazed *faïence utchat* ⟨eye⟩.

Length, 1⅜ in.

843. Blue glazed *faïence utchat* ⟨eye⟩.

Length, 1½ in.

844. Blue glazed *faïence utchat* ⟨eye⟩.

Length, 1¼ in.

845. Green glazed *faïence utchat* ⟨eye⟩.

Length, 1 in.

846. Green glazed *faïence utchat* ⟨eye⟩.

Length, 1⅛ in.

847. Blue glazed *faïence utchat* ⟨eye⟩.

Length, ⅞ in.

848. Blue glazed *faïence utchat* ⟨eye⟩.

Length, ¾ in.

---

* Originally inlaid with red colour.

849. Blue glazed *faïence utchat* 👁 .

Length, ⅝ in.

850. Green glazed *faïence utchat* 👁 .

Length, ⅝ in.

851. Black glazed *faïence utchat* 👁 .

Length, ⅞ in.

852. Blue glazed *faïence utchat* 👁 .

Length, ⅞ in.

853. Green glazed *faïence utchat* 👁 ,

Length, $\frac{7}{10}$ in.

854. Green glazed *faïence utchat* 👁 ,

Length, ⅝ in.

855. Blue glazed *faïence utchat* 👁 .

Length, $\frac{9}{16}$ in.

856. Green glazed *faïence utchat* 👁 ,

Length, ½ in.

857. Green glazed *faïence utchat* 👁 .

Length, ½ in.

858. Green glazed *faïence utchat* 👁 .

Length, ½ in.

859. Green glazed *faïence utchat* 𓂀 .

Length, ½ in.

860. Green glazed *faïence utchat* 𓂀 .

Length, ½ in.

861. Green glazed *faïence utchat* 𓂀 .

Length, ½ in.

862. Green glazed *faïence utchat* 𓂀 .

Length, ⅝ in.

863. Blue glazed *faïence utchat* 𓂀 .

Length, ¼ in.

864. Blue glazed *faïence utchat* 𓂀 .

Length, ⅜ in.

865. Red glazed *faïence utchat* 𓂀 .

Length, ⅝ in.

866. White glazed *faïence utchat* 𓂀 .

Length, 1 1/16 in.

867. Carnelian *utchat* 𓂀 .　　Length, 1½ in.

868. Carnelian *utchat* 𓂀 .　　Length, ½ in.

869. Carnelian *utchat* 𓂀 .　　Length, ¼ in.

870. Carnelian *utchat* .   Length, $\frac{5}{8}$ in.

871. Carnelian *utchat* .   Length, $\frac{5}{8}$ in.

872. Lapis-lazuli *utchat* .   Length, $\frac{1}{2}$ in.

873. Green stone *utchat* .   Length, $\frac{11}{16}$ in.

874. White stone *utchat* .   Length, 1 in.

875. Onyx *utchat* .   Length, $\frac{5}{8}$ in.

876. Red glass *utchat* .   Length, $\frac{9}{16}$ in.

877. Green glass *utchat* .   Length, $\frac{9}{16}$ in.

878. Red stone *utchat* .   Length, $\frac{1}{2}$ in.

879. Blue glazed *faïence utchat* .

          Length, $2\frac{1}{2}$ in.

880. Blue glazed *faïence utchat* .

          Length, $1\frac{5}{8}$ in.

881. Green glazed *faïence utchat* .

          Length, $1\frac{3}{4}$ in.

882. Blue glazed *faïence utchat* .   Length, $\frac{7}{8}$ in.

883. Blue glazed *faïence utchat* .

          Length, $\frac{13}{16}$ in.

884. Blue glazed *faïence utchat* 𓂀. Length, $\frac{6}{8}$ in.

885. Blue glazed *faïence utchat* 𓂀. Length, $\frac{5}{8}$ in.

886. Blue glazed *faïence utchat* 𓂀. Length, $\frac{5}{8}$ in.

887. Green glazed *faïence utchat* 𓂀.

Length, $\frac{6}{8}$ in.

888. Blue glazed *faïence utchat* 𓂀. Length, $\frac{1}{2}$ in.

889. Green glazed *faïence utchat* 𓂀.

Length, $\frac{7}{8}$ in.

890. Blue glazed *faïence utchat* 𓂀. Length, $\frac{3}{8}$ in.

891. Green glazed *faïence utchat* 𓂀. Length, $\frac{1}{4}$ in.

892. Carnelian glazed *faïence utchat* 𓂀.

Length, $\frac{3}{4}$ in.

893. Carnelian *utchat* 𓂀. Length, $1\frac{1}{8}$ in.

894. Carnelian *utchat* 𓂀. Length, $\frac{6}{8}$ in.

895. Onyx *utchat* 𓂀. Length, $\frac{3}{4}$ in.

896. Red stone *utchat* 𓂀. Length, $\frac{9}{16}$ in.

897. Red stone *utchat* 𓂀. Length, $\frac{9}{16}$ in.

898. Black stone *utchat* 𓂀.   Length, $\frac{3}{4}$ in.

899. Blue stone *utchat* 𓂀.   Length, $1\frac{3}{8}$ in.

900. Blue paste *utchat* 𓂀.   Length, $\frac{1}{2}$ in.

901. Glass (?) *utchat* 𓂀.   Length, $\frac{6}{8}$ in.

902. Blue glazed *faïence* shrine ; on one side is a figure of Sekhet in relief, and on the other is inscribed 𓎛𓋹𓊽 "Nephthys, life, and protection." From Abydos.   Height, $\frac{3}{8}$ in.

903–997. A miscellaneous collection of beads, pendants, amulets, etc., in carnelian, amethyst, glazed *faïence*, glass, etc.   From Abydos.

998–1004. Blue glazed *faïence* beads.
                Lengths, $\frac{6}{8}$ in. to $\frac{1}{2}$ in.
1005–1015. Green glazed *faïence* beads.
                Length, $1\frac{1}{4}$ in.
1016. String of glass, glazed *faïence*, and other beads.

1017. String of glass, carnelian, and glazed *faïence* beads.

1018. String of green glazed *faïence utchats*, beads, etc.

1019. String of green glazed *faïence* beads in the form of *utchats*.

1020. Necklace of green glazed *faïence* beads.
Length, 2 ft. 6 in.

1021. Necklace of green glazed *faïence* beads.
Length, 2 ft. 1 in.

1022. Necklace of green glazed *faïence* beads (with *utchat*, etc.). Length, 1 ft. 6 in.

1023. Necklace of green glazed *faïence* beads.
Length, 1 ft. 1 in.

1024. Necklace of green glazed *faïence* beads.
Length, $10\frac{1}{2}$ in.

1025. Necklace of green glazed *faïence* beads in the form of lotus flowers. Length, 2 ft. 3 in.

1026. Blue glazed *faïence* menât, the upper part of which is in the form of the goddess Nut. From Abydos. Length, $4\frac{1}{4}$ in.

1027. Light green glazed *faïence* pendant, having on it in relief a figure of the god Harpocrates seated on a lotus flower ; on each side of him is a winged uræus. From Ṣaḳḳâra. Length, 3 in.

1028-1158. Necklace of green and blue glazed *faïence* pendants, beads, etc.

1159. Network of blue and green glazed *faïence* beads which originally formed the outer covering of the mummy.   Length, 1 ft. 7½ in.; width, 8¼ in.

1160. String of white glazed *faïence* beads.
Length, 1 ft. 1 in.

1161-1166. Green glazed *faïence* oblong beads.
Length, 1⅜ in. to 1¾ in.

1167-1173. Green glazed *faïence* beads in the shape of lions' heads.   Length, ½ in. to ¾⅙ in.

1174-1179. Green and blue glazed *faïence* beads in the shape of lotus flowers.   Length, ⅛ in. to ¾⅙ in.

1180. Blue glazed *faïence* stamp; the base of which is in the form of a cartouche 〔〕, inscribed   Length, 2¼ in.

1181. Rectangular blue glazed, hollow-work *faïence* plaque, pierced with seven holes. On one side are the hawk of Horus wearing the double crown, two *bennu* birds, two uræi crowned with the crowns of

the north and south, etc., and on the other are
Harpocrates seated on a lotus, winged uræus, Rā, etc.
Length, 1¾ in.

1182. Rectangular blue glazed *faïence* plaque,
pierced, with figures of deities in hollow-work on
each side. Length, ⅘ in.

1183. Blue glazed *faïence* ægis of Bast.
Length, 11/16 in.

1184. Green glazed *faïence* pendant ; vase.
Length, ¾ in.

1185. Blue glazed *faïence* pendant ; Bes wearing
plumes and standing upon serpents, with *utchats*
in relief. Length, 1½ in.

1186. Blue glazed *faïence* quadruple *utchat*.
Length, ¾ in.

1187. Green glazed *faïence* vase. Height, 1⅛ in.

1188–1190. Blue paste baskets. Length, 9/16 in.

1191, 1192. Blue paste pendants. Length, ¾ in.

1193. Blue paste ring. Diameter, 1 1/16 in.

1194. Lapis-lazuli pillar surmounted by the head
of a hawk. Height, 1½ in.

1195. Green glazed *faience* pillar surmounted by a lion's head, upon which is a disk.   Height, $1\frac{7}{8}$ in.

1196. Lapis-lazuli lotus pillar surmounted by a ram's head upon which is the ⚏ crown.

Height, $1\frac{6}{8}$ in.

1197. Green glazed steatite stamp, inscribed with a bull's head ✡.   Diameter, $\frac{6}{8}$ in.

1198. Green glazed steatite stamp, inscribed with a sistrum ⚱ having pendent uræi.   Diameter, $9\frac{0}{16}$ in.

1199. Green glazed steatite plaque, pierced; on one side is a figure of Thoueris in relief, and on the other are inscribed ⚲ and lotus flowers.   Length, $\frac{1}{2}$ in.

1200. Green glazed steatite plaque, pierced; on one side in relief is a hawk, and on the other is inscribed Àmen-Râ ⌇⊙.   Length, $\frac{3}{16}$ in.

1201, 1202. Green glazed steatite cylinders inscribed with emblems of "life," "good luck" ⚕⚶⚕ ⚶⚕, and lines.   Length, $\frac{8}{16}$ in. and $\frac{9}{16}$ in.

1203-1205. Green and blue glazed *faience* shrines with figures of a goddess on two sides of each in hollow-work.   Height, $\frac{7}{16}$ in. to $\frac{3}{4}$ in.

1206-1207. Lapis-lazuli stamps with the words "Temple of Âmen" on the base.

Diameter, $1\frac{1}{2}$ in.

1208. Green glazed steatite stamp, inscribed with a hawk and winged uræus. Diameter, $\frac{7}{12}$ in.

1209-1214. Green glazed *faïence* draughtsmen.

Height, $\frac{5}{8}$ in. to 1 in.

1215. Bluish-green glazed *faïence* ring with scarab of the same material. Diameter, $1\frac{3}{8}$ in.

1216. Green glazed *faïence* plaque with a dog-headed ape in relief. Length, $1\frac{1}{4}$ in.

1217. Green glazed steatite bead surmounted by three frogs. Length, $\frac{3}{4}$ in.

1218. Portion of a green glazed *faïence* ring; a lotus flower surmounted by an ægis of Khnemu.

Length, $1\frac{1}{2}$ in.

1219. Light green glazed *faïence* pendant, having , cat, etc., in hollow work. From Abydos.

Length, $\frac{11}{16}$ in.

1220. Dark blue glazed *faïence* pendent figure of Bes. Length, $1\frac{1}{2}$ in.

1220a. Red glazed *faïence* pendent figure of Bes.
Length, $\frac{3}{4}$ in.

1221. Greenish-blue glazed *faïence* pendent figure
of a sow. Length, $\frac{3}{4}$ in.

1222. Greenish-blue glazed *faïence* pendent figure
of a sow. Length, $\frac{1}{2}$ in.

1223. Greenish-blue glazed *faïence* pendent figure
of a sow. Length, $\frac{1}{2}$ in.

1224. Greenish-blue glazed *faïence* pendent figure
of a sow. Length, $\frac{1}{2}$ in.

1225. Green glazed *faïence* pendent figure of an
altar. Length, $1\frac{1}{8}$ in.

1226. Green glazed *faïence* pendent figure of a
serpent. Length, $1\frac{1}{4}$ in.

1227. Blue glazed *faïence* pendent head of Hathor.
Length, $1\frac{3}{4}$ in.

1228. Blue glazed *faïence* pendent head of Hathor.
Length, $1\frac{1}{2}$ in.

1229. Blue glazed *faïence* pendent head of Hathor.
Length, $\frac{3}{4}$ in.

1230. Blue glazed *faïence* pendent head of Hathor.

Length, $\frac{9}{16}$ in.

1231. Blue glazed *faïence* pendent figure of Sekhet.

Height, 1 in.

1232. Light green glazed *faïence* frog, with suspending loop. From Abydos.   Length, $\frac{1}{2}$ in.

1233–1237. Blue glazed *faïence* vases in the shape of lotus flowers.   Height $5\frac{3}{4}$ in., $5\frac{1}{2}$ in., $4\frac{3}{4}$ in.

1238, 1239. Green glazed *faïence* aryballi.

Height, $3\frac{1}{2}$ in., $2\frac{3}{4}$ in.

1240. Blue glazed *faïence* vase with two handles.

Height, 2 in.

1241, 1242. Blue glazed *faïence* vases with two handles.   Height, 5 in., 4 in.

1243. Blue, thick, semi-transparent glass vase.

Height, $3\frac{7}{8}$ in.

1244. Blue glazed *faïence* bowl.   Diameter, $5\frac{1}{4}$ in.

1245. Blue glazed *faïence* vase with two handles.

Diameter, $1\frac{3}{4}$ in.

1246. Blue glazed *faïence* vase with serrated edge.

Diameter, $1\frac{3}{4}$ in.

1247. Blue glazed *faïence* hollow-work ring.

Diameter, $\frac{3}{4}$ in.

1248. Brown glazed *faïence* ring, having four figures of Rā, 🔱, etc., in hollow-work.

Diameter, 1 in.

1249. Brown glazed *faïence* ring, having four figures of Rā, 🔱, etc., in hollow-work.

Diameter, ⅞ in.

1250. Brown glazed *faïence* ring, having four figures of Rā, 🔱, etc., in hollow-work.

Diameter, 1 14/16 in.

1251. Brown glazed *faïence* ring, having four figures of Rā, 🔱, etc., in hollow-work.

Diameter, ⅞ in.

1252. Brown glazed *faïence* ring, having four figures of Rā, 🔱, etc., in hollow-work.

Diameter, ⅞ in.

1253. Brown glazed *faïence* ring, having four figures of Rā, 🔱, etc., in hollow-work.

Diameter, ⅞ in.

1254. Brown glazed *faïence* ring, having four figures of Rā, 🔱, etc., in hollow-work.

Diameter, ¾ in.

1255. Brown glazed *faïence* ring, having four figures of Rā, 🔱, etc., in hollow-work.

Diameter, 1 1/16 in.

1256. Brown glazed *faïence* ring, having four figures of Rā, 🗿, etc., in hollow-work.

Diameter, $\frac{11}{16}$ in.

1257. Brown glazed *faïence* ring, having four figures of Rā, 🗿, etc., in hollow-work.

Diameter, $\frac{11}{16}$ in.

1258. Brown glazed *faïence* ring, having a figure of Rā 🗿 and lotus flowers in hollow-work.

Diameter, $\frac{7}{8}$ in.

1259. Blue glazed *faïence* ring, having a figure of Rā 🗿 and lotus flowers in hollow-work.

Diameter, 1 in.

1260. Blue glazed *faïence* ring, having a figure of Rā 🗿 and lotus flowers in hollow-work.

Diameter, 1 in.

1261. Blue glazed *faïence* ring, having a figure of Rā 🗿 and lotus flowers in hollow-work.

Diameter, $\frac{7}{8}$ in.

1262. Blue glazed *faïence* ring, having a figure of Rā 🗿 and lotus flowers in hollow-work.

Diameter, $\frac{13}{16}$ in.

1263. Blue glazed *faïence* ring, having a figure of Rā 🗿 and lotus flowers in hollow-work.

Diameter, $\frac{7}{8}$ in.

1264. Blue glazed *faïence* ring, having a figure of Nephthys, ⍦, and lotus flowers in hollow-work.

Diameter, ⅞ in.

1265. Green glazed *faïence* ring, having a figure of Isis, the boat of the sun, lotus flowers, and a serpent, in hollow-work.   Diameter, ⅞ in.

1266, 1267. Lapis-lazuli spirals. Diameter, 1¼ in.

1268. Part of a wooden spoon, with the figure of a frog.   Diameter, 2¾ in.

1269. Wooden spoon with handle in the form of a lotus.   Length, 3½ in.

1270. Wooden spoon.   Length, 5¾ in.

1271. Bronze surgical (?) instrument.

Length, 3¾ in.

1272. Flint saw.   Length, 5¾ in.

1273. Bronze eye-lid for the right eye of a mummy case or coffin.   Length, 3⅛ in.

1274. Green glazed *faïence* bezel of a ring, with an *utchat* 𓂀 in relief.   Length, 1 in.

1275. Green glazed *faïence* pendant, with the head of the goddess Hathor in relief. Length, 1¾ in.

1276. Green glazed *faïence* quadruple *utchat*.

Length, ¾ in.

1277. Mother-of-emerald *utchat* 👁.

Length, 2½ in.

1278. Mother-of-emerald pendent hawk 🦅 .

Length, ⅝ in.

1279, 1280. Two carnelian *nefers* ‼ .

Length, ¾ in.

1281. Blue glazed *faïence* buckle 🔱 .

Length, 1¹⁄₁₆ in.

1282. Green glazed *faïence* stamp, inscribed on the base with the figure of the god Horus and an uræus.

Length, 1⅛ in.

1284. Green glazed steatite *utchat*, on one side of which are uræi and the head of Hathor.

Length, ½ in.

1285. Green glazed steatite fish 🐟, on the base of which is inscribed ⌷ Åmen-Rā.

Length, ₁₅⁄₁₆ in.

1286. Two green glazed steatite crocodiles on a pedestal, on the base of which is a linear device.

Length, ₉⁄₁₆ in.

1287. Carnelian cowroid.   Length, $\frac{7}{16}$ in.

1288. Green glazed *faïence* cowroid.

Length, $\frac{7}{16}$ in.

1289. Green glazed *faïence* cowroid, on the base of which are inscribed "life" and "good luck".

Length, $\frac{1}{2}$ in.

1290. Green glazed steatite cowroid, on the base of which is inscribed a cluster of lotus flowers.

Length, $\frac{7}{16}$ in.

1291. Green glazed steatite cowroid, on the base of which is inscribed the hawk of Horus.

Length, $\frac{11}{16}$ in.

1292. Green glass bead.   Roman Period.

Length, $\frac{1}{4}$ in.

1293. Round glazed steatite bead (?), on the base of which are uræi, etc.   Diameter, $\frac{7}{16}$ in.

1294. Green glazed steatite cartouche, on each side of which is inscribed a cluster of lotus plants.   Length, $\frac{3}{4}$ in.

1295. Glazed steatite plaque from a necklace, having upon it, in relief, a figure of the goddess Isis

suckling her son Horus, and symbols characteristic
of an early period.   Length, 1½ in.

1296. Blue glazed *faïence* plaque, with 🔲 *ḏet* in
relief.   Length, 2 1/16 in.

1297. Blue glazed *faïence* pendant.   Length, ½ in.

1298. Blue glazed *faïence* pendant.   Length, ¾ in.

1299. Portion of a frame of a box covered with
ivory, upon which are inscribed the prenomen and
nomen and titles of Rameses X., King of Egypt,
about B.C. 1150. The text reads :—

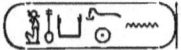

  ka   neχt   χā   em   Uast   suten net
The powerful bull, crowned in Thebes, { *King of North* }
                                      { *and South,* }

Rā-nefer-ka-setep-en-Rā   *king of the two countries,*

  us   χepeś   se-ānχ   taui
mighty of valour, *making to live* *the two lands,*

son of the Sun,   { Rameses, crowned in Thebes, }
                       {   beloved of Aman,   }

sa Râ   Râ - meses χâ Uast Âmen merer

Heru   nub   us   renpit   mâ   Râ   t'etta

the golden Horus, mighty of years like the Sun for ever!

The number of monuments inscribed with the name
of Rameses X. is small, and this fragment of a box
is therefore of considerable interest.   Length, 6⅜ in.

1300. String of *faïence* and other beads.
                                        Length, 9 in.

1301. Votive bronze altar with a figure of the
deceased pouring out a libation.   On the altar are
two hawks, two obelisks, two jackals, and a frog.
                                        Length, 2½ in.

1302. Wooden figure of a jackal, painted black.
                                        Length, 3½ in.

1303. Bronze polytheistic figure with the body
and wings of a bird (Horus), the head of a ram

Plate XXV.

CIPPUS OF HORUS.

(Åmen), the arms of a man, etc. ; he wears the triple
crown and stands between two crocodiles.

Height, 3¾ in.

1304. Fine green stone cippus of Horus.* The
lower portion of this remarkable object projects and
forms a kind of plinth upon which lie two crocodiles.
Above, in relief, is a figure of Harpocrates standing
with each foot on a crocodile ; the god is nude and
wears, as usual, a lock on the right side of the head.
Above him is the head of Bes. To the right, also in
relief, are an *utchat*, a scorpion, the hawk of Horus,
Isis (?), lotus standard with hawk, etc. ; to the left are
an *utchat*, a scorpion, a bird with two pairs of wings,
Horus spearing a serpent, a standard with plumes, a
bull, a snake, Nephthys, etc. On the sides and back
and plinth are twenty-one lines of lightly-cut hieroglyphics. On the back is a deity, with four rams'
heads, seated under a canopy of light ; at each side
are two apes making adoration, and close by is a
figure of the deceased worshipping.

Height, 7¾ in. ; width, 5½ in.

1305. Glass oval, pierced. Length, ⅜ in.

---

* See Plate XXV.

1306. Black basalt amulet of the heart pierced with holes whereby to sew it to the bandages of the mummy. On one side is a figure of the goddess Nut with outstretched arms, beneath each of which is a hawk-headed deity, and on the other is a version of chapter 30B of the Book of the Dead. The space left for the name of the purchaser is blank.

Length, 1⅞ in.

1307. Hæmatite pillow.   Length, ⅓⅔ in.

1308. Hæmatite amulet .   Length, 1⅜ in.

1309. Hæmatite ram inscribed on the base

𓊪𓂝𓈙𓃀𓃭.   Length, ⅞ in.

1310. Large bronze bowl.   Late Period.

Diameter, 7¾ in.

Plate XXVI.

BLUE GLAZED FAÏENCE FIGURE OF VENUS ANADYOMENE.

Nos. 1311—1340.

OBJECTS OF THE GRÆCO-
ROMAN PERIOD.

1311. Blue glazed *faience* figure of Venus Anadyomene.* Height, 1 ft. 2½ in.

1312. Terra-cotta figure of a woman suckling her
child (Isis and Horus). Height, 6¾ in.

1313. Terra-cotta figure of Eros. Height, 6⅝ in.

1314. Pair of silver earrings. Diameter, $\frac{4}{16}$ in.

1315. Pair of silver earrings. Diameter, $\frac{9}{16}$ in

1316. Silver earring. Diameter, ½ in.

1317. Silver earring, with projecting nob.
Diameter, $\frac{10}{16}$ in.

---

* See Plate XXVI.

1318. Gold ring with lapis-lazuli bezel whereon is cut a figure of Venus Anadyomene.

Diameter, $1\frac{1}{10}$ in.

1319. Green glazed pectoral with a pierced projection at each end for attaching it to the bandage of the mummy. On one side, in relief, is the god Anubis standing by the bier and the letters **L I C** and on the other the inscription

C I C Y I C O K A I
C A P A Π I ω N
C ω T H P E B I ω

Length, $4\frac{7}{8}$ in.

1320. Hard stone Gnostic amulet inscribed on the obverse with a figure of Khnoubis, **ΠΠΠ** and $\underset{\text{m}}{\overset{\text{w}}{\rule{0.5em}{0.4pt}}}$

and on the reverse with nine rows of Greek letters arranged in magical order. The edge is bevelled.

Length, 1 in.

1321. Large variegated glass bead.

Length, $2\frac{1}{8}$ in.

1322. Red terra-cotta ostrakon, inscribed with eleven lines of Demotic.   Length, $2\frac{3}{8}$ in., width, $2\frac{1}{8}$ in.

1323. Brass ring.   Diameter, $1\frac{1}{4}$ in.

1324. Copper coin, illegible.   Diameter $\frac{7}{10}$ in.

PAINTED PLASTER HEAD FROM A COFFIN OF THE
GRÆCO-ROMAN PERIOD.

Plate XXVII_A

PAINTED PLASTER HEAD FROM THE COFFIN OF A LADY OF THE
GRÆCO-ROMAN PERIOD. ABOUT A.D. 300.

1325. Painted plaster head of a young man,* with obsidian eyes inlaid.

1325A. Painted plaster head of a woman,† with obsidian eyes inlaid.

These heads were found upon rectangular wooden coffins together with plaster models of the feet. The Greeks first attempted to perpetuate the memory of the features of their dead by inserting painted portraits of them over the face of the mummy, but subsequently they placed painted plaster models of their heads and faces on the covers of the coffins.   About A.D. 300.

1326. Red terra-cotta lamp.   Length, $7\frac{1}{4}$ in.

1327. Red terra-cotta lamp with a seated figure in relief, on the top.   Length, $5\frac{1}{4}$ in.

1328. Red terra-cotta lamp with a figure of Hercules, in relief, on the top.   Length, $4\frac{1}{2}$ in.

1329. Red terra-cotta lamp with a figure of a man playing pipes, in relief, on the top.   Length, 4 in.

1330-1335. Red terra-cotta lamps with figure of a lion slaying a stag, in relief, on the top.

Lengths, $4\frac{1}{2}$ in., $3\frac{3}{4}$ in., $3\frac{1}{2}$ in., 3 in., $3\frac{1}{4}$ in., $2\frac{3}{8}$ in.

---

* See Plate XXVII.   † See Plate XXVIIA.

1336. Handle of a red terra-cotta lamp.

Length, 2¼ in.

1337. Head of a red terra-cotta figure of a woman.

Height, 2¾ in.

1338. Head of a red terra-cotta figure of a woman.

Height, 1¾ in.

1339. Bronze figure of Aphrodite as Isis* on a pedestal. The goddess wears on her head the plumes, disk, and horns of Isis. On her right wrist and on her left arm she has bracelets; the right hand rests on her chest, and the left on her left thigh. Græco-Roman Period.   Height, 9¾ in.

1340. Bronze leg of a box in the form of a Cupid.

Height, ⅝ in.

---

* See Plate XXVIII.

Plate XXVIII.

BRONZE FIGURE OF APHRODITE, AS ISIS.
OF THE GRÆCO-ROMAN PERIOD.

Nos. 1341–1391.

ALABASTER VASES AND VESSELS, AND MISCELLANEOUS OBJECTS.

1341. Alabaster jug 🝆 for holding unguent. From Thebes.   Height, $6\frac{7}{8}$ in.

1342. Alabaster stibium pot. From Thebes.
         Height, $4\frac{1}{2}$ in.

1343. Alabaster stibium pot. From Thebes.
         Height, $2\frac{1}{2}$ in.

1344–1348. Five alabaster spoons, or ladles. Lengths, $7\frac{1}{2}$ in., $7\frac{1}{4}$ in., $4\frac{1}{4}$ in., $4\frac{1}{4}$ in., and 4 in.

1349–1353. Five alabaster vases.
Diameters, $3\frac{13}{8}$ in., $3\frac{7}{8}$ in., $3\frac{1}{4}$ in., $3\frac{1}{4}$ in., and $2\frac{1}{2}$ in.

1354. Alabaster vase on stand 🝕 .
         Diameter, $5\frac{1}{2}$ in.

1355. Alabaster vase on stand ⬘ .

Diameter, 5¼⅛ in.

1356. Alabaster bowl.

Height, 3¼ in., diameter, 6¾ in.

1357, 1358. Two alabaster vases.

Diameters, 5⅛ in. and 3¾ in.

1359. Alabaster vase.   Height, 6 in.

1360. Alabaster vase.   Height, 3½ in.

1361. Alabaster vase.   Height, 5¼ in.

1362. Alabaster vase.   Height, 4½ in.

1363. Alabaster vase.   Height, 5 in.

1364. Alabaster vase.   Height, 2⅜ in.

1365. Alabaster flat bowl.   Diameter, 12 in.

1366–1375. Ten miscellaneous alabaster vases.

Heights, ¾ in. to 5 in.

1376, 1377. Two diorite stibium pots.

Heights, 3 in. and 2½ in.

1378. Calcareous stone kneeling figure of a man holding a shrine, upon the front of which is the figure of the god Osiris in relief.   Height, 8¼ in.

1379. Stone figure of the god Osiris, wearing the *atef* crown and holding whip and flail.   Height, 4¾ in.

1380. Stone figure of the god Osiris.
Height, 8¾ in.

1381. Calcareous stone seated figure of the god Osiris wearing the *atef* crown, and holding whip and flail.   Height, 8¾ in.

1382. Wooden pillow, or head rest, for the dead.
Height, 8 in.

1383. Green stone hawk of Horus with gold crown and beak ; the eyes are inlaid with some kind of precious stone.   From Abydos.   Height, 1⅜ in.

1384. Green glazed *faïence* cat with kittens.   From Abydos.   Height, ⅘ in.

1385. Wooden model of the serpent Nehebka. From Abydos.   Height, 2⅝ in.

1386. Silver pendent figure of the god Amsu,   From Lower Egypt.   Height, 1½ in.

1387. Green glazed *faïence* pendant with figures of Isis, Harpocrates and Nephthys in relief.   From Abydos.   Height, 1¼ in.

1388. Light bluish-green glazed *faïence* seated figure, portrait of a boy. Very fine, clean work. XXth dynasty. From Abydos.   Height, $1\frac{5}{8}$ in.

1389. Red and black opaque glass head of a woman. XXth dynasty. From Abydos.

Length, $1\frac{1}{8}$ in.

1390. Fragment of a light green glazed *faïence* vase with the figure of a crocodile in relief. From Tûna.   Length, $1\frac{3}{16}$ in.

1391. Fine veined alabaster vase, inscribed with the name and titles of Pepi I., king of Egypt about B.C. 3233.

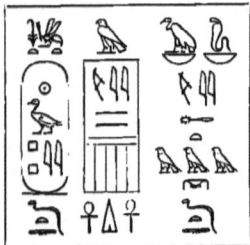

From Ṣakḳâra.   Height, $5\frac{3}{4}$ in.

1789. Painted wooden coffin belonging to the Græco-Roman period, length 6 ft. 2 in. On the outside are painted figures of the four genii of the dead, or children of Horus, and other deities, and the ordinary sepulchral formulæ which, however, are sometimes incomplete. On the breast is a figure of the goddess Nut, and at the foot are figures of various amulets, the ṭeṭ, etc. The inside of the coffin is very rough, and is without paintings and inscriptions. The coffin is made of rough pieces of wood pegged together, and lacks the finish and good work of the best periods of Egyptian sepulture. Inside the coffin is the mummy of a woman which is remarkable for its elaborate bandages, which are very narrow and are closely folded in a diamond pattern; these suggest that the mummy belongs to the late Roman period, and also that the coffin was not made for it. Presented by Sir Francis H. Laking, 1896.

HARRISON AND SONS,
PRINTERS IN ORDINARY TO HER MAJESTY,
ST. MARTIN'S LANE, LONDON.